20

the Light

John

C'mon the
Montrose !

Cheers,

the Light

Jim Alexander

Planet Jimbot

Edited by Kirsten Murray

For LC

Contents

1. Shoebox   *1*

2. Lilac   *21*

3. First Day On Earth   *41*

4. Event Horizon   *60*

5. Viking Funeral   *75*

6. Call Me Al   *93*

7. Church Of The Last Day   *110*

8. Gossamer   *134*

9. Panda Panda   *158*

10. Eighty Per Cent Water   *173*

11. Cry For Me Argentina   *182*

12. The Goodish Samaritan   *194*

13.	A Very Russian Hacking	*217*
14.	Opposite Of Light	*238*
15.	MD	*251*
16.	World Shut Your Mouth	*265*
17.	Turnberry	*288*
18.	Last Day On Earth	*305*
19.	Look To the Light	*315*
	Acknowledgements	*333*

1

Shoebox

He opened his eyes. It was different this time.

It was five in the morning. Geoff had hit the snooze button once already before finally, irrefutably coming to his senses. It was as much of a reprieve as the world could muster. There was a feeling originating from the pit of his stomach, travelling through the extent of his gut. He knew that something was up. Today of all days. Today of any days.

In some respects the morning was no different to any other. Geoff's undergarments were arranged on the dresser in his bedroom. Suit and shirt for the day, hung from the night before, were perched on the curtain rail. Watch and wallet rested on the second top shelf of the tall bookshelf which came with the flat as way of fixtures and fittings, gobbling up precious space, its presence made doubly conspicuous by the scarcity of books on display.

Upended there like two lonely, slightly off-tilt sentries were Jilly Cooper's latest and a Jack Reacher novel. Both were intended as birthday presents for his ex, only for the relationship not to last that long. Now they were uncomfortable, incidental, fictional reminders of what might have been, consigned to the gathering of dust.

Shaver and foam each occupied the designated place on the bathroom shelf next to toothpaste and toothbrush. It was a Tuesday and Geoff as a rule always shaved on a Tuesday. He was the kind of fella who made sure everything was where it should be, so he could sleepwalk his way through morning ablutions with no need to engage the brain. Get dressed, get ready for work. He would wake and everything was where it should be—as it should be—except that this was the morning where it wasn't.

He woke with a strange tingly feeling moving up and down his arm. There was a rhythm to it, more psychological than physical in impact. It made him feel sick. He knew what this meant; who wouldn't? In a flash, body swivelling, moving from the horizontal to the near-vertical, he climbed out of bed. The soles of his feet, moving downwards, made a slapping sound on impact with the wooden floor, disturbing the morning silence. To be fair, this early in the day you could argue the world hadn't started yet. At least, not one he recognised. The heart hadn't fully started beating. The pulse was still to quicken.

What more was there to expect from a slap on a wooden floor? The sound of flapping fish on the deck of a fishing boat? The energetic patter of bath water? The sound of a glass eye falling from the heavens making impact with the ocean surface? The noise you'd associate across all genders with overenthusiastic masturbation?

The thing was he couldn't feel the floor; couldn't feel the solidity of it. Take away the reality of the wooden slats below him and there was no sensation to go with the sound. No thunder with the lightning. The soles of his feet were numb to the fact, numb to the world. If he closed his eyes and wished away his surroundings, for all he knew his unreliable feet could be standing on quicksand. Or hot burning coals. Except for the fact he wasn't sinking, or burning.

His chest, on the other hand, felt the strain like it was broken. Like he was on a rollercoaster, on a straight hundred-and-eighty degree drop; the metal bar designed to prevent you from falling out doing its job only too well, overcompensating, crushing against you and pulverising your breastbone. He was giddy. He couldn't tell if the room was spinning or he was spinning, or both. There was no feeling in the soles of his feet and the rest of his body seemed to want to compensate for this wildly. But this in itself wasn't necessarily something to worry about. You would think.

Who was he kidding? Geoff closed his eyes and fought the temptation to moan, fearing if he started, he might not stop. *No time like the present then*, he thought as he lunged towards the curtains, opening them in theatrical fashion, only to be greeted by the all-pervading gloom, the darkness of late winter. He knew it was cold outside. It was that time of the year. He held up his hand. He pushed apart his fingers, establishing a good gap between digits, before diligently placing his palm against the window pane. Against a sheet of glass bereft of condensation, he pressed with force, or so the logic functions of his brain dictated was the case. But for all that, he could not feel its coolness. He could not feel the actual glass.

The thing was he was feeling fine. He was fit. He'd run a half marathon last year, with blisters on his feet the size of a small planet to show for it. He hadn't taken a day off sick for something like eight months. The *Dear John* text he received from Brenda—the Jilly Cooper/Jack Reacher fan—complained about many things, but personal stamina was not one of them.

For something better to do, Geoff grunted loudly. It was a short-lived outburst which was no kind of mercy at all, the ensuing silence coming across as stark and undernourished, worse than before. His mind was a cluster of stinging nettles. What to do? This wasn't happening to him. This *was* happening to him and he better do something about it. He was mistaken, his instincts were wrong; he'd made some kind of error. He wasn't mistaken. He was still asleep. He was awake. This was fucked up. This was *really* fucked up.

A thought popped into his head, a terrifyingly volatile one; the kind that made you wonder whose side your brain was on. Was it possible to die standing on your feet? Literally standing on your feet? How could you stop your body from folding in on itself? Your feet from buckling under the weight of you?

His mind was racing, racing, racing while ever conscious of the fact he needed to calm down. Taking deep breaths in rapid succession, shallow and deep, which began to overlap, utterly befuddled, struggling to distinguish inhalation with exhalation. The only way to bring all this to a close, he decided, was to stop breathing. What was the point, he thought? He held the thought along with his breath; crystallised; caught in a loop, seizing his brain, whirling, maddening, like the satellite images of a storm, signifying overwhelming threat, an impending doom.

Was this ever going to end? Don't answer the question. His palm was still up at the glass, limbs locked and fused. A statuesque idiot, hoping for divine providence that, get real, was never going to happen. Each of his thoughts picked up an echo, flitting around inside his skull like a succession of trapped birds. His body not moving, his mind refusing to stay still, was this how he intended to spend his last day on earth?

'What's the point?' he finally said aloud. Popping into his head, he felt like he was a magician conjuring up a cliff face, something he could hang onto to stop him tumbling into the abyss. 'I still have my voice. Christ, some might say that's my biggest asset.'

It was that—and the fact he'd started breathing again.

'Only asset,' he added, snorting in jest. And suddenly his mind started to adjust to something like normality—breathing more regular—bordering on the blissful.

He thought about going back to bed and just sleeping it off. There was a theory going round if you recognised the signs and avoided taking the *Light,* introduced a liberal measure of self-denial to the mix, that you could rewire the brain and kick-start the physiology and so avoid the inevitable. He'd heard the stories just like everyone else, but mere hours ago he would have happily scoffed at them. Helpings of withering scorn dismissing them as urban myth with a flourish of a hand and enlarging of the eyes.

'I need to work superfast,' he said. 'Don't have time and whose fault is that?'

An answer was not forthcoming. The sense of bliss from just seconds before had already burned itself out. Slowly, mournfully, he withdrew his hand from the window. His mind was still trying to keep up with events, the unfolding raw materials of reality, but once it did so, he shook his head furiously. Lethargy was a luxury right now he could ill afford.

He knew he shouldn't. He knew his yammering brain had wasted enough time as it was. What was the expression? *Hope springs eternal.* As if to emphasise the point, Geoff dropped to all fours. He stuck his head under the bed. With both hands he scrambled around furiously. He'd only recently put it in there, but as things stood he would have been as well burying it at the bottom of the Bermuda Triangle. Fingers and thumbs, inert and devoid of feeling, did their best to scurry and search through all the crap which had accumulated there over the last two years, starting the day he moved in. An empty bin; bedside lamp with no bulb; used batteries; a couple of plastic bags full of magazines, the majority still in their original wrappers; a ceramic ashtray; a small artificial Christmas tree; a hand-carved chess set; an old pair of trainers; a packet of condoms, bashed but unopened; a Bon Jovi t-shirt. Signs of a wasted life.

Conscious of time—always conscious of time. Time an unconstrained animal, something had to give; perhaps it would be his sanity. Hands formed as fists pushed into both sides of a block of cardboard. He had his reprieve.

Revelling in its pliability he let out a victorious yelp. Hands so compelled, in the shape of claws, dragged out the shoebox. Secured in his line of sight, he took off the lid which he tossed, spinning elegantly, over his shoulder. He peered in, his face a strange combination of agony and ecstasy switching from one to the other; expecting miracles in an age where such things were no longer considered fashionable.

Point proven, inside the box was a platoon of tiny, half-chewed, dark green plastic toy soldiers. Their only function, it appeared, was to keep guard over an emaciated bundle of notes. If the shoebox was a cupboard, it was enough to make even a battle-hardened Old Mother Hubbard weep. Hope; he was blinded by hope, and hope in this instance came in the guise of an old cardboard box. It was the kind of hope that dug him out of a hole only to subsequently throw him back in again. And now without hope, the only thing on hand to fill the vacuum was sick realisation. He stared slack-jawed at the meagre savings on display in front of him. He had been deluding himself and not for the first time. He'd tricked himself. He had only himself to blame. He had fucked himself.

Maybe he was mistaken in his prognosis. Perhaps he'd misread that troublesome feeling in his gut that greeted him as he awoke. It was there, then it was gone; ephemeral; the dispersal of dandelion seeds in a light breeze. It had happened once before. He'd come to and thought that was it, curtains for the Geoffster. (The other type of curtains.) Back then there was no feeling in his arms, but that was a night where he'd slept on his front in the grip of a deep sleep, one that wouldn't seem out of place in a mausoleum, hands tucked under his hips, effectively cutting the circulation from the elbows down. He thought he was going to die, but he was mistaken. He'd dropped the ball. The first of nine lives, he remembered thinking, as the feeling reluctantly, jarringly returned to his hands. He made the seesaw staccato transition from distressed to calm, swallowing back his anxiety and gathering up his composure like the folds of a favourite shirt. A false alarm, thankfully. It was only his arms that had been dead.

If that was the first of nine, then this would be his second. He still liked those odds.

He could just check and then he'd know for sure. Extinguish the doubt. Exorcise the ambiguity. But to do so he'd need to steel himself and overcome his natural default position as the cowardly lion. He'd need to face that very special type of terror. The thing that stops you from finding out, real or imagined, what's lurking around a corner in the dark; or from peeking through sweaty fingers at the nerve-shredding reveal in a horror film; or stopping you, despite the pain, so regular and severe, from making that doctor's appointment. The terror of certainty.

The shoebox was his 'mattress fund.' The idea was to save enough cash to allow you to whore, drink, smoke, gamble, and gorge the whole day through. Or that's how it should have been. In fact, that's what it was only months previously. Safely tucked inside the box, there was several thousand easy. But he needed a new catalytic converter for his *Fiat 500 Abarth 599* convertible. And how could he refuse her? It was love at first sight; bowled over by her design and attitude; sporty, compact, bijou, and fruity. Clean, but could get dirty if she wanted. It was true love. It was man/machine love. Right from the off, smitten, he had a name for her: *Vera*.

And what were the chances? One month a catalytic converter, the next Vera needed a replacement gearbox. It was a personal badge of honour, one of several, to drive in the city centre as fast as he could. To cut corners, sometimes literally. He hated the idea of having to slow down. All that yanking, turning, and skidding at full speed had a cost, though. Sometimes, as he swerved in front of another car to claim the one parking space available over a growled whisper of 'fuck you-fuck you-fuck you,' he could hear the scrunching, screaming metal of the car's insides. Small car, high maintenance; Vera, the shiny love of his life, was crippling him. Nothing made Geoff's eyes water more than the phrase 'monthly instalments.' To pay for the repairs he could have asked for an extension to one of his personal loans, but he just couldn't face the medicals. So what else was he to do, buy a fucking Panda? What it came down to was that he needed someone to look at his car over a number of weekends and no self-respecting streetwise mechanic would allow anyone to jump the queue for anything other than hard cash. This was Leytonstone, East London, after all; a law to itself. A mini-universe.

For as long as he could remember (as a rule, he discounted any memories from before the age of twelve) he'd always wanted to live in the city. And he had followed his dreams all the way to a cramped flat in Leytonstone with its unloved bookshelf, which at least gave his cleaner something to dust and make him feel he was getting marginally more value for his money in return for his services. The irony of this wasn't completely lost on him, but he didn't care much anyway. The rent was extortionate for a place too small to swing his ex-girlfriend's cat. Not that he could be persuaded to keep swinging for long. He had this thing about cat hairs getting into his eyes, mouth, every orifice you could think of. It was intolerable, made him want to scratch to the point of requiring a tranquiliser. In fact, thinking back, on one of the rare occasions he found himself back at hers, the act of propelling the furball in a fit of pique at the wall (to be fair, it had been a particularly bad day at work) may well have proved the final straw; the catalyst for her *Dear John* text. In the blink of a watery eye (a cat hair had got in it) his current had become his ex. Tough outcome, especially considering, apart from a broken claw, the cat was perfectly okay.

Living and working in the city meant everything to him. Any decision worth making—politics, finance, commerce—was made here. He could feel the power of the place vibrate through his feet, shuffle inside his shoes (when his feet still had feeling, that is). He was part of a monster, a socio-financial complex; a nation state in all but name; a Garden of Eden for a modern age; a city landscape to form the perfect backdrop for any self-respecting pop video. Stuff your New York. When London farted, the rest of the world, nostrils flaring, knew about it. He was a tiny component, sure; a particle, a corpuscle, an ant—and not an important one at that—but part of the fabric nonetheless. Part of the colony. For Geoff, living in the city was worth the premium; worth swallowing up all he earned and then some more. Even the air—the gritty, shitty, dirty city air—he'd take a moment to breathe it in. It was that simple, made even the bad stuff bearable; better than bearable. Residing in London made life worth living.

But what about death? Where did that fit in?

He should never have needed to dip into his shoebox, that shouldn't have mattered at all, but his bonus was postponed for what seemed like the hundredth time. Another fall in the markets was the reason. Fucking banks. Gutless. And it was a thousand times worse, he lamented, his cross to bear, working for one of them. His bonus should have been paid by now and used to refill the shoebox without fanfare. Mattress fund replenished. But these days it was never about now, always a case of jam tomorrow. It couldn't be helped, so his manager would tell him. It wasn't the right time. He needed to be patient. But for Geoff it *was* the right time. It was no use to him tomorrow. He needed funds desperately. More than what he had, the bare bones, which was scarcely enough to buy a date and walnut muffin and grande (venti at a push) cappuccino.

He'd spent it. He was spent. He hadn't saved nearly enough, and now he was beyond saving. He'd fucked up. He was the kind of guy who fucked up a lot, but not one to apologise for it or learn from his mistakes. The fact he never gave to charity was another badge of honour. It was something in his own mind he could happily justify. It was a choice, a brutal one. A brutal life choice. Deep down, if put to the test, he'd probably agree with the assessment he wasn't a particularly likeable person. He rooted for the bad guy at the movies. More Joker than Batman. But still, this wasn't a reason for anyone to deserve to die.

'This can't be happening to me,' he said. 'It's so unfair,' his voice again, this time agreeing with himself. He was sobbing, knew he had to do something. He slapped his face with his hand. It wasn't a hard slap, no conviction behind it. He felt a tingle move up and down his cheek in the shape of radio waves. In contrast, there was nothing in the way of feeling emanating from the palm of his hand. It was like part of him was cut off from the world already. People spent their whole lives preparing for this, but this didn't mean they were ever truly ready for it. 'I'm going to die,' he wailed. 'This is the day. This is the day.'

Then from the depths of his despair there blossomed a solid, unexpurgated thought. Maybe, he reflected, there was still time. 'It's early,' he said, 'it's still so fucking early.' It was as if by saying the words out loud made the day all the fucking earlier.

There was a square panel fitted to the living room wall in its customary position next to the door. From it came a mauve glow. It was unavoidable, but Geoff wasn't ready to face it just yet. His was a ground floor flat, two rooms, and for now, in the grip of stultifying indecision not sure what to do next, he was staying put in the bedroom. His routine would have to be the first casualty of the day. He'd bypass a shower. Although it was Tuesday, there would be no shave today. In any case, today of all days, he didn't relish being in close proximity to a razor—or shaving cream, strangely, for that matter. At least his stubble would enjoy a stay of execution.

'The early bird,' he said. He had to keep talking. His voice, its timbre, was something he could rely on. But even this strategy, basic as it was, was not without risk. He heard a noise he did not immediately recognise before realising it was his own laughter. This was a situation where rationality, like ready cash, was not a given.

All he could do was wait until the laughter—not loud, an audible tickle trying to break out of the back of his throat—subsided. He started to count inside his head from one upwards. Every number was a sledgehammer cracking open his hopes and dreams. He thought if he reached one hundred he would scream, which at least would replace the laughter. He thought he'd collapse to the ground, froth at the mouth, and start chewing on the carpet. At the count of thirty-one, mercifully, the laughter stopped.

Geoff got dressed in record time, taking advantage of where everything should be, but ruining everything by having to halt, bend over, and redo the tying of a shoelace which flopped in his defective hands like boiled spaghetti. He was aware, always aware, of that unobtrusive, inconspicuous square panel in the next room. Its dampened iris light was burning a hole through the wall and into the back of his skull. It was the *Light* and wasn't for getting out of his head. It came with the flat. What was he supposed to do? It was the elephant in the other room.

He was dressed and almost out of there. He dashed into the living room, animated, a collection of jingly jangly limbs. But that all stopped as he stood motionless at the door. It had been a morning of fits and starts, now he needed to take a moment and expunge the thought, fight the compulsion to place his palm on the *Light*. His body spasmed; it shrank and shook as it resisted a lifetime of conditioning. The global crash that was the First Day happened when he was seven years old. To take the *Light*

13

was as much a morning ritual as a five-second yawn or ten-second scratching of his rear-end. All three would have to wait. He willed himself into movement, his frame unfolding, as he hauled himself out of the door.

He had panicked but he could take the *Light* at any time, or so the voice at the back of his head was telling him. But he knew; he really did know. Except that he really didn't know.

In a flash, the clinking of keys, he darted back indoors to face that square panel once more. There had been enough drama in his life, more than enough that morning, so without fanfare—or at least without any more unnecessary grief—he placed his palm on the *Light*. In return, up on the screen there would be a tick or a cross. It was as simple as that. No thumbs up or emoticons, nothing that could pass as social media. You either passed or failed. You hoped to pass many, many times and live a long and full and at times fulfilling life. You only failed the *Light* once.

He was blinking too much, so barely registered the screen, not that there was much in the way of information to absorb. Moments later, he was back out the door and on his way. He could feel the invisible umbilical cord between him and his precious flat stretch perilously. He heard the door behind him slam shut. It was such a final sound. Unhappiness enveloped Geoff like a shroud.

At one point in the recent past, he thought Brenda was going to move in. Right up to the extent he couldn't sleep with worry, wondering where she'd put her stuff, how much space he'd need to free up to make room, terrified at the prospect of having to downsize his seventy-five-inch TV screen. And if that wasn't enough, she wouldn't be alone. The reality hit home, setting off endless scenarios in his head, plotting events which would lead to the euthanizing of Public Enemy Number One—her tabby—while minimising the risk of any blame being attached to him. But that was all over, it was never to be. Brenda was out of his life and now he was going to die alone.

'No,' he admonished himself, dragging him out of his self-pitying stupor. 'Not throwing in the towel yet. Still have a Plan B.'

He was outside, feet placed firmly on terra firma, or so his brain was telling him. He was only in his suit, no coat, despite the low temperatures. Whatever was going to kill him, he'd decided it wouldn't be the cold. His head spun. He breathed in the petrol-tinged air. It was raining; a shower; a light one. Down the street, not too far, he could see where the shower started (or ended). He drew breath and focussed on the twenty feet or so in front of him where no rain was falling. It was impermanence in action. The world could be so different, one of marked contrasts. One side wet and the other side dry. On the one hand shimmering and treacherous, and on the other safe and unchanging. He was next to a road and cars passed by, moving from one state to the next, dry to wet, wet to dry, between both worlds; testimony that transition was possible. He couldn't recollect ever having seen anything like it, not in all of his twenty-nine years. Or perhaps instead, it was the first time in his life he'd considered such a thing significant enough to notice.

Twenty-nine, that was the key. No one ever died as young as twenty-nine. That was it; he had to be dreaming. The rain, the shoebox, the *Light*, they were all the stuff of dreams. But could he really take the chance? Didn't people die in their sleep? In their dreams?

He awoke from his reverie and focussed on Plan B. A short, hurried walk took Geoff to Sainsbury's Local, still early, but showing stirrings of being open for business. More to the point, there wasn't a queue at the cash machine outside. He strolled, back straight, setting his sights on that hole in the wall. He couldn't help but experience a rush; an anticipation of the fact, hallelujah, that his luck was finally for turning. Once there, utilising finger and thumb, he slipped his debit card into the card reader. There were some gentle clicks and clacks as the machine accepted his plastic with unfussy motorised ease. He entered his PIN, thinking that this was such a blatant, brazenly obvious and audacious thing to do that it just might work. That somehow, while he may not have been the first to consider such a course of action, he was the first not to immediately dismiss it out of hand. Ominously, from the cash machine there came a swishing, clattering din. A message popped up on the screen saying 'Verification Void,' and despite the wild optimism of moments before, Geoff knew it wasn't referring to the validity of his PIN.

With an iron pyrite gargle down the metallic tunnel, the machine swallowed his card. Frustrated, beyond frustration, Geoff swore under his breath but wasn't of a mind to stop there. Undeterred, he produced several more cards, repeating the same action while hoping for a different result. The machine took no time in eating all the plastic in his possession, company credit card included. All the while, Geoff, if not mad (and it was a big 'if'), painted the picture of an increasingly agitated man.

'Why don't you just swallow me up as well, you bastard?' he wailed, bringing both hands down with an almighty thump on the non-cash dispensing cash dispenser. He then stood rigid, wide-eyed, every muscle in his body frozen, terrified that it might just do that. It had devoured everything else. After the morning he'd had he was due a few flashes of insanity. The odd brain fart. Now having subsided there followed moments of clarity. He was content to accept that nothing of the sort was going to happen, another urban myth he might have heard (or imagined) where people who failed the *Light* were eaten up by cash machines. His mind was hostage to fortune and fairy stories.

There was no one around, but the feeling he was surrounded was all he could think about. He was twitchy, ready to turn to face his nemesis in the shape of a nearby streetlight. But this was no ordinary streetlight. There was the regular LED lighting, perched in its customary position up top forming a near forty-five degree arch to light the way when dusk falls. Where there's a head there's also a heart. Halfway down the column, occupying a central position, was a box which emitted sangria or mulberry light, or some such purple hue. This was the *Light*, readily available twenty-four hours a day as way of public service. It was universal, although less so on the streets where some were vandalised or awaiting maintenance, which usually came down to something as straightforward as the application of a screen wipe from an employee at Waltham Forest Council.

Its prevalence did not stop there. The *Light* for the

most part was in people's homes and offices. It was in hotel rooms. Every eventuality was catered for in case you'd simply left home and forgotten to take it, or were away on a business trip, or who knows, maybe on a dirty stop out. There could be no excuse, the *Light* was everywhere.

Before going on holiday, in addition to making sure you have your traveller cheques, plug adaptor, the correct documentation, travel insurance, and the right vaccinations, you needed to make arrangements for the *Light*. You needed to apply for a *Light* visa, which came in the form of a barcode and only worked alongside a biometric passport. If you were visiting a country that didn't extensively offer the *Light* (for whatever reason) you had to ensure you took sufficient currency to see you through the holiday, then resign yourself to the pain of sorting things out when you got back.

The stipulation was clear, every day you needed to place your palm on the *Light*. It was accepted, the social norm, the first thing you did (or as near as) when you awoke. For an external reading outside your home or place of work, additionally you'd input an ID number, more than likely your National Insurance number, more than likely using a key fob, or just as likely a chip implanted in one of your fingers.

The *Light* measured the level of electrolytes on the palm of your hand. It didn't matter if you built up a sweat, generated any kind of heat, there was no getting around the fact that a reading of no electrolytes equalled *Last Day*.

Doubly so, there was no getting around the fact you

had to offer up a human palm. There were many instances of people—desperate people—begging, bribing, and threatening friends, family, and the vulnerable; a sacrificial lamb to offer up a hand. The living imitating the soon-to-be-dead. But this was illegal and the penalties severe (at least for the living). There were numerous police and government departments dedicated to combatting *Light* fraud. The ultimate sanction was to be barred from the taking the *Light* entirely, effectively ostracised and cut off from society.

Could it be considered acceptable no matter the circumstances for someone with no future to jeopardise another's future? Social norms were built up, the establishing of taboos; the favours, requests, threats; the one thing you could not ask for.

Not that this was of concern to Geoff. He could have phoned and tried to persuade Brenda to put her hand forward in place of his. Just maybe she might have said yes if he'd settled for being friends and hadn't posted all those nasty things about her on Facebook. She would have been his knight in shining armour, like that was going to happen. But he was an anxious man, full of frantic thoughts. Brimming with desperate yearnings, he was a dam with a structural weakness which threatened to overflow and burst open.

There were no loopholes, or was it simply that people had stopped looking for them, afraid of what they might find instead. That life was a secondary concern. That everything that led up to the here and now was ancillary and superfluous. Meaningless. Geoff was not alone in facing a day like no other, frightened out of his wits; matters made worse by the real possibility that his Last

Day was closer to the finishing than the starting line. It was the realisation that scared him half to death.

Over half, as was likely the case.

2

Lilac

Everything has a centre.

From the centre of the streetlight, the *Light* shone lilac. Geoff stood stupidly staring at it for quite some time. Its main role, it seemed to him, was to taunt him, sneer at him, belittle him. Its other primary function was to reject him with the sure knowledge of never having to do so twice. The streetlight could have been part of an alien invasion force; one of the tripods from *War of the Worlds* by HG Wells.

The reality of the situation began to bite and leave its mark. This was happening to him—not to someone else.

With the onset of every waking day, the onus was on you, citizen of the world, to verify the fact you'd see out the next twenty-four hours. Put simply, to prove you'll live another day. Failing this your savings were frozen, credit cards blocked, wages stopped, leases terminated.

From a financial perspective you were persona non grata. You'd dropped off that cliff face at the edge of the world. Joint bank accounts were illegal. Having someone else hold money in trust on your behalf was forbidden. Unlimited financing of someone else's final day was unlawful. There could be no reliance on anything in kind, not on your Last Day. The legal position was, strictly speaking, that you had no legal position. Mattress funds could in theory be shared or pooled, but such actions were not without consequences for the living.

The fact was in the cold light of day—*this* day—you had to take what you could. When you could. If you could.

There was no definite cut off, but the longer the period between taking the *Light* the more problematic things would become. Anything over twenty-four hours could see you at risk. You were as good as dead. And even if you weren't—if it was an oversight, if you were ill—you'd still need to spend the best part of a day on the phone or online, or both, self-certification to hand, on a wing and a prayer trying to get yourself—and your accounts—reinstated.

Take the everyday scenario of taking the *Light* at 6.30 a.m. on Monday and at 6.31 a.m. on Tuesday. You'd have strayed one minute over the twenty-four hours. It would be unlikely, and really, really unlucky, that your cards would be frozen so soon, but that didn't mean it couldn't happen. It could only take a minute. Best to be regular, then, where the *Light* was concerned.

But what happened if you weren't regular? If there was no good reason for it? Where there was no oversight...?

The world had turned its back on you. All you had

to see you through whatever part of the day you had remaining, the only possession worth a damn, was your mattress fund. You may of course chose to spend your last hours with friends and family, or tearful farewells on Skype, or staring at a wall, or screaming at a streetlight, or somehow managing to get through to your insurance company only to be asked if they could call you back later. You could volunteer at a food bank, or rarer still throw yourself off a tall building. Alternatively, if you wanted to go out with a bang, that's where the mattress fund came into play.

In the here and now, all Geoff had was himself, the paltry contents of his shoebox, and a discredited Plan B. Machinations that seemed to him so ridiculous now. The hope that he could draw out money from a hole in the wall before anyone had noticed he had failed the *Light*. The system could have been down, he supposed. There could have been a glitch.

The system was never down. He wondered how he'd got to be so brainless; have the same intellectual capacity as stainless steel cutlery.

Geoff had always hoped, always fancied the notion that if there ever was a need for a Plan B, his would be an elegant, meticulously hatched one, too clever by half. He hoped that his workmates, cockroaches every one of them, might hear about it after the fact and joke about it and give him his dues, and maybe even raise a toast to him. 'He was a slippery one, the Geoffster,' they'd say, 'a real stand-up guy. He showed them, he really showed them. Went out all guns blazing. Cocked his leg and pissed on that lamppost.' Instead it was none of those things; it was just desperate. A massively naïve, amateurish schoolboy effort. He could have continued contemplating how poor a plan Plan B was, but equally aware in his present predicament that he could not do so indefinitely.

He experienced a pang of self-loathing, which had to wriggle and squirm and find a place alongside the sense of loathing he already felt for life in general.

It had stopped raining, at least for a short while. It was late January and rain wasn't the worst that could happen. Water on the ground streaked like translucent small snakes heading towards a drain situated at the side of the road.

Geoff watched on, a swelling in his chest, white residue having formed at the corners of his mouth, burgeoning with desire, wanting so much to occupy the space between someone's legs while snorting cocaine from another's bare chest. Wanting his balls tickled with a feather duster. A proper send-off. Was that really so much to ask for?

Reality reasserted itself and he was aware of footsteps in the wet heading in his direction. He stuck a hand in his pocket with the sole purpose of juggling an electronic box with serrated hook. He released it, letting it slide down the pocket, before plunging his hand in to grab it again. He repeated the action several times. He didn't have to feel its impression in his palm to know it was there, a habit acquired from before he could remember, the act of pocket shuffling with your car key. It was the dose of normality he needed, reset button hit. Formulating once more, everything was in place. Him, his pocket, his car key. Satisfied, he was ready for Plan C.

The approaching figure was male, carrying an

unopened umbrella. In and around his forties, without doubt older than Geoff—Geoff was certain—the bastard.

'Excuse me,' Geoff said, standing a foot away or so from the man, opening up his shoulders, making his body big, effectively blocking his path. He smiled and hoped on balance, body language included, he came across as unthreatening. Still, not shy about coming forward, which was wholly appropriate considering the circumstances. 'I need money,' he opined.

There was something in the man's eyes. He swung his umbrella up into a horizontal position, two hands gripping the folded canopy, which he held against his chest.

As way of follow up, Geoff waved his hands frantically like they were trying to assist in the landing of a Boeing 737.

'No, no, no, no,' he said. 'Sorry, you're misunderstanding me. I don't want…' Fingers trembling, his hands made a downwards fanning motion. 'No intention of…'

Geoff made a grab for his pocket. The man didn't lower his umbrella. Geoff, so committed, revealed his car key.

'All I'm asking for is a trade,' he said, dangling the key fob enticingly, or so he hoped was the case. 'My car, *Fiat 500 Abarth*, wait for it,' he mouthed more than spoke the words, *'599.'*

'You heard it right, immaculate, new—as good as new—recently serviced at great personal expense, up to date and tip-top. It's yours, my friend, in return for all the money in your wallet.'

'Rest assured it's not a fucking Panda,' Geoff added,

ever hopeful, seeking to crowbar a zippy one-liner into proceedings to lighten the mood.

But zippy one-liners were not Geoff's and today of all days the last thing he needed was to be reminded of the fact. Thoughts and counterpoints invaded his brain furiously. *Maybe the guy is a big fan of the Fiat Panda. A 'nan's car', surely not? Takes a full five minutes to take a left? Half your lifetime to reach the end of the road?*

'Goes by the name of Vera,' Geoff said, arm a little too outstretched, too close, passive aggressive, shaking the key in his hand perhaps a little too enthusiastically. His head was a train crash. He was veering off-script. Man and umbrella continued to face him, unmoved.

'At least...' Geoff croaked, still trying to build a rapport, knowing all the while that particular bird had flown, built a nest, incubated several eggs, eaten a thousand worms, devolved back to an archaeopteryx, '...tell me your name.'

The man realised what was happening. He knew exactly the nature of the predicament which unfolded before him. There was only one scenario where a man much younger than him would offer his car (and if it came to it, probably wouldn't stop there) in return for any loose change on his person.

'You don't need to know my name,' Umbrella Man said. His tone was careful and deliberate; poised, not wanting to appear unsympathetic. 'I'm sorry, but that is something you cannot ask me to do. There are laws.'

Geoff had a wild-eyed look about him. He held the other man's stare.

Even if he wanted to look away, avert his gaze, he could not. He wanted a lifeboat, but instead was cast horribly adrift, abandoned to the rapids; the breaking of relentless, overpowering, deadly waves.

Hopeless. Unprepared to offer a helping hand. The *Good Samaritan*, another urban myth Geoff had heard about.

Geoff was lost to the world. A world which had rejected him out of hand. He thought maybe he could go buy a packet of cigarettes (if he could afford it), return to the flat and set fire to the place. He'd squat on his bed, all part of a gloriously grotesque final act, a literal smoking of himself to death. He'd ensure the irony wasn't lost on him. And he'd wait until the flames tore into him, dismantling him with a pain so agonising and indiscriminate, pushing him beyond the capacity of thought. Reduced to a mass of gelignite limbs, hot boiling blood, scorched retinas, liquefied kidneys. The palms of his hands and soles of his feet would blister and peel, but desensitised, unfeeling, still defiant to the end. Hoping the smoke got to him first. Smoking on the outside, smoking on the inside...

He thought of his dad who slipped and fell in the shower, cracking his head open. He did so while getting ready, the poor sod, wanting to look his best on his Last Day. Geoff thought maybe he should grab a baseball bat from somewhere and vandalise all the cars up and down the street, and maybe even crack open some heads as well, starting with the prick standing in front of him. He wanted to march all the way to Hollybush Hill and knock down the obelisk that stood there restored from Roman times. But genuinely, who had the time? He thought about phoning Brenda, he still had credit, and apologise for all the terrible things he'd said about her.

He'd then more than likely, he thought, break down and cry. Hopefully touched by this, overwhelmed by this, she'd respond in kind. He would confess his sins. It didn't matter whether they were true—no time to think first, to fact check. He'd blurt out the first thing that penetrated his bloated head—and she would forgive him all the same.

'There are laws.'

He thought of all of those things, but the reality was he was standing in front of a man who wasn't prepared to put his hand in his pocket. He thought of punching him really hard. He wondered how his stupid, well-meaning, going-through-the-motions face would feel against his knuckles. He still had feeling in his knuckles, he was sure of that. And he wondered if he moved on, walked some more, there'd be some arcane rite, something ancient and magical he'd somehow stumble upon, which could rewrite the laws of nature? Of life and death?

Leytonstone was such an old town. Beyond its modern trappings, it had its secrets. This was a Roman town.

Not thinking straight, he was suffering here. He really was suffering. He still needed to get past the umbrella. He needed to give up on it, just like its owner had given up on him. He wasn't ready to be that brave, though.

To be fair to the guy, none of this was worth the hassle. Geoff had approximately thirty-six months of payments still to make on the car. Legally speaking, the moment he opened his eyes that morning, Vera was no longer his to give away.

'Look just take the keys, huh, and thanks for just standing there and taking the time. Seriously. Appreciated. I'm not being sarcastic here. Parked about four hundred yards thataway.'

Geoff directed a thumb over his shoulder before tossing the key in Umbrella Man's direction with his other hand. The key's trajectory formed a gentle arch. The man, reflexively, relinquishing his two-handed grip of the umbrella, snatched the key out of the air with a flourish. So that's how you got past the umbrella, Geoff thought, feeling partially enlightened.

Geoff didn't wait for a response. He brushed his way past. All that mattered to him now was to put as much space between him and man and umbrella as possible. From behind him, he got his response anyway. It was the sound of a car key on the way down, hitting the metal gridlines that form part of the roadside drain. He heard the bounce-bounce-clatter that signalled further descent. Going all the way. He kept walking, shoulder joints popping. It was as much as he could do to brace himself for the final hurrah. He didn't hear the splash behind him that signalled rock bottom, or whatever they called the lowest point of a drain.

An unedifying spectacle Plan B may have been, Plan C was by comparison an unmitigated fucking disaster. Despite all this, because of all this, brewing away in his dislodged brain was Plan D. He was stuck. He was sinking. He still believed the earth was flat. While there was a way, and the clock was still ticking, there was time for Plan D. Geoff hadn't got as far in the world of banking as he had in a relatively short time (he could afford a flat in Leytonstone after all) without having a Plan D. He'd love to say Plan D was a place, a location, a calling, but the reality was that this was another half-baked notion sluggishly pieced together in his mind. First thing first, he set himself the task of a brisk ten to fifteen-minute forage off High Road, leading him to the gentrified embrace of Bushwood. That would do for now.

It occurred to him that this would be the last time he'd walk through London, and only this part of London. East London caught in the shadow of proper London, the centre of London. It was *too* East. He couldn't help but mentally demarcate; to dwell on the variances. There seemed no life to the buildings around him, like they were paintings. The sound of traffic coming from the main road was noise trapped inside his head. He was originally from Blackburn, Lancashire. When he first arrived, everything seemed so new and shiny. You could tell straight away that this was where the wealth was. It was on the roads, in the infrastructure, there were diamonds in the hedgerows. Every car was less than three years old. The reasoning was if you were seventy grand in debt then another twenty on top really didn't matter. The prospect of a last day on earth didn't change anything. Except for the need for monthly health checks, sometimes weekly, dependent on proportion of debt set against income; the taking of blood pressure and testing of reflexes. Sessions increasing in frequency to one every second day was not unheard of. It wasn't important he was part of the London sprawl. It appealed to his nature, his sense of being. It was a beautiful, gargantuan thing to be part of.

Twenty-nine was so fucking young. He didn't feel like he was a whole person, not yet. He hadn't earned it. Hadn't lived a life, built a legacy; wasn't even sure what they meant by this. He hadn't existed long enough to have a lifetime of regret. And yet here he was, the opposite of feeling special. He couldn't jump the queue. Dare he even think it—the feeling that London had let him down.

Geoff realised his face was wet and this wasn't all down to the intermittent rain. He became aware there was a whine emanating from his lips. Nothing too loud or obvious; it wasn't the sound a cat made when you stepped on its tail, or when thrown against a wall. He felt the weight of injustice coming down hard on his chest and shoulders, beating the spiritual shit out of him. He was pissed off, seeing red, ready to grab someone by the throat, ready to kill someone. Although given current developments, chances were he'd be the one who ended up murdered.

Unless of course there was a murder pact to be arranged. The notion violently, appropriately enough, took hold of him. He faced some flats, cupping his hands around his mouth. 'Anyone going to die today,' he hollered, a little surprised at the deepness of his voice. 'If so, I have a proposition for you. Honest I won't bite—unless you want me to.'

There was no answer. Not that he expected one. All the windows remained unopened. He started laughing; guffawing with such force he took bites out of the air. It left him feeling breathless in no time at all.

He wasn't hysterical, not yet, in as much as he could still self-diagnose himself. In as much as his survival instincts had kicked in, instructing him on the need to keep his act together. His survival instincts, he thought, the good this would do him. He remembered a feature on the news, a study into futile suicide attempts. Each case was depressingly similar in a harrowing way. Utilising various firearms, they'd shot themselves at close range, in the head, around the mouth, but crucially not on their Last Day. Timing was everything. Not to die, the intervention of fate, matters not going according to plan, although quite a few ended up in a vegetative state. It was never a case of cheating death—that was never on the cards. Now Geoff was questioning how he would die. Now he was thinking he didn't want to know the answer. He waved at a street CCTV camera which was hanging over him. He put his hands in empty pockets. Head down, leaning forward, shoulders hunched like the condemned man he surely was, he resumed walking.

When the mood took him Geoff would show an interest in what his colleagues at the bank were up to. In the absence of any meaningful domestic setup to call his own he'd happily indulge in small talk. He'd make the odd enquiry: 'Living with anyone?' 'Kids?' 'Problematic father-in-laws?' 'Looking forward to your nephew's birthday party?' He'd keep it superficial, no real interest in scratching below the surface, but still the basics were always good to know. He liked to think this meant he was off the hook, there was no pressure. The fact everyone else was getting on with their lives meant that he didn't have to.

One of his colleagues was Simon Fletcher, usually shortened to Si. Si worked alongside Geoff in Compliance, who he discovered—while chatting at a crappy work do which dispersed on cue at 8.30 p.m.—had a husband, who was a junior doctor, euphemistically referred to as 'between jobs.' They had two young kids. As it happened they lived pretty damn close to Geoff. A twenty-minute or so walk away. He'd taken a look; the width of half a fingertip on Google Maps.

Outside the rituals of hello and cheerio, they'd only talked a couple of times, but that was enough for Geoff to pick up on something; something underlying; something that most definitely scratched beneath the surface. Si seemed happy enough with his life, loved his family. However, there was the time when Geoff reflected, not triumphantly, on a world of drink and knock-backs, punctuated by an indeterminate number of hangovers and broken promises. In response there was a glimmer to be found in Si's eye. Barely susceptible, but there it was all the same. It was as if part of him was envious of Geoff; resentful of the trappings of an obviously throwaway life. It stirred up feelings of nostalgia inside him just maybe for wilder days. It didn't mean Si was about to do anything drastic—he had responsibilities, he had ties—but Geoff was sure there was an aspect of him, a longing; a feeling that refused to be banished at least completely. He hadn't fully turned his back on those crazy drug and alcohol-fuelled times (Geoff assumed booze and drugs were involved; made more sense than carrot juice and strawberry and banana smoothies). And perhaps, just perhaps, if the opportunity arose, like the opening of a vault, maybe on his last day on earth for example, then he owed it to himself, or that part of himself, to be prepared. Or at least to keep his options open—even though, really, years ago, he'd well and truly left that old life behind. To have something stashed away. A mattress fund, even.

There was a word; it had been used by one of them. He couldn't remember who had said it, not that this mattered. At a work night out Geoff would drink as much as the rest of his team put together. It wasn't difficult. Si in comparison, nursing a vodka and coke, was a figure of nervy restraint. It was a word, a throwaway word, as inoffensive as words go. One of them said it and as a result they exchanged glances. For a brief moment, so brokered between them, there was a shared understanding. There was a common bond.

'Shoebox.'

That was then. This was now. With no further verbal outbursts to his name, Geoff arrived at his destination on foot. A Bushwood residence situated in the middle of a row of semi-detached houses, modern brickwork; a much nicer place than his, must have cost an absolute fortune. Valuations so high, if the streets were paved with gold it wouldn't make a blind bit of difference to the property prices.

Geoff knocked on Si's door. As knocks on the door went, these were loud and purposeful, but he hoped didn't come across as too loud or too purposeful. A stabbing pain emerged in his ribs. It was a stitch from walking, not having walked far, but evidently far enough. It occurred to him maybe his problem was congenital, nestling there, insidious, a Trojan horse placed from birth. He could be like one of those marathon runners who inexplicably dropped dead in their prime.

Maybe he had a bad heart. Destined to amount to nothing much at all. Maybe he should have taken more time to have more health checks. But, come on, he wasn't spineless. Not some hypochondriac. He was too young to harbour serious thoughts of mortality. He could go and see a doctor, but where would that get him? Aged twenty-nine and no ties, nothing to show for it. None of us wanted to grow old. Some of us didn't have to.

Everything was old for its time, especially his surroundings. The Romans had built this town, but it wasn't resistant to the onset of time; brittle, long tarmacked over. The streets were built on the roots of trees that had nowhere to go except through concrete. The streets were built on Roman dust.

It was Si who answered the door. The first thing he noticed was Geoff's suit, showing signs of damp especially around the shoulders. This wasn't the only thing that alerted him that something was up. He stared at the bedraggled, dank figure standing on his doorstep. A man up until now he only recognised from work.

'Isn't it Tuesday?' he asked. To underline the point, he directed a finger towards his chin, which he stuck out for added emphasis.

In their conversations, as sparse and routine as they were, in return for modest tales of Si's domesticity, Geoff would repay in kind, divulging personal nuggets such as shaving on a Tuesday—and only on a Tuesday, every Tuesday without fail. Today was Tuesday. The radio had confirmed as much when Si woke that morning. Si also recognised week old stubble when he saw it.

'Can I be straight with you?' Geoff said. 'Not been myself lately. Honest, mate, head's all over the place.'

This was indeed a Tuesday and Geoff was unshaven. Si was unshaven, too. The comparisons didn't end there. In terms of body type they were pretty similar.

Geoff grabbed Si by the throat, using his bulk deceptively well to push him back into the hall. There was no feeling in Geoff's hands, but he could tell from

Si's reaction that the power and severity of the grip had surprised him. Geoff's whole demeanour reeked of desperation. He shoved Si against the wall.

Fuck morality. Fuck taboos. Fuck your nan's car. Fuck the right thing to do. What use was any of this to a dying man?

'I'm scared,' Geoff said, deeming some kind of explanation necessary.

Si tried to push back too many times, repeatedly having to adjust the position of his hands, losing vital momentum.

Geoff never lost focus. 'I know you have kids, let's not involve them, huh?' he said. 'You have something I need, under a mattress, in a shoebox. This is my Last Day; for me there's no going back.'

'Please…'

Si put both hands up in a show of supplication. Geoff acknowledged this by releasing his grip. Adam's apple set ablaze, Si massaged his throat, using both hands coming in from both sides. He fought a cough, conscious of the fresh wave of pain such a thing would elicit.

Geoff wanted to give his work colleague some space. He took a step back. Up on his heels, he peered over Si's shoulder. The front door held his gaze, standing ajar, adjacent to the bottom of the stairs. He hoped the worst was over. He hoped that normality would now impose itself. Si would lead him up the stairs and reveal the bounty that was his secret stash. He'd be at the Church in no time at all.

'Look, I'm sorry I came on so strong,' Geoff said, trying to smile, mouth crooked as if he had broken teeth. He was at a loss as to what else to do.

Si was down to a single hand massaging his throat.

Geoff braced himself for some harsh words, he'd give him that, but Si had to come around. He just had to. He was out of options. Only in the final moments did he realise Si was peering over his shoulder, too.

A knife went through Geoff. It was a knife in the back. Seized by momentum, but strangely no pain, body stricken, hands flapping, he fell forward. Si, returned to employing both hands, pushed Geoff back as way of an automatic response.

Geoff's body flipped the other way, before slamming down back first on the floor. He still had the strength if not the poise to keep his frame tensed; still alert despite the pain that shot through him.

Si's husband Sofiane peered over him. He had the face of someone crazed, someone frightened out of his mind. There were two of him. Geoff was seeing double, he decided. The thought process bequeathed him a welcome if short-lived diversion from the pain.

From Sofiane, at least from one of him, his expression had now lessened in severity into something humane. 'The children,' he said in hushed tones. He was still leaning, staring. It was ridiculous. The whole scene played out in Geoff's addled brain like something out of an old Agatha Christie movie.

Si took control of the situation, giving orders, careful not to raise his voice too loud. 'Sofi, go back and check on the kids. Don't let them see this. Phone the police, then an ambulance.'

Geoff was now feeling numb all over. It was like the lack of feeling was catching. It was contagious. The outside world, the environment that surrounded him, seemed so very far away. It was as if the blood had flown from his brain, but if this was the case he didn't want to think where it could possibly have gone to. The adrenaline coursing through his body, instrumental in helping him see out his last few dreadful, pitiful minutes, was no longer in plentiful supply.

His vision was shot, hyperopic, but he convinced himself he could still make out the end of the hall. And next to the front door, situated there, an achingly familiar purple light. He was certain this would be the last thing he'd see and couldn't decide whether to regard it as poetic or a plain kick to the balls. He fought to hold onto the thought, as imbecilic as it was, knowing that with its passing he'd be gone too. He didn't see the need to say anything, grimacing ever so slightly, conscious of his failing, dying body shutting down, falling back in tiny increments against the handle of the knife still lodged in his back. He experienced the sensation of floating over a cold wooden floor. There was no carpet, he suddenly realised for no particular reason.

There really was no excuse, unless of course there was an excuse. He groaned out loud before lamenting the act as such a waste of energy. So many haphazard thoughts, half-shaped and achingly familiar, fighting for attention in his head. He thought of his personal trainer outside the gym who ignored him when he said hello in the middle of the street. He thought of the morning while walking to work, some random guy in his twenties shouting out to him without provocation from the other side of the street, calling him a wanker. For the first time in many years he thought of his granddad who died from a stroke. A stroke from God, so his nan called it. Jumbled thoughts continued like a disturbed beehive;

like microwaved kernels transformed into projectiles of puffed up corn. Of the time he didn't spot another car indicating a left turn at a roundabout, ending in a dented right rear door for his trouble. Having sex with Brenda, culminating in the shooting of lifeless sperm inside her. He had been tested for it; he'd been tested for everything. He had a low, next to negligible sperm count, as lifeless as the rest of him.

'No need for an ambulance,' he said, his mouth feeling squishy, rubbery, tasting of copper coins. The damp had spread under his skin. He couldn't be sure if Si, or anyone, was still with him. His eyes were struggling to take in his surroundings. All he could see were dark flaps like burning paper, which amounted to seeing nothing at all. 'No point,' he wheezed.

The tension had left his body entirely. He lay back uncoiled and flat against the handle, the blade having followed through, nicking his heart. He opened his eyes wide, a final cursory act. The terror of certainty.

Still aware of it across the hall, where it had tormented him, now it seemed to beckon him, the light at the end of a tunnel. A panel attached to a wall next to the front door. The light that was the *Light*.

He expected to see lilac, wanted to bathe in it, for it to carry him along, was completely at ease with this. Instead, in his mind, it was violet, which flooded what remained of his ruined optics, the colour of beautyberries.

'That's so…'

Si was still there; close enough to catch Geoff's whisper. Instinctively he bent his knees, lowering himself, answering the alluring call of a man's last words.

There was silence. That might have been it, Si

thought, ears attuned to another man's destructions. It was a fitting epitaph, perhaps. Broken words from a broken man.

'…certain,' the whisper continued after an elongated pause, accompanied by a gasp, barely passing muster as a last breath, but would have to suffice.

No one should die alone.

That was Geoff's Last Day. There was no better way of describing it. It had come to an end.

3

First Day On Earth

There has never been a popular saying ending with the words 'as reliable as the World Death Clock.' To be fair, up until one day in 1998 it was pretty spot on, not too shoddy, projecting the death rate around the world for every day of every month of every year. Consistently clocking off at the one-hundred-and-fifty-thousand-mark, year by year, on an upward trajectory. Always in line, the more born on the planet, logic and genome dictated, the more will die. You couldn't expect an exact figure, but something to the nearest thousand was pretty damn accurate. Every tick and every tock announced another swing of the scythe from the Grim Reaper. The World Death Clock, you could swear by it.

At least you normally could.

As has always been the case, it is the living who are left to come to terms with death. Some angry and devastated that a life should ever come to an end; others grateful for the blessed finality of it all. Some in denial, while for others something to be quickly negotiated and thankful for. The way we react to something as predictable as death was unpredictable. In Thailand, one hundred days of mourning were declared for the dead king, while on the same day, in another part of the world, a nameless baby daughter was abandoned to a ditch in Xixiashu. They died before their time and yet reason determined it could never be anything but their time. This was an essential fact, this was how death worked. It was an end. It was *the* end.

There was the afterlife, of course; various ideas of god, heaven, and hell thrown into the mix to muddy the waters. From time immemorial, there has been always been the question of faith. This time was no different. What was conclusive was the event that took place on the 7th of January, 1998. That's when the World Death Clock lost its shine. That was the day the nature of death was changed forever.

Ironically, up until that point, it was the question of birth rate that got everyone in a tizz. Here was a world petrified by the prospect of unchecked population growth. A case of human beings complaining about other human beings whose crime was the audacity of having being born. Population levels in 1998 were close to the six billion mark, estimated to grow by a quarter in twenty years. As soon as we arrived, from the first baby reflex motion, the first flop of the head, some anonymous statistician was already charting our departure. Mortality rates—investment streams predicated on how long you might live for—were big business. Once the world got over the shock of your being born, it was the milieu of death that took main billing. Perhaps the fascination with birth was not so ironic after all. You couldn't have one without the other.

1998 also signalled, incidentally, the arrival of the Nokia 6120 and Google.

It was a Fleming—but not the famous one who invented penicillin—who first sliced the world into time zones. Sir Sanford Fleming came up with the concept; you could be standing somewhere and at the same time somewhere else in the world would be eight hours behind or six hours in front. The workings of the world punctuated by two dozen midnights. And in 1998, the spectre of death, like the elongated shadowy fingers of Nosferatu, stretched across the world in a way that was unprecedented. As much as three million worldwide died that day, beginning with the Polynesian kingdoms of Samoa and Kiribati, through to the very last time zone, Baker Island, set adrift of the outlying United States.

Forty days of death rolled into one. Five and a half million souls. The equivalent of the total population of Denmark or Paraguay.

It measured in the tens in Tonga, unusually high. A woman died of haemophilia. A man died of old age in his sleep. There was a case of accidental poisoning. On a global scale, not earth shattering, not illuminating, but without the first snowflakes there could never be an avalanche.

Both New Zealand and Australia had their own quintessential disasters in the shape of earthquake and plane crash respectively. Coming in, the first reports of people having lost the sensation of touch in their feet and hands. Death from natural causes was unnaturally high. There were several incidents of fatal dog attacks.

The same day; a new set of crises. In Japan, a spike in deaths due to stomach cancer; starvation in North Korea; malignant neoplasms in South Korea. Around the same time, truly upsetting news stories were emerging; an awareness in people that they were about to die. Financial soothsayers warned of runs on the banks; markets susceptible to collapse. On a global scale, anxiety and fear piled up on anxiety and fear.

When China woke up, all bets were off. It was at this point that commentator Al Baumann infamously remarked that 'the 糞 had hit the fan'.

Infectious and parasitic diseases, rampant bird flu, an attempted military coup, purging of prison populations, diseases of the ear and mastoid process. Bodies piled up high on the sides of roads. Baumann would later go on to comment, which some found confusing at the time, 'death does not do irony.' But the more the phrase was repeated, by him and others besides, the more sense it began to make.

Circulatory diseases, natural disasters, stillbirths, acts of genocide, terrorism, fatal accidents, being struck by lightning. Nepal, India, Pakistan, Russia, Europe. Border conflicts, air pollution, endocrine, nutritional and metabolic diseases, complications during pregnancy, the extreme cold. South America, Canada, USA. Cancer of all kinds, respiratory diseases, victims of gun crime, skin disease, exposure to narcotics and hallucinogens, traffic accidents, hypothermia, snowslides. State-sponsored executions. A spate of fatal stab wounds to the neck.

It was a tidal wave. And yes, people died as a result

of tidal waves. In terms of cause it wasn't as if death had reinvented itself, but in terms of effect it was seismic. The usual instances of death applied, but to every forty instead of one. To this day, experts still collate data; constantly revisiting, endlessly revising; going back to the start of it all. A start with a time, location, and date, which was twelve midnight in Kiribati on the 7th January 1998.

'That was the day,' they'd say looking back and everyone knew what they meant by this. 'That was the day.'

People were quick to ask the question. Commentators would ask why death was behaving in such a way, phrasing the query as if they expected an answer. It was as if death was announcing a new radical way of doing things. Death was always a player. Now it seemed intent on becoming an even bigger one. It got greedy. It wanted a larger slice of the cake. As for the citizens of the world, what were they to do? They were unprepared. A few intrepid souls apart, no one was ready for death. When you pared it down, stripped out the criss-crossing lines of mess and confusion, boiled it down to the basic ingredients, nothing had changed even though everything had changed.

Not measured in terms of twenty-four but of twenty-six; the sum total of time zones that make up the day, such were the vagaries awaiting you, stretching from one point on the globe all the way round as you crossed countries, borders, and continents. A dozen twice over becomes twice the baker's dozen. But as peculiarities go, this was the least of them.

And the country arguably most affected—that felt it deepest—was France, taking into account the overseas territories which covered twelve separate time zones. Twelve Maginot Lines in total for death to lumber across.

The global economy relied on people acting in a certain way, markets following tried and tested parameters, but death was not behaving. It was disastrous. The dying emptied the banks and the living clamoured to take what was left. The financial markets collapsed. People took to the streets. It was inevitable, flawlessly predictable, that rioting would follow on a global scale, seemingly without end. Not that the world's security forces escaped unscathed, the prospect of looming death did not discriminate in this respect. It punched a hole through them, too.

The great serpent Ouroboros spanning continents swallowed itself, and then coughed itself back up only to devour itself once again. Looking down from space, if you squinted hard enough you could see a world mottled with fiery dots. It was only a matter of time before they were joined.

Was this how it was to be? If the apocalypse was to arise from something, then why not this? On the back of a worldwide phenomenon where members of the human race wake up one morning to find staring back at them their imminent demise? Not a bang, but a whimper—but a wave of them—a well of tears. Cockroaches were on standby, ready to inherit the earth a little earlier than planned.

It seemed that way. Betting odds on the end of the word were slashed, which begged the question, what kind of person would place a wager on such an outcome? What would they hope to gain?

It was only then—at that point—that something

wonderful happened. Something truly miraculous, something of wonder. A woman named Jennifer Coutinho walked into her local Baptist church in Kalamazoo, Michigan, carrying in her arms her dying baby.

She hadn't walked far in the biting cold, but far enough for her hands to tremble. She sat on the third last pew of an otherwise empty church. It was a Wednesday, the early hours, and her part of the world was stirring to life. Everyday things, contours and ships, were shifting, sharpening.

She was dignified and silent. The baby, named Daniel, only a few days old, was wrapped tight in an off-white shawl. His breathing was rasp, erratic; an insufficient presence, unable to form an echo to reverberate through the chamber. She tried to get her baby to suckle from the teat, but the child was struggling to drink. Mother's milk simply dribbled out of his mouth. She gently rested her pinkie on his bottom lip and hoped she wasn't imagining his breath on her finger.

A member of the church staff named Eric approached mother and baby. He did not recognise her as a regular worshipper, but could tell that something was wrong. 'Can I help you?' he said. This close, this still, he picked up on the ragged breathing. 'The child, does it require medical attention?'

Jennifer stared at the man. Their eyes met but she did not motion to speak. To Eric she appeared in a blissful state and he immediately suspected she was taking drugs. He waited some moments longer and was about to ask the question again when she responded. Her words were measured, not slurred. Eric relaxed at this and smiled a smile of reassurance. He did what anyone would do who prided themselves as a good listener.

She told him that an angel had come to her that night in a dream. She knew he was an angel even though his features were obscured, enshrouded in a ball of light. The light was intense. She could not tell if it was blinding as she had no desire to gaze in its direction. She didn't have to look at it to know it was there.

The angel told her that death intended to take her baby. With baby Daniel's fate set, there was nothing she could do to prevent or frustrate the course of events. But what she did have was the gift of one last day to spend with her child as she saw fit.

Was she only dreaming? It was unlike anything she had dreamt before. So vivid, so powerful, it was as if some of the light had snaked around and entered her, spread inside of her, filling her up with a kaleidoscope of emotions, raw and distilled, personal, beyond easy recognition. Her every nerve was a tripwire. She harboured no compulsion to view angel and message as anything but the truth.

Awake, she then decided to enter the church and spend what little time she had with her baby boy in a place where she hoped she would not be disturbed. 'A place of peace,' she said. She was not especially religious and could understand why people feel uneasy and take exception to a place such as this. But on the occasions she had cause to enter the church, she'd found it comforting. She'd found it safe.

Eric had been a church custodian too long to be easily shocked, but the strength of conviction in the woman's voice was something he had rarely heard, not even within the church's hallowed walls. Gently but assertively, he questioned her further, tried to persuade her to take action, but throughout she sat completely still. There was a small cry from the baby which caused her to adjust position slightly to rock her son. He settled quickly, but the intermittent breathing remained; there was always the breathing.

Eric, dictated by conscience and a sense of public duty, phoned the cops. They responded within the hour. But it was a small town, closely-knit when the mood took it, and word got out. Meanwhile, the strange phenomenon involving death was well underway, threatening to push the world to the brink. Rumours were rife. Uncannily accurate accounts of what was happening swept the earth, quickly followed by appallingly inaccurate ones. Panic in its purest and most unadulterated form had set in. And yet there was something in stark contrast about Jennifer and baby Daniel's story which struck a chord. Perhaps its only purpose was to act as a diversion. A thing of whimsy. Perhaps something in her frankly fantastical account of an encounter in a dream with an angel fascinated a populace facing up to something new and terrifying with no rational explanation close at hand. Nothing terrestrial; nothing to call their own.

'Where is God?' someone screamed in Buenos Aires for hours on end.

For many, Jennifer's story resonated. People needed something to believe in. If not an outright miracle, something they could at least equate with a miracle.

By the time the police arrived outside the church in Kalamazoo a crowd had already gathered.

For the most part, the crowd remained outside the

church. An occasional caller would walk in to offer hushed words of support; to perhaps glean some wisdom from mother or in some cases (admittedly a tiny minority) baby. No one stayed long. It was as if Jennifer and Daniel had become an enlightening force, transcendent, other-worldly. Their presence quickly took on the form of something oppressive and overwhelming, igniting a desire to not outstay your welcome and rejoin the growing masses outside. A vigil had formed and the police, also growing in numbers, kept to the sidelines, attention split between the woman and child within and the makings of a potential mob without. If reports were to be believed, this was the only church not stuffed to the aisles with humanity, as elsewhere, apostates turned true believers.

Word spread like wildfire, piercing the crowd, that the cops fearing for the baby's safety were about to storm the church. Civilians in response started emptying their pockets, picking up stones and bottles, whatever they could lay their hands on. Some had guns, which remained concealed for now. Whatever it took to protect sanctity of mother and child. The authorities had undergone a change, too, having somewhere along the way acquired full riot gear.

A voice rose above the din, yelling, booming, causing everyone to stop in their tracks. 'They got tear gas, they got tear gas!'

'They got tears!'

Inside the church, baby Daniel's heart stopped. It took a few moments for his mother to be sure he had stopped breathing, then for the grief to strike. Her chest tightened, stomach convulsed, she gasped for air around her that no longer seemed in ready supply. But she never cried out. She just needed a moment to remind herself, knowing her sweet baby could not be saved, that this was the path she had chosen.

She placed her hand on Daniel's cheek. He seemed so tiny. He was still warm. 'My beautiful baby boy, so grateful,' she said. She kissed his cheek. 'For this precious day.'

Outside, it was like everyone had a shared experience. Everyone took stock. The consequence of following any other course of action was too daunting, too oppressive. Calm was restored, positions were maintained.

It was four hours before midnight on the First Day on earth. Helicopters flew overhead, carrying camera crews in their bellies.

All eyes fell on the church exterior, which now commanded a captive world audience. Where previously there was only despair, if not hope there was now something else. The crowd had grown; a burgeoning bustle of race, age, and gender, filling the whole of West Michigan Avenue, pushing out, a diaspora, an urban sprawl. Local people gave out food and water. They handed out clothing to others not equipped for the dipping temperatures.

Nightfall descended and tightened its grip. From above, helicopter searchlights reached down to streetlights which combined to shed light on the behemoth below, otherwise subdued and engulfed in the steady darkness.

A man in the crowd keeled over clutching his chest and people reacted, rushing to his side. Someone grabbed his hand and he responded with some last words of his own. 'It's cool, man,' he said. 'I just knew. Really glad to be here.'

Others watched on, stunned, mouths wide, tears in their eyes, some with clenched fists. There had been numerous false starts, but no one was sure which way the mood might turn.

A police lieutenant, who could no longer stand the tension, shouted into a loudspeaker. 'What do you want?' He repeated, upping the amplification, even though it wasn't needed. 'What do you want?'

No one had an answer.

Word came down from someone high up in authority. It sparked and fused and filled the air. 'For the love of God, don't engage with the mob—I repeat do not engage…'

By midnight, it was a case of more and more, who hailed from far and wide, just to be part of it. An influx of Exodus proportions. Previous rumours surrounding Daniel's passing were officially confirmed. The crowd stood silently, not wanting to move, not wanting to have to make a decision.

To be there was enough, even though the majority were situated miles away from the church, such was the size of the gathering. The global television and social media audience counted in the hundreds of millions, soon to be billions; viewers taking solace from the permanence of the picture of a church standing on solid ground with the knowledge of a grieving mother inside. The stillness of the moment reflected back at them perfectly, an image of immobility.

'We're all in this together,' a voice piped up, reverberating from somewhere, picked up by a nearby microphone. Multiple ears pricked up at the sound, but the spell remained unbroken. The vigil continued.

All around there were tendrils, shockwaves stretching from the epicentre to the four corners of the globe. The fact was that people were dying and kept on dying.

Journalist Heather Carlson steeled herself. Earlier she had sought out the local library, sourcing a reference book which included designs of local churches. She found what she was looking for. Always looking to go against the trend, she took it upon herself to seek out a little-used side portal, not wanting to attract unwanted attention in the act of entering the church. She passed a small anteroom where a man was kneeling, eyes closed and lips moving furiously. Moving into the main part of the church, she saw Jennifer seated, her eyes shut as well. She was clutching baby Daniel. Both mother and child seemed impossibly still, caught in time, like a photograph. Heather edged a little closer, but her footsteps, elevated by the acoustics, gave her away.

Jennifer's head moved, her eyes opened, as she immediately awoke. She couldn't have been sleeping long. 'You got the time?' she said, not missing a beat.

'Ten minutes past the hour,' Heather said, before hurriedly adding, 'Midnight, the hour is midnight.'

'While I was sleeping—oh, I only closed my eyes for a minute—the angel spoke to me.'

From Heather there was a sharp intake of breath, which seemed to her, even as she was doing it, a ridiculous thing to do. She tried to hide it, stymie it, but you couldn't conceal anything, not in this place where every sound above a whisper was made a prisoner. 'Jennifer, what did he say?'

'He told me I was going to be taken, same as my baby, same rules. That's how it goes. If it's to be my last day, I can do what I want. Do as I please.' As she spoke there was a quiet, steely determination about her. She chose her words like she had all the time in the world. She wasn't going anywhere. 'Can I … I know this sounds crazy. Please, can I touch your face?'

'Way I see it,' Heather said, 'it's the rest of the world that's turned crazy. You're the only sane one left.'

Heather did as Jennifer asked. Still on her feet, she placed a hand on the back of the pew shifting her weight forward. She stretched her neck muscles.

Jennifer reached out, shifting position, holding Daniel in close with her other arm. She rested her hand on Jennifer's cheek, her thumb stroking her face. 'I can see you. You are very beautiful. But I can't feel your face,' she said. 'I can't feel a thing.'

Jennifer leaned forward a little more, causing Daniel to slip out of his shawl. She quickly reacted, wrapping him back up. His lips had turned dark blue.

'It was before.' Effortlessly, given the circumstances, she flashed the journalist a smile. 'Yesterday. I put my hand on my baby's cheek and left it there feeling his warmth slowly be taken from me. It's a blessing, don't you think, to have hands that no longer feel?' Her eyes never seemed more alive, more full of hope. 'I don't want to go. I don't want to leave here. I want to stay and be with my Daniel.'

What was it to be a journalist named Heather Carlson? To be present in a near-empty church (one remarkable thing in an endless chain of remarkable events)? In a time of tumultuous and terrifying change, she found herself alongside the person of the moment. This was a woman with the world's eyes on her. And by way of one last uncharacteristically civilised act, the world had kept a respectful distance.

How had it come to this? How had Heather Carlson earned this? She was with the *Chicago Sun*, no longer a junior reporter, but still the conviction gnawing away at her that the assignments she was given were something of an afterthought.

She was nothing special. She hadn't changed the world. She didn't enjoy the taste of alcohol in any form, in fact she detested it, which made her unique among her peers. Still, this was her defining moment. She had walked into the church where more seasoned reporters had not (and there were plenty of them around on the ground and in the air).

Afterwards, the reasons offered from those reporters to explain the oversight (if that's indeed what it was) were plentiful. They didn't think they'd be able to get in (there were a lot of riot cops around). They were ordered to hang back by news agencies not wanting to break the moment. To let things be, not break the spell, now *that* was the story. They didn't want to risk the world's ire by being the one who interrupted a mother's grief. Simply put, they were experiencing what everyone else was feeling—a need to be there, but not too close. It was as if the stakes were that high. It was a chance of a lifetime, any lifetime, to come close enough to God; to comprehend life, the meaning of existence, through the prism of death. Why all things must die. On a basic level, even for the most grizzled of world-weary journos, it was overwhelming. It was Millennium hysteria come two years early. It was the big question—too big, too much for any one individual to deal with.

One could offer a multitude of reasons. A multitude of sins. The truth was no one knew why they did it, or more to the point why they didn't do it. At the time they couldn't make sense of it. It was only after the event that they were able to piece it together, and in so doing piece themselves together. And that was a story in itself. It added to the mythos where the predatory tendencies of journalists were stripped bare and everyone shied away.

Everyone bar one.

It was Heather Carlson who did not look away.

'Jennifer,' she said, 'you can stay here as long as you want. I'll set everyone straight.'

'You promise?'

'I promise.'

It was well after midnight. It was the start of the second day on earth. Heather, fingers pressed so tight, reached out for a moment. She considered touching the woman's shoulder, but just as quickly dismissed the notion, awkwardly withdrawing her hand. She had nothing more to say and so extracted the rest of her, never to look back.

Heather took the most expedite route, walking out the church's front doors, so announcing her presence to an unsuspecting world. Instantly, she regretted not taking more time. It would take more than a deep breath to properly compose herself. She wanted to pop back into the church and only come out again when she was ready. But with the eyes of the world on her, as unreal a situation as it was, this was not a realistic option.

She looked out onto a crowd of epic proportions and

could not see an end to it. Hundreds of booms, mikes, and cameras like pop-ups from a children's book, never-ending, were thrust in the air. Accompanying flashlights took a firm grip of the ether, creating a retina-skewing, shifting landscape. She spoke coherently, although it was unlikely her voice carried far. She had no idea how long her pauses were between sentences (she never listened back to the recordings). Still, she had promised. She would see this through.

'My name is Heather Carlson. The reason I'm here … It is my privilege. The woman I just met is the most extraordinary person I have met in my life.'

'As you know earlier tonight, before midnight, baby Daniel died. Mother has asked to be left alone. You've respected her wishes. Now I must tell you, I don't quite know how to tell you, but tonight, the early hours of a new day, she is dying as well. Yes, I … dying. She wishes to be left with her Daniel in this church in Kalamazoo. She believes this to be her right.'

'This is her right; her privilege. A loving mother and citizen of the world. This is her Last Day and she knows this to be true. This is the path she has chosen for herself.'

'So please respect her wishes. Give her some space. Her name is Jennifer. Everyone go home—I'm going home—and leave her the fuck alone.'

It was the second day on earth. Death having announced its transformation in a massive way now reverted back to normal figures—but never to return to *normal* normal.

That was 1998, the beginning of it all, where everyone would know on the day of their death that they were going to die. Vivid dreams, a premonition, would announce someone's Last Day. For those who did not die in their sleep, they'd wake with a lack of feeling in the palms of the hands and soles of the feet.

There were still exceptions to the rule. There were false alarms. There the ones caught unawares, insensitive to their external and internal environments, failing to pick up on the signs. It would take another five years to see a massive step in removing such anomalies and ambiguities with the release of the first batch of household Verification Units, colloquially referred to as the *Light*.

Back then, if the world was facing a turning point, it had now turned back. The revelation that Jennifer was dying too—a day after her child—offered an outlet, a process, a platform for the world to grieve and heal and adjust.

Some of the Kalamazoo crowd stayed and continued their vigil but the majority followed Heather Carlson's advice and left. Officially, it was pneumonia that took the child. It was a congenital heart condition, an abnormal narrowing of the aortic valve, which took the mother. It was the combination of both that allowed the world to take stock and step back from the abyss.

There was the obligatory head count. A final tally of fatalities was itself inflated by the global rioting sparked off by the First Day phenomenon. Fear of death was the perfect vehicle, a self-perpetuating truth. The irony was not lost on anyone. Nor was the rawness, the brutality, the terrible, gaping sense of loss. An unprecedented spike during peacetime in daily mortality figures, although it could be argued for twenty-four hours the world was at war with itself. Death begot death. It had the final say.

Now the dust had settled, the image of a church in Kalamazoo gave way to more familiar global landmarks on screens. Times Square, the Eiffel Tower, the Taj Mahal, Westminster, the Kremlin, the Forbidden City. But there was nothing reassuring about the familiar. The legacy of Jennifer and Daniel Coutinho was set to continue, no more apparent than their posthumous naming as First Mother and First Child of the fledgling Church of the Last Day. The topography had shifted. The nature of death had changed and the world would never be the same again.

On the third day, life reasserted itself and people buried their dead.

4

Event Horizon

Si lay in bed. He couldn't sleep but was consumed by lethargy. Everything, even the thought of movement, the simple act of shifting position in bed, seemed too much for him. Work had given him two weeks of compassionate leave. At the time his first thought was that he couldn't stay cooped in the house for two days, never mind two of anything else, but still, as of this moment, he couldn't get up on his feet either. To do so constituted in his mind a gargantuan task; unpalatable; unbearable. He was instead inanimate; unresponsive. Pinned down by a cartoon anvil, unfeasibly and comically heavy, centred on his chest. He wanted to twitch his big toe like John Wayne in a film he remembered watching on TV in his youth, where the Duke played an oil rig worker recovering from a near fatal fall, willing life back into dead legs, endlessly repeating the same thing for what seemed like the whole of the movie, '*gonna move that big toe, gonna move that big toe.*' Si wanted to prove that he could do it, but it was as if his mind had pulled down the shutters, protecting him from something. His mind was layered, a ball of iron wool. It took so long to unravel, once done he had forgotten why he had wanted to do something in the first place. Guarding him against his own thoughts and memories. There was something bad lurking not far away, lumbering around the recesses, but that was okay, because the way he was right now, any kind of *far* was far enough.

The *Light*, he thought. Sometime soon, he would have to take the *Light*.

In the meantime, he had done enough to think that he was made of stone; weighted down by imaginary boots filled with concrete. His body was so heavy, so useless, his mind had to detach itself, ascend and become ghost-like. But he couldn't maintain this for long. The higher he soared, the more inevitable the crash to follow. The salt pinprick of the first bead of sweat made itself known on his brow.

Incessant banging came from downstairs. The source was Sofiane no doubt tidying up the tidying up.

There was no hope, no religion, no second opinion, and no referrals. There was only the *Light*. He couldn't focus on anything unless it was right in front of him. Nothing else to look forward to the way things were shaping up, or look back on. But that was Si, a glass half empty kind of guy.

They'd sent the kids, Alex and Julia, away to Brighton

to stay with Sofi's sister. For a couple of days, their home was decreed a crime scene, which meant the adults needed to call in a favour and claim a cousin's boxroom for the duration. Si was surprised at how soon they were allowed back into their own home; was taken aback by how courteous and professional everyone was to them. He shouldn't have expected anything less, but still it was good to see.

Sofi dreaded their return and the state of the house, hallway in particular, which awaited them, but surprisingly there were no nasty surprises. The blood was gone, or at least expunged from that part of the floor they could see.

There was only the *Light*—the *Light* Purple—a chemical process for verification. He was fully aware—how could he not be?—but he wasn't interested. Why bother? What did it matter if he'd see out today or any other day? If not tomorrow then he'd die at some point. He'd cease to be anything; a flatline; a sack of stagnant water. Just like…

…on his back…

It was a little too early—still a little too raw—to think his name.

The police had already indicated a couple of times that it was a cut-and-dried case. Death, the imminent prospect of it, made people crazy. Si and Sofiane were to be commended for dealing the way they did with such a dangerously volatile situation. All Si remembered was a guy from work, who he pushed over. He pushed really hard. He remembered splaying his hands, making them as wide as possible to gain more purchase, to cover as much of the area around his attacker's chest as possible and push all the harder. He remembered how Geoff swayed back; how balletic a moment this was. His mind pictured him falling frame by frame, caught in mid-thought, mid-process. He would have hit reverse it if he knew how to. He would have called it back. Stopped him from falling back onto a big fucking knife. He could not distinguish them. Seamless, conjoined, one action could not exist without the other. The outcome was all the same.

If only he could concentrate better; not let the motion sickness get the better of him. He allowed a living, breathing man into his house and—it didn't matter who—they'd knifed him in the back. This was how Si remembered it. It was clinical and haphazard, jumbled and cold. Context was all in this instance—they were in danger, under attack—but this required a level of thinking that made him want to vomit.

And scream. Vomit and scream.

The *Light* was in the same room as him. There was no escaping it. He'd need to take it—take himself to it. There was something eminently human about taking the *Light* and in so doing finding out the essential fact whether you live or die. But what happened to the ones who didn't want to feel human? Who didn't want to know? Not today, maybe never? What was to be done with them?

He couldn't lie in bed forever. He wasn't even properly tucked in. His feet, big toes and all, were cold, sticking out from under the duvet. Since they'd got back Sofi ruled the downstairs, making the upstairs Si's domain by default. But upstairs only made sense if there was sleeping and lovemaking to be done. These days the former was in short supply and the latter was non-existent (Sofi was sleeping in the kids' room). He couldn't stay in exile forever. That was never his style. He knew he would need to gravitate downstairs at some point.

Decision made, no point drawing it out any further, so up out of bed he got. He dressed quickly. There was one remaining act to be negotiated, though, before he'd leave the relatively peaceful surroundings of his current environment and face the terrors rumbling beneath in the guise of a traumatised and deeply disgruntled spouse.

The *Light*. He was of the opinion the shade he encountered would determine—in addition to the obvious—the type of day he could look forward to. The lighter the hue, the breezier and easier the day which awaited him. He liked to be greeted by lavender or periwinkle, while eggplant or wine, and especially raisin, was a definite no-no. Plum was borderline, not too light, not too dark; nothing much to speak of either way.

He rarely used the one downstairs at the end of the hall next to the front door, referring to it many times over as an unnecessary expense. '*You can never be too careful,*' was the response. '*But we already have the Light in the bedroom,*' he would counter. Didn't they find its presence reassuring to the point it helped them sleep? Wasn't this enough? Wasn't it overkill to have one at opposite ends of a flight of stairs?

The irony was the *Light* situated both upstairs and downstairs suited their current living arrangements; this uneasy peace. The partition of the family home. Even in his present listless state his mind was buzzing.

Being able to take the *Light* on his own terms and in his own space, however forced upon, now took the form of a tiny victory. Such a consideration shouldn't have mattered when compared to the horrific nature of recent events. It was trivial beyond belief and life was too short, but right now this was all Si could think about.

All this thinking, against his better judgement, wasn't getting him anywhere. No longer lying down but still in the bedroom, he took a step to the side and faced the *Light*. He duly deployed his hand, pressing his palm against the screen. It wasn't an action that felt remotely odd to him. He'd been doing it every day for as long as he could remember. In return the *Light* gave him a big tick. It glowed boysenberry.

'At least we're still alive.'

Having made the long climb down, Si stopped short and sat on the third bottom stair. Sofiane was scrubbing the floor in the hall for what seemed conservatively like the hundredth time. As smells went, Si was indifferent to the one of disinfectant, which was just as well. He would have offered to help, but the mood Sofi was in, he'd be instantly rebuffed. One more rejection to join all the others. They weren't in each other's line of sight but were aware of one another, a glimpse to be found in the corners of their eyes. It was enough to hold a conversation.

'We need to move,' Sofi said.

'Move?' Si reacted. 'After all it took to buy this place?'

'We don't do anything here except live and sleep, if you can call it living. We're not happy here, and now we're not even a family. We could go anywhere. Where we are isn't convenient for anyone except you.' Sofi's voice began to fade, but a sudden injection of resolve, and volume, spurred him on. 'It's not suitable for Julia or

Alex.' Sofiane stopped scrubbing the floor. 'What am I saying? They're not here anyway. My sister has them and I don't want them back here.'

While accepting fault lay with him, Si wasn't prepared to convict himself, not quite prepared to put himself in front of a jury. He still couldn't explain why *he* turned up at their house. He didn't know anything about him. He didn't attach any importance to the fleeting conversations they'd had. There was nothing to feel out of place in an otherwise opaque and murky universe. There was the comment about shaving every Tuesday, but that only stood out because he was describing himself and it was such a bloody mundane thing to start with.

There was one other thing, even more trivial, if such a thing was possible. It nagged at him, pinched his temples with no realistic prospect of ever letting go. It came in the form of a single word.

The senseless violence—the horror—could it really all have come down to the utterance of something so innocuous? So insignificant? Something on the lines, maybe, he could neither confirm or deny, of *shoebox*.

That's just preposterous, just crazy, he assured himself. Si craned his neck, allowing him to snatch a proper look at Sofi through the bannisters. 'We can't let this beat us. Come on, how are we to blame here?'

'Wasn't he your friend?'

Tolerance levels breached, the disinfectant fumes began to nip at Si's eyes. 'A work colleague,' he protested. 'It's not as if we…'

'Didn't he say you had something he wanted? Why would anyone say that unless they know you? Was it a … a shoebox?'

66

The word was out and now it didn't appear innocuous at all. It left in its wake a big ugly stain that no amount of bleach could ever wash off.

That was the point that Si walked out the front door. He didn't need to be read fortunes to foresee where the conversation was going, and for him it was inconceivable that any of it could possibly go well. He was out, wearing a plain beige pullover. It was chilly, the dying days of January. Tree branches twitched in the wind, showing Si's big toe how it was done. So much, he decried, for childhood memories of John fucking Wayne.

Preferably, he would have had his fleece along for the ride to bump up the layer count, but that remained upstairs in the house just vacated. The kingdom he had just bequeathed. He looked back forlornly at the front door, now very much closed behind him, and concluded lamentably that this would have to remain the case. There was no going back, not yet at any rate. Thinking about it, he probably needed to cool off, literally as was now the case in the biting cold.

There seemed little prospect of Sofi running after him, either. That may have been Si's style on occasion, but it wasn't Sofi's. There was fifteen years between them and it was the oldest who was the impulsive one.

Si thought he could take the car. This proved a wild thought—another one—as the realisation sunk in the car keys were back in the house. As good as entombed, he lamented.

He walked briskly without much thought for the direction he was taking. He had lived here for two years now, but the well-worn route to Leytonstone tube station (and less often Leytonstone High Road for the

Overground) aside, he didn't know the area at all. Home was very much seen as a base. It amounted to a reasonable commuting distance to One Canada Square for work purposes and a launching pad for all the other places they wanted to be for non-work purposes, but crucially it was never about being *here*. It was public transport on weekdays; car on the weekend for those little breaks away. On his commute he was inward-looking, nose rarely deviating away from his phone; a Spiral G8, top of the range, no less (well, at least it was back in October). He'd look up and occasionally indulge in people watching (fellow passengers only), but seldom if ever to peer out of the window. The outside world held no real interest for him. Which brought him to the present and the realisation let loose on his own two feet if he kept his head down, it wouldn't take him long to get completely lost.

Instinctively he shied away from High Road. Si had a natural aversion to crowds, which was unfortunate because London was chock-a-block, absolutely teeming with humanity. Normally he'd just grit his teeth. He'd reluctantly rub shoulders and block everything out and just get on with it, but not today. Today was different. He was out and about, a cavalier. A free spirit in a brownish yellow pullover.

It wasn't even if Sofi would have the mind to call or text him. Sofi was stubborn. They both were stubborn. Si would declare that his better half was significantly more stubborn than him, sure in the knowledge that Sofi would claim the same about him. As points go it was a moot one anyway, riding on the wave of a familiar theme. He didn't currently have possession of his phone, which resided in the zipped pocket of his fleece back home.

If Sofi did phone and followed the ringtone (currently a rousing refrain of La Marseillaise) it would lead him upstairs, the fallen kingdom, which was nowhere at all.

There was a mental leap as Si's thoughts turned to Geoff—he could say his name now. They turned to the steps Geoff took bringing him closer to his own personal oblivion.

The act of forming his name gave Si a jolt, made him think that maybe he should pay more attention to his surroundings. Here was a place of joined up distances, taking him past a street of plush apartments arranged in octagonal blocks, followed by creaky old houses, remembrance of the old town, facades renovated and buttressed against the weight of time. There followed inelegant, crammed terrace flats displaying evidence of damp, post-industrial, pre-financial, with allegedly real Londoners hidden somewhere inside. He kept on walking in the biting cold, alternating between feeling younger and then much older, immersed in a place of changing and discombobulating landscapes; a city of haves, have-nots, and wouldn't and shouldn't haves.

Could this part of the world be dissected any less effectively, less flimsily? There were threads but they were gossamer. The only detail was surface detail. He was afraid he wouldn't need to look too hard and for too long until he saw the cracks. These were the fault lines. London was coming apart at the seams, this he already knew. He didn't need reminded of the fact. If London was calling—and it was always calling—he wasn't interested in answering.

He made a concerted effort to focus the mind. Acutely aware of the feel of the inside of his jeans against his thighs as he walked. He questioned the whole point of it, quickly concluding any idea of karma or Zen or whatever they called it was overrated. *What kind of hell was this*, he asked himself, *to be so alone with your thoughts.* He passed a row of Bed and Breakfasts. He zigzagged though a traffic island with a blind turn. Navigated a street that reminded him of Bedford Way, up until the point that it didn't. At one juncture, breathing too heavily, conscious of a hollow discomfort in his lungs, he forced himself to slow down. Still, despite himself, he found the unfamiliarity of his surroundings invigorating. His head began to clear. He was finding himself, or so he was telling himself, insisting to himself, and in so doing breaking the spell. *It's just walking,* a voice inside him emerged irritably, determined not to leave any feelings of worthiness unchallenged, *something everyone does all of the time. It's not spiritual. It isn't the equivalent of meeting up for a cup of tea with the Dalai Lama.*

'You're not going to ruin this for me,' he said quietly to himself. The authority in his voice diminished under his laboured breathing. Normally he'd run as way of exercise on a treadmill in a gym. He wasn't a natural walker, at least not by choice.

As he moved against the flow, there seemed to be less people around, but the streetlights, a more regular occurrence, made up for that. The *Light* was everywhere. He wondered if he was supposed to find this reassuring.

He was in his late thirties when he first met Sofi. He was in his late forties now. '*Who are you?*' he asked when he first set eyes on him. '*What are you?*' was Sofi's response. It was a period in Si's life that coincided with a flourishing desire to settle down. It was like pushing a button despatching the hellraising to the past, throwing it down the rubbish chute. He loved Sofi and the kids, but he was only human. He wouldn't go as far as portraying himself the victim, but the occasional recipient of a random flashback. His mind would hark back to those wild nights of yore; the drink, drugs, and flesh. They'd stick in his head, spicing up the domestics when clearing up after breakfast or wrestling with the hoover. The thing was he and Sofi had promised each other, if it came to it, when the time came for either of them, they would see it through together. As a family. And Si was fine with this, more than fine. He couldn't imagine any kind of alternative that came close to this. He had worked too hard to build something worthwhile to then casually piss it away up against a wall.

And yet for all that there was a flip side. Was it so much of a shock for part of him to still hanker after the past? He couldn't expect to wholly erase his former self, especially the mistakes he'd made, the ones he'd learned from, had helped inform him and make him the better man he was now. Nostalgia was fine, remembrances of a past life. So long as he could draw a line, keep the past to the past. So long as he could pull back from it anytime.

The line was blurred the day he acquired a box of thirty-five centimetres long, twenty-five centimetres wide, and thirteen centimetres high, having unburdened it of a pair of trainers. A box then used in the intervening months and years to deposit various amounts of cash. When he had the house to himself, he'd remove the floorboard under the bedside table. He'd carry out the deed, swapping larger denominations for smaller ones, before dropping the box back into the gap. He'd return floorboard, carpet, and table to their original positions with hubby left none the wiser.

So it became a secret. He was afraid of how Sofi would react. Si was deeply unsure himself of his motives why he kept it. It seemed easier at the start just to try to hide it. And like every little, innocuous secret, it grew many arms and legs over the years.

Below the floorboards, the biggest fucking cliché of them all, but it suited him to spend the minimum amount of time necessary deciding on a hiding space.

And he paid the shoebox a visit only sporadically when the opportunity arose, both appeasing and burying the past; the wild man he would never again be, but all the same could not totally give up on.

'Couldn't resist revealing its existence to some non-entity from the bank called Geoff, though, could I?' He was chuntering, which was fine; it was for his ears only. Even though the jury would have to deliberate some more, he still refused to convict himself. 'The fucker who threatened my family.'

'Who bled out in my hall…'

He maintained a comfortable pace, clearing his head only to clutter it up again. He was on a slope, which didn't stop there. It was at the start of a steep hill. It threw him off kilter, but he plodded on regardless, his breathing a little too heavy for his liking. For a moment, he thought *time out*. He'd reached the point where he was ready to retrace his steps (or, more than likely, hail a black cab to take him back home).

Out of the blue, a shiny red Vauxhall Corsa, tyres screeching, drove past him, guzzling up the incline. Si was singularly unimpressed by all the unnecessary squealing. His annoyance didn't begin to subside until the car was swallowed up by the other side of the hill. Before he was even aware that his lips were moving, a '*hmph*' had escaped his mouth. He channelled his irritation and packaged it up, shaping it into the motivation to push on. He'd give himself, maybe, he hadn't fully decided yet, another five minutes, and then that would be it; time to turn back.

Leading with his elbows, he picked up the pace. On the hill he noticed the houses seemed a little larger than usual; Edwardian probably. He decided this was a good time to check out the name of the street, but couldn't locate the street sign. Not that it had ever bothered him up to this point, but it struck him that the street names were never in the place you expected them to be and never in the same position as the one on the street before.

He'd only negotiated a few more steps when another roar announced that the red Corsa was back, this time erupting from the opposite direction. It sped past him, tyres shrieking, dicing the air, if anything more frenetic than before. The few moments it was in his sights, he looked for the driver, but couldn't get a fix on them. With the car's reappearance, Si's irritation returned also. Starry-eyed, having just designated himself as the only lost soul in East London, he didn't appreciate some tosser, confused and bewildered, cutting up and down the streets like a wailing, burning banshee.

It occurred to him that this adventure wasn't turning out to be the wholly karmic, cleansing experience he might have hoped for. Overhead, as if to confirm the change in mood, he noticed black smoke which hung in the sky. The smoke was like ink splashes, spread out and misshapen, hastily dispensed on blotting paper. From the angle, peering up, it appeared to Si like the smoulder was physically attached to the top of the hill, like it belonged there.

He was shaking, but not because of the cold. All he wanted was a sign of life. All he had was smoke. A sign of danger? Of distress? Something gripped him; a fierce, fanciful thought, an agonising need to reach out and help. It didn't matter who he was helping. He continued walking towards the smoke, which continued to dab at the sky. Part of him was repelled by it, so part of him was compelled by it.

He was the light and this was the event horizon.

5

Viking Funeral

Si was sweating now. Much to his alarm and disappointment, he felt the strength give way around his legs. The black smoke continued to preoccupy him. It couldn't have come from the Corsa's exhaust, could it? The car looked too new and shiny to be responsible for such a gloomy discharge. Mind you, the way the driver hurled the thing around, showing it zero respect—no one looked after anything these days—maybe the vehicle, internally at least, had aged before its time.

He placed his hands on the front of his legs, confirming that they weren't in fact made of lead, and kept climbing. He would reach the top, he decided, inspect the smoke, bestow a cursory glance to check that all was well with the world, no doubt uttering a '*tut tut*' along the way. He would then go straight home, not collect two hundred quid for passing go, and while not apologising outright to Sofi for walking out, he'd suggest they order a takeaway. It would be Sofi's choice, knowing that no matter how pissed off he was, he couldn't help but crumble at the reference, however obviously shamefully shoehorned in, to everyone's favourite classic Meryl Streep movie. (Actually, it was no one's favourite—top three, maybe top five—but he had to work with what he had.) It was just a daft couple's thing they shared that reminded them of just that; they were a couple. And Lord knows both of them needed reminding sometimes. On his less than triumphant return, all going to plan, Sofi would unleash a verbal onslaught on him, prominently featuring the words *irresponsible* and *selfish* with the odd swearword thrown in for good measure, before coming to a decision; although Si couldn't rule out using what influence he still mustered to steer matters towards ordering a curry.

Si had reached the top of the hill. It hadn't in fact taken forever to get there. He peered down and stretching out before him at the bottom, occupying both sides of pavement and spilling out into the road, were various items of household furniture. They were all set aflame.

On one side, on the slope down, was a dresser, a stacked set of kitchen stairs, and a wardrobe with one open door revealing clothes still inside. He could smell the fumes, caught upwind. Everything had been doused in petrol and set on fire. On the other side of the road was a kitchen table and chairs, cardboard boxes piled up one on top of the other (the fire was making short work of those), and a sofa. Beyond this, so many more household items: lampshades, curtains, trays of cutlery, a TV, some board games, a fridge freezer; it made no sense to dwell on it all or cast his gaze further. The flames spread quickly. It was all a blackened mess. Sparks from the electrical goods only added to the malaise; the sheer disordered stupidity of it all. Dirty smoke writhed skywards like so many hungry, desperate hands. Soot and acridity now percolated the air which made his eyes water, made him pine for the relative straightforwardness of the disinfectant back home. He was telling himself, instructing himself, to go back the way he came. The driver of the Corsa from earlier was now elevated in Si's mind to that of great sage—a Gandalf of our times—assessing the situation and getting the hell out of there. It was time for Si to do a one-eighty and turn on his heels and follow suit, make some screeching of his own.

But wanting to leave was only part of it. Another part of him wanted to make sense of it. He was afraid that if he left now, all he'd have to take back would be disjointed, demented images. Blackened, melted fabric, corruption of the ordinary, the stuff of nightmares for years to come. A crowd had formed at the bottom of the hill, mostly adult, some drinking from cans. In among them were children, their low bopping heads giving themselves away. Some were as young as eight or maybe twelve. The young, the old, the indifferent; Si had never been great at guessing someone's age. Sometimes he couldn't remember his own age; purposefully so, he'd be the first to admit.

In the middle of the road, at the centre of the maelstrom, was an armchair. The chair was enveloped in a shimmer which spewed out orange-black curling plumes. There was something sitting on the armchair, crackling, turning, charred. Some kind of showroom dummy? It was difficult for Si to tell through the murk; a combustible mattress close to the chair producing a thick funnel of smoke.

He had been walking aimlessly for something like forty-five minutes. Life had seemed so uncomplicated then despite his best efforts to make it appear otherwise. And now he was feeling enraged at the unedifying spectacle played out in front of him. His body shook with the sheer indignation of it all. How could this be happening? This wasn't suitable for kids. What would happen—how would he feel—if his children just happened to be passing?

Struck by a bout of self-righteousness, a need for action, a yearning to just see this crappy day out, he marched down the hill. A feeling of giddiness came over him.

'Oh, the grand old Duke of York,' he began singing to himself, while not one hundred per cent sure of the tune. With every step he felt less in control of his legs, swept along by gravitational forces, hips grinding, taking the brunt of each conspiratorial step. 'He had ten thousand men.'

The closer he got and the less it appeared so, the greater the determination to convince himself that, yes, it was a dummy in the chair. A torched mannequin. This close, he could feel the heat coming in waves from various directions. He was no longer feeling the cold; that sensation belonged to a half-remembered life from a long time ago. Hot ashes hit the back of his throat and he found himself fighting the need to gag. He was now eye level with much of the crowd. Another maddening thought—it occurred to him that he was the only one not wearing a coat.

'This isn't right. It's not suitable,' Si blurted out the words. He held out his hand like a Shakespearean actor and barked out an order to no one and everyone in particular. 'Hey, give me your phone. I'm reporting this.'

Faces from the crowd checked him out, trying to decide whether the guy was serious or taking the piss, but coming to the rapid conclusion it didn't matter either way. The figure remained sitting up on the armchair, its head flopping to the side. From what he could see, face and forehead were beginning to peel, exposing what looked like blackened porcelain underneath. *Like discarded dirty orange peel*, Si thought furiously to himself. To think anything else would be to champion a lost cause and he hadn't the patience or guile for such a thing. He knew—*he knew*—the burning figure was a real person. They didn't make mannequins that looked that old.

He was aware of a crackling noise, and now the sound was inside his head, he couldn't shut it out.

'That's sick,' he said. 'That's just sick!'

Someone from the crowd, a man wearing a Parka, hood up, stepped forward, mobile phone clutched in his hand. Eyes fixed on the communication device, Si appreciated the fact it was a similar model to his, so he never saw it coming. He heard a bang signalling a punch from another direction, landing on his ear. Another punch, a meaty one, from the same source followed, this time square in the face.

Before he knew it, Si was flat out. It was surprise more than anything that did it for him. Only the second time in his life he had been punched in the face. The first was from his brother at his other brother's wedding (to be fair, he had started it by trying to punch his brother first). He didn't remember back then, though, feeling quite so fuzzy in the head. It was like the blood had rushed *from* his head. He was aware of something warm trickling down his nose. He felt a tepid glow embody him and was worried he might have wet himself. Once more he was struck with a determination to wriggle his big toe. If he couldn't do it now, while the blood was flowing from his top half to his bottom half, then he'd never be able to do it.

He wasn't afraid of death. It wasn't his time. The *Light* had given him the all-clear for the day, but that didn't rule out the prospect of an ugly crowd beating him up, breaking his body; it ending for him badly. Maybe they would leave him in a coma? Maybe he would die tomorrow as a result of injuries sustained today? There was movement around him, but he didn't want to focus on anything; didn't want to make the moment any more real than it already was. Maybe they would set him on fire, too? And he would somehow live through it, body in constant agonising pain. What had he done? What had he walked into?

'Sorry,' he said, stifling a sob for no one in particular, except perhaps himself.

He felt the warmth from the collective fires sweep over him; insulating him, lulling him into a dreamlike state. He shivered despite the heat.

He was aware of many things. A woman in her twenties was crouching over him. She wore a duffle coat with wooden toggles and belted cuffs. Her eyes were half-closed with the smoke. A scarf was wrapped around the bottom half of her face. She placed her hand over Si's mouth to check for signs of breathing. Si duly obliged. Her hand shifted forty-five degrees, as she now offered to help him up.

She spoke up for the benefit of the crowd. 'I'll take him with me. That way you get rid of both of us. Two birds with one stone.' She smiled at Si as way of confirmation her offer was just for him, 'Pub?'

He took her hand.

'You're over the worst of it,' she said. 'At least we're still alive …'

***

It was later, morning breaking into afternoon, and Si had no recollection of how he'd got here. But got there he had, seated inside an old stuffy pub called (if the beer mat was to be believed) The Gadfly. He sat at a round wooden table; all types of lurid suggestions had been scratched into the surface, choked with profanity thanks to various penknives, biros, and cutlery. The back of Si's chair was wobbly and loose, so swinging and pushing his whole weight back on it seemed out of the question. His cheeks reddened.

Next he checked his crotch for signs of leakage, but thankfully there was none.

The right kind of relief washed over him and he visibly relaxed and became better aware of his surroundings. The woman from before was sitting across from him. Her scarf was down around her neck revealing a lightly freckled face. She was ash blonde; had an undercut hairstyle, hair swept to the side. She was young, but something told him she had already lived a life. Her eyes danced and picked up the light.

She gave him another minute to acclimatise to his new surroundings.

'You can either read the table graffiti about some guy called Tom who—apart from having never met you before in his life—is up for sucking your cock,' she said, 'or you can go to the bar and buy me a drink.'

Si got to his feet. His was a bewildered expression; the lines on his face tried to configure into a man-of-action expression, but so far had failed miserably.

'I should complain to the manager about it. Chair's not fit for purpose, either,' he said. 'Maybe we could sit somewhere else? The pub is empty.'

She looked up at him, and realising he wasn't joking, shook her head. 'Christ, live a little, will you?' *Now here was a guy*, she was thinking, *who didn't make a habit of drinking locally*. 'I'll have a pint of Stella,' she said, 'preferably in a Stella glass.'

As he sloped off to the bar, he was aware of the smell of smoke still clinging to his clothes. It was like reliving your worst memory, at your most vulnerable, except for the fact that, already forming, *this* was his worst memory. He had been at his most vulnerable. He grimaced and could feel the area around his nose had swollen up. Checking his watch, he noticed it wasn't much past lunchtime. Normally as a rule he didn't drink before five, but *normally* seemed the pertinent word here. And this was anything but normal.

'Alfie,' the barman said as way of greeting. 'I own this place,' the barman-turned-bar-owner added.

'Simon.' For a second he nearly forgot why he was

standing there, his mind a complete blank. An empty canvas. He gathered himself and breathed out slower than he thought he'd be presently capable of. 'Or Si, if you like. A pint of Stella, thanks, and a bottle of Peroni.'

As he waited for the drinks, he turned his head to take in more of the pub and noticed a small portable TV tucked away on a top shelf attached to the wall. Considering he didn't think such a thing as a portable TV existed anymore, at least in a functioning capacity, the picture on the screen was remarkably clear, although the volume was turned right down. On screen was a news story featuring a clump of black and white fur which, once untangled, Si saw were two panda bears. The pandas gave way to an angry man-of-the-country-type seated at a glass table, having removed one of his shoes in order to bang it on a table.

'I never change the volume,' Alfie said, 'always on silent. That way you ignore the shit comes out of their mouths, read their expressions instead. You'll know exactly what those arseholes are really thinking.'

Si's head spun back. He surveyed both drinks, present and correct, on the bar. He handed over a tenner, half expecting it not to be enough, only to be pleasantly surprised when handed several coins back in change. Drinks in hand, he made to return to the mystery girl who by some twist of fate was now his new drinking partner.

Twist of fate—he didn't much care for the expression. Didn't much care for the word *twist*, or for the word *fate*.

Over his shoulder, Alfie continued to commentate on the world at large. 'Fucking pandas,' he said.

Si glanced back at the TV. The news had moved on,

now showing footage of the sinking of the Argentinian warship *General Belgrano* way back in 1982 during the Falklands War (or so the caption up on the screen, diminutive as it was, informed him).

Which was from before his time. Well, almost…

Si, feet shuffling, left the foul-mouthed barman and returned with drinks back to the profanity-strewn table. His companion and possible saviour (the jury, a second one, was still out on the latter) remained seated, her eyes not having strayed from the approaching pint of Stella. The fact he didn't know her name but here he was buying her a drink didn't sit well with him. Unlike the rambunctious Alfie, it didn't seem like she was going to volunteer the information anytime soon, which was fine with him. He'd take matters into his own hands.

'What's your name?' he said. 'What is any of this about?' He blinked. He was feeling better, his wits slowly returning to him. 'I'm going to phone the police. Or the fire brigade. The police fire brigade. If I can borrow someone's phone.'

She noisily took a slurp from her pint. 'Easy question first,' she said. 'Ollie.' She exhaled loudly and a rattle escaped from her throat. He could have sworn he heard her lungs creak. 'We can go into more detail if you like, but before we start—for your information, it's what the old bastard wanted.'

She took out a packet of cigarettes and began to tap the packet softly, metronomically, against her temple. 'Old Charlie, it was his Last Day. He lived on the street for fifty years, along with everything he owned; he wanted to burn it all. You'd only expect it as standard in modern builds, but he could have applied to the council for the

Light to be fitted. Because of his invalidity could have asked for a hand-held. Just like he could have applied for a bank account or asked for fucking Wi-Fi, but he didn't want any of those things. Wasn't interested in protecting his money. He just wanted to know when he was going to fucking die.'

'So instead he insisted we push him to the *Light* at the end of the street. This time he got his wish and on his final day, obviously, he could do as he bloody pleased. Even if you've been living under a rock you know this. Even if the police turned up, what do you think they would have done about it?'

Si was a fish out of water. It was like he had indeed been living underneath something heavy and flat. He really wanted to ask why, after recent events, she'd even consider smoking a cigarette, but the prospect of hearing a reply left him less enthusiastic.

'At least tell me it'll make the news,' he said.

'It needs to be news to make the news,' she said. She was surprised she hadn't lost patience with him, but then again, there was nowhere else she needed to be.

Si, not for the first time, questioned what he was doing here. Was he in shock, or concussed, or both? He took a drink from his beer and it seemed all right, so at least his sense of taste was okay. Actually, this early in the day it tasted like the assorted chemicals it was, but this served to back up rather than contradict his previous assertion. Not that this should have mattered, but he was of a mind to take any assurance going. All the while, there was a dull pain at the back of his head, which he did his best to ignore. He felt dehydrated. It had been a long day already.

Ollie waited patiently until Si exhausted his full range of facial tics as he tried to work out what was happening to him. She could have told him—of course she could have—but he needed to ask first.

'Just so you know, I like older men,' she said.

'Married,' he said.

'So?'

'Gay.'

'Oh.'

She got to her feet, a cigarette wedged between two fingers. 'Well, don't mind me, I'm going out for a fag.' She made a little face, expectant, hopeful of some kind of reply, but Si wasn't in the mood for verbal jousting, if that's indeed what this was intended to be.

She went outside.

He was utterly pissed off. He'd been punched really hard and now, rubbing salt in all too obvious wounds, comments about his sexuality. He couldn't even begin to process that he'd just watched a man burn alive. Burned alive? Could he truly have been alive when the fire started? Si wasn't there, not right at the start. He pursued a state of mind, one that assured him, yes, he was dead beforehand. There was every chance of it, and he'd be certain of it, right up to the moment he was told otherwise.

How could that be possible? Was he still in the real world? *Or is this just fantasy?* (How did the song go?) Was he, up until a few days ago, so completely unaware of what was happening around him? Ignorance was no excuse, but bloody hell, it was the only one he had. When Geoff knocked on his door—what seemed like an eternity ago—did he bring with him some kind of virus or infection? Such was the intensity, the desperation, the explosion of violence; it had an effect, changing and contaminating the world around him. And with Si it didn't stop there. Something had changed inside of him, too.

The pub door opened and having witnessed the medieval atrocity that was old Charlie's Last Day, in shuffled many of the crowd from before—including some of the children. Si tensed up at the sight of them, an already wounded animal caught in the spotlight. The man in the Parka with the phone still had his hood up. Si must have seen him from the corner of his eye during the (admittedly one-sided) scuffle, because he also recognised the bloke who punched him. The bloke seemed no less threatening despite carrying in both arms, bent at the elbows, a folded, bumpy pile of thick matted fabric. Head darting and animated, he was searching for someone already in situ in the pub. All Si's fears coalesced as the guy, locking eyes with him, began to move, legs gobbling up the short distance between him and Si. He stood for a moment at the table, motionless and emotionless, before holding out the folded clothing.

'Here,' the bloke said.

'Here?' Si said. He felt nauseous. The last thing he anticipated was idle chit-chat.

'Here,' the man repeated. He extended his arms, thrusting out the pile of clothing so it was near brushing against Si's face.

Si sniffed. The easiest thing would be for him to take it, so that's exactly what he did. Such was its weight, the fabric unfolded quickly to reveal itself as a winter coat.

'We rescued it from the fire, right,' the man explained.

Not that an explanation was required or indeed desirable. 'Thought you might need it more, right.'

'That's very ... very...' Si was spared the agony of having to finish the sentence. Glancing up, he saw that his coat-bearing nemesis had already forgone the table in return for the sanctity of the bar.

Speedily, stealthily, Si got up, careful as he did so to push back the chair with the minimum of noise. He made a beeline for the pub door, leaving the coat refolded and unwanted at the table. He opened the door in stages; then out into the bitter icy air, turned even more bitter and icier, he went.

A now-familiar voice came from behind him. 'You know this death thing? Knowing the day you're going to die?'

He turned. Standing there was the young woman named Ollie, taking a blink-and-you'd-miss-it drag on her cigarette.

'It's all a load of shit,' she continued. 'It's all a great big fat government conspiracy. Forget the *Light*, that's what I tried to tell Charlie. He didn't want a corner to crawl into, he wanted spectacle. He wanted a Viking funeral. That's how he described it.'

The temperature seemed to dip even more around Si. He brought his hands up to cover his arms. He fought as best he could the compulsion to let his teeth chatter.

'And on the day Charlie knew he was going to die, he agreed to hear me out, to let me explain what a big lie it all was, but in return, there was a price to pay.' She took another draw of her cigarette as truncated as the last one.

'What...?' he said. He wanted to cough; the need was psychological rather than physical. He dreaded asking the question because again he feared the answer, but he had come this far. 'What price?'

She drew on the last remnants of her cigarette. Her hands stayed still enough for Si to register that she wore fingerless gloves. 'He would hear me out, that was the deal,' she said, 'and in return if he still wanted to go through with it, it would fall to me.'

For Si, this was the first time he'd detected an openness; a softness to her. She came across as almost human.

'I had to strike the match.'

Something was ringing in his ears. It may have been her voice.

He turned, walked away, upping the pace, heading for the incline that would take him closer to home and more importantly, further from the barbarous, grotesquely played out insanity presented before him. A world that was not his own. To spend a moment more with these people, he would need his head examined. He'd need a brain transplant.

'He marched them up to the top of the hill.' Still not sure of the tune, which was maddening in itself, he began walking up the incline, but such a course of action didn't fill him with optimism. He looked again and again but still could find no street sign. His mind was reeling; every element of his surroundings seemed ready and willing to collapse in on itself. Through sheer force of will he doggedly kept at it. 'And he marched them down again.'

Appearing at the bottom of the hill was a black cab creeping along the road, its light on. He on the other hand started to move faster still. He willed his arms to move, to flap like the wings of a bird, as he squealed like a fattened pig led to the slaughter, yelling, 'Taxi! Taxi!'

The cab promptly came to a stop, engine still running. He ran the last few yards towards it as if his life depended.

He flew into the backseat of the taxi, landing on all fours. He straightened up and spurted out his address to the driver; words so terribly rushed he needed to repeat them twice. The cab set off and Si, straightening himself up to a seated position, could feel his body ripple and undulate with ecstatic delight. He didn't think it brave, only foolish, but he peered out of the rear window anyway. He looked up and could see wisps of dark smoke bending and scurrying ever upwards towards the atmosphere. At that precise moment he promised himself, a forty-something, that he would never leave home again.

'It's a mad world,' he heard the taxi driver say. He could have been referring to anything in particular, and that was probably the point.

In the back of the cab Si gathered himself and began to take proper breaths once more. The outside world was once more reduced to a blessed blur. Textures, shapes, and settings all merged into one. It was like his brain had reached saturation point, it couldn't take in any more. It was a blessing. The taxi took one turn after another and Si became anxious, longing for a straight line. The ride in total was a smidgen over fifteen minutes. Fifteen minutes, he reflected, that's all it took; the return to sanity.

Si was so grateful to be home. Vacating the vehicle, he wanted to hand over the total contents of his wallet, but settled on an amount where the tip came to double the actual fare. The driver took a moment to check the notes he'd been handed. 'It's a mad world,' he was heard to say again before pulling away.

Si stood and waved off the cab. It was like he was a four-year-old. It occurred to him he had never done anything so dopey in his life (even when he was four years old). He was just so relieved and delighted; a little light-headed. Standing on familiar pavement; a terrific feeling, just to be back on safe ground. That said, he wasn't quite home, having been dropped off at Number 58 and not Number 38—maybe he should have repeated the address a third time—but really it was no hassle. After what he'd been through, he was happy enough to face the prospect of a short, familiar walk. He was certain each step homeward would bring with it a profound and crystallised thought, a deeper understanding of the lurid, treacherous parallel universe located little more than a fifteen-minute drive away.

Much to his disappointment his mind went blank. Perhaps it was too soon to start processing things?

He kept walking. The street took a noticeable bend before him. From this vantage point he could see the side of the house, a segment of his back lawn. For a second he thought he could see smoke. He was experiencing a flashback. For a horrifying, stomach-churning set of moments he was somehow back in that other place.

He stretched his neck out as far as it could go. He shook his head, seeking to dispel the mental interference, drag some sense kicking and screaming back to proceedings, but it could not be denied it came from his house all right. At an angle, there was no doubt, there was smoke.

He was aware of a figure close by, almost at his shoulder, but he didn't look around.

He edged a little closer to the point he could make

out Sofi standing over something burning in the garden. There was a chance it could have been anything, of course, but that didn't stop Si knowing full well what it was. The burning object could have been a box. And there was sufficient smoke to suggest it wasn't some empty box.

He didn't need to see any more. Sofi was still obviously dealing with his demons, having moved on from disinfecting the floor for a hundredth time to searching the house top to bottom before finding, then burning, Si's shoebox.

Yes, that word again—*shoebox, shoebox, shoebox*—the biggest mistake of his life.

How dare you! How fucking dare you! Sofi, obviously deep in thought, wasn't for turning around and Si, in stark contrast to only moments before, was not for announcing his return.

Si's head was spinning, full to bursting, a slew of accusations. He felt betrayed, crushed. He immediately about-turned and was confronted by his old, deceased colleague Geoff. Si put his head down, opting to stroll past. To keep up, Geoff's ghost had to widen its stride.

'Go away,' Si said, 'don't make me push you again.'

It had been a day of aimless ambulation and look where that had got him. Undeterred, unwilling or unable to deviate from the rule, Si kept on walking. He didn't dare to think where to. All he knew, the only certainty was he was alone now, with only ghosts for company. He was cast adrift.

6

Call Me Al

'The 粪 had hit the fan.'

These days Al Baumann spoke the words with a touch
of whimsy. Not as much a case of look at how bad things
were then, but look at how good things are now. His
grasp of Mandarin had grown more assured over the
years. Not that it mattered to the adoring Massachusetts
crowd, sitting, stamping and whooping in assorted
fashion before him. He was speaking at the Worcester
Memorial Auditorium. As ever his words, looking back,
looking forward, were ones of assurance. Such was the
concordant nature of the relationship he had with his
audience; no matter what had changed, what will
change, in the end the message was always the same—that
everything would be okay.

'Death does not do irony.'

These days he phrased his most famous lines in a

wholly different way. Back in 1998, the words were spoken in a clipped fashion, nuance rushed, reflecting ongoing feelings of dread at the continuing situation. Everyone knew of *death* of course, but not as something quite so idiosyncratic. It was tantamount to a new set of rules, terrifying in itself. Baumann not only described the fear and confusion, he reflected on and made sense of it. The more times he said it, the more others repeated it, the more sense it made. And as his voice had changed over the years; the timbre much deeper; it complemented the changing tone. It was an invocation. In the here and now, no matter how softly spoken it was, it was a clarion call. 'Death does not do irony.'

'What do these words say to me now?' he said. 'That change is constant—to properly come to terms with change takes generations—and it will take more generations to come to finally embrace it. New voices emerged for a new age to help try and guide us. There was Jennifer Coutinho. There was Heather Carlson. There was baby Daniel. He had a voice, too. And what these voices said to me—and continue to say to me to this day—is that we are all unique in this world. I believe we are unique in the universe. Because as human beings we understand and we can adapt and we can change. Because we know on *this* day of all days, it will be *our* day.' He shook his head slowly, purposefully. 'More than any other.'

At this point he took a moment. He tapped his index finger twice on the lectern. It was the easiest action in the world and he revelled in the simple things. 'On a day that eclipsed anything we had seen before, including any single day of fatalities attributed to the Great War or World War II. Despite the fear, the confusion, the anarchy, we have shown we have come out the other side; that everything would be okay. That everything *is* okay.'

'We remember.'

Baumann pursed his lips. He took the glass of water from its designated position on the lectern and took a sip. The crowd at first sat in silent reflection. One beat, two beats, the ebb and flow, and at last there was rapturous applause. An explosion of exultation.

With both hands he gripped the lectern securely fixed to the stage. His sight was failing him due to macular degeneration. A combination of wearing lenses and the bright lights of the auditorium helped alleviate the symptoms, but as much as Baumann was up for the fight, he knew it was a losing battle. He was an old man. He had lived a life.

The people were too far away, too small and delicate to define. He was standing in a vast old interior, an echo chamber, sloping in at him from all directions like converging mudslides. Even so, it didn't stop him studying the splashy blobs that made up the crowd. As ever, he was looking for one face in particular. He imagined if he could see her she would somehow come sharply into focus. He imagined her hair these days would be more silver or platinum than blonde. Despite the sheer pointlessness of wanting something so hopelessly improbable, he still wanted it. He wished he could see her one last time.

He raised a hand which instantaneously exerted a calming effect over the raucous crowd. 'The fight continues,' he spoke softly into the microphone, a little croakily at first, but less so as he hit his stride. 'Three days ago, I was in Riyadh arguing for official acceptance of the Church. Middle-East authorities continue to resist. There are pockets of individuals trying to do their best in challenging times and still to this day it pains me to report they live under the constant threat of persecution. And yet *Light* Verification devices are used as much in that region as any other. But still they do not recognise the right of the individual on his or her final day to follow their heart's desires, and do so freely under the sanctity and auspices of the Church of the Last Day.'

'We have our angel.'

'It is not as if the *Light* is going to go away. It has become part of us; as important to us as the air we breathe. And we are its custodians. We are—every one of us—the keepers of the *Light*.'

The crowd continued to interact when required, on one hand contemplative, at other times noisy. For Al Baumann, the act of looking was no longer enough. He could not make out a soul. And it wasn't just his sight that was failing him. He was losing his strength. Every day his mind, his body was so much weaker. Somewhere along the line he was losing his soul as well. Shapeless, formless, he could hardly feel a thing.

***

Back in 1998, a handful of days after the event—the First Day as many were now calling it—Baumann undertook a whistle-stop tour around the world. He was in his fifties, but pretty fit for his age. His new role was certainly a change, a massive step up from his last job as political pundit waxing lyrically on gubernatorial elections in New Jersey. He had an easy manner about him, but covering local elections aside, in the cut-throat, dog-eat-dog world of political commentary, this was never going to be enough.

On the First Day, while the cameras were rolling in a Washington-based studio, execs desperate for a sound bite, something to best express the tension, the fluidity of the situation, it was Al Baumann who grasped the nettle. He demonstrated the right type of awareness. He was winging it, but at this point so was everyone else, making it a level playing field. He was the first to use the word 'change' in the context of what was happening. The first to coin the phrase 'global shake-up.' He talked of his family and spoke of the daily vigil spent at the bedside of his dying grandmother. He described in detail the range of emotions experienced while watching a loved one hold on to life. Love and despair bundled up with pain, anguish, and suffering. Every day he would see with his own eyes a different stage of death, not knowing if this was to be her last day; never to truly know until it was too late. Never to know it was her time until it *was* her time. Al Baumann may not have been the first to claim something new was happening with death, but quickly he became the voice to rise above all others. His was the voice of authenticity; the one that people latched onto. The First Day phenomenon may have turned out to be a one-off; a tragic series of global events, yes, an aberration of nature, but a temporary blip all the same. It could have passed, fizzled out, leaving Al Baumann, fifteen minutes of fame gobbled up, ultimately a forgotten man.

But that's not what happened. He had made his mark.

His place on the mount was secured. By the time the church in Kalamazoo took prominence over him—and everyone else besides—Al was happy enough. He had hogged enough of the limelight without suffering the fate of being too overexposed. He was beginning to repeat himself anyway.

On the third day, they began to re-open the airports. Baumann remarked that it was pretty amazing how quickly the human race had reverted back to normal, at least on the surface. For the most part, to play the part of a normal, outwardly functioning human being, the surface was all that was required. Baumann took one of the first flights to London where he interviewed Emily Carmichael, who spent the First Day with her sister Jacqueline. Jacqueline woke having experienced vivid, portentous dreams. She'd lost the feeling in her hands and feet. She didn't feel unwell, a little warm perhaps, but nothing to merit causing a fuss. She couldn't recount anything from her dreams except the sense that they contained a message, something really important and she knew that she would never dream again. Emily without hesitation accepted Jacqueline's words—they were sisters after all. They held hands, never letting go, right through to around seven that evening when Jacqueline lost consciousness and died.

He spoke to an anonymous mother in Copenhagen, whose son Tobias complained of terrible headaches and somehow knew he was dying. Suddenly he attacked her, punching and kicking one moment before dying in her arms the next. He talked to Mariana in La Paz, Bolivia, on being told by her terminally ill daughter that this was her Last Day. She reacted to this by suffocating her using a pillow. As she explained, she could not stand the thought of her suffering for another minute, never mind what remained of the day. Mariana was currently on trial for murder, but her defence team was mounting a special plea of 'global hysteria.' He talked with Amr, a Cairo-based businessman, who offered another perspective. Despite being given a clean bill of health, Amr was convinced that he was not only going to die that day, but had indeed died and had subsequently returned as a ghost.

But it was the less lurid, smaller, more intimate stories that had the most impact. The quiet deaths, the ones surrounded by loved ones, connected the most. As he listened, absorbed, and reported on them, Al Baumann felt part of a brand new world community. Those who were affected first-hand by the events of the First Day, all woven into the same great tapestry. But that was only so much window dressing. If you looked hard enough—or in fact looked at all—you'd see a big crack in the surface. The impression of normalcy was in fact nothing more than an uneasy peace. People hadn't simply got over it. The scars hadn't suddenly scabbed over. There were wounds that still wept under the skin. It seemed inevitable, such were the fault lines that the world community would erupt again, and the consequences this time would be a whole lot worse for everyone. It seemed to Al Baumann that everything, something as crucially precise as world order, was being held together by the most fleeting of circumstances, the flimsiest of string. Preventative measures, he was certain, were called for.

At no point did he think he could ever change things on his own. He always saw himself as a cog, a facilitator at best. He would accumulate extremely capable people along the way, but back then, right at the start, he needed someone at his right-hand side—or perhaps he could be at her right-hand side, whatever the situation demanded.

He made enquiries into the whereabouts of Heather Carlson, the journalist in Kalamazoo who interviewed Jennifer Coutinho. She had been keeping a low profile, although wasn't particularly difficult to find. Many of her colleagues in the press and media had mercilessly rounded on her. They did so out of petty jealousy; the fact she shunned publicity made her appear an easy target (which explained why they lined up to gobble her up and spit her out while simultaneously leaving Baumann well alone). The only thing that interested Baumann was what the general public thought of her and broadly speaking they were sympathetic towards, and equally as importantly, intrigued by her. He was desperate to speak to her, but delayed doing so until he had something to offer. Something juicy enough to lure her back into the public eye.

And he was pretty damn sure he had just the thing. He had secured exclusive access to a bona fide, confirmed Last Dayer (as they were now euphemistically called) based relatively close by in Quebec. A series of voluntary tests had uncovered, under ultraviolet, the lack of electrolytes in the palms of his hands. This represented a major breakthrough—the closest anyone had got to a scientific process to detect a Last Dayer's lack of touch. The electrolytes test was still in its infancy and clinically untried, but Baumann had only to set eyes on the man called Jack Pelletier to know it was true. He could read it in his face, see it in his eyes. Baumann hated uncertainty, but his instincts in this case were correct. These days they were rarely anything but. He was on a roll. He contacted Carlson and offered her the interview. Because of time constraints, an obvious one in particular, she had to come to a decision on the phone right there and then. There would be no second chances.

And she took it.

Of course nothing was certain. Heather Carlson was on a flight, still up in the air, still hours away. Pelletier could die at any time. Medical staff were put in place, unsure how to react with the adult in their care; who, no matter the extent of their administrations, was definitely going to die sometime that day. They were there primarily to try to prolong matters.

'Just keep him alive for as long as possible,' Baumann said. 'That's what you people do, isn't it?' Before hurriedly adding, 'Although he's no use to us if he loses consciousness.'

The location was the Quebec newsroom in Westmount, more commonly used by the Royal Canadian Mounted Police. Heather Carlson arrived with the minimum of fuss; no airs and graces. She had applied her own make-up on the way there. On meeting face to face for the first time, Baumann noticed her mop of blonde hair and the tiniest of noses. She was twenty years his junior.

'No time like the present,' he opined and took her straight to Pelletier.

Pelletier was in a room with a modern reclaimed wooden table, florid curtains, a vase of flowers, and two comfortable chairs. Baumann described the room as 'sympathetically lit.'

As soon as she hit the seat, she motioned to the cameras

to start rolling. Everything around them clicked effortlessly, seamlessly; a shamelessly controlled environment. The temperature in the studio was raised a notch, a mixture of body heat and electrics.

Heather Carlson began the interview. 'I've just met you. I know your name is Jack Pelletier. You have a wife and two children, both in their teens. I can't imagine how difficult this must be for you. But please know how grateful and humble we are that you should agree to talk to us. In the course of this interview I—everyone who is watching—we're hoping to get to know you.'

Pelletier nodded too many times than was natural. He was nervous. He did not look well. Heather Carlson leaned forward. She gave him a little smile, a glancing touch of the hand.

'You and me, we're going to do just fine,' she said.

The interview unfolded. Pelletier just wanted to tell his story, one of frustration, incapable of truly comprehending what it was to have, at most, only hours left. He still had aspirations; still had so many things he wanted to do. Run a marathon, climb a Scottish mountain, write a novel, build a car up from scratch. It was just that there was no time. He spoke mostly in English, but sometimes strayed into French, and so helped the worldwide audience understand—if that was indeed the right word to use—that he was dying; that he was flesh and blood; that he was human. There was nothing new in his words, nothing revolutionary, no fresh insights to be offered, and that was the point.

Pelletier was fifty-three years old. He didn't know what he was dying from. He had been plagued by respiratory problems, but today of all days he felt fine. He had only told his family of his fate hours beforehand and yet here he was bearing his soul in front of a worldwide audience.

A fascinated Al Baumann watched from the sidelines. Pelletier looked up at an angle as he talked, staring at a tile on the ceiling. Heather withdrew, faded into the background and let him talk. He was the man of the moment after all. She knew this, even if he did not.

Baumann could only judge Heather Carlson in terms of her profession and how she had grown in this regard. In his eyes, she was no longer the rookie opportunist as labelled by her peers over the preceding weeks and months (he was happy to admit he had harboured one or two doubts himself, now decisively dispelled). She had grown older and more assured over such a short period of time. She was using her instincts, too. Baumann saw in her a butterfly bursting out of the cocoon. The spotlight was on Jack Pelletier, quite rightly of course, but he wasn't the one Baumann couldn't take his eyes off of.

Pelletier began coughing and could not stop. He was breathless and visibly distressed. Heather twirled a finger to signal for the medical team to be brought in. She looked directly into the camera, her face filling the screen, taking it upon herself to bring the interview to a conclusion.

'Mr Pelletier, we just want you to be comfortable,' she said, her gaze never wavering from the camera lens. 'Your family are here. You'll be with them soon. This is a Fox & Friends News Network production in conjunction with the Canadian Broadcasting Corporation. Take care everyone and hold your loved ones close. Thank you. Thank you.'

Unlike the time she stood outside the church in Kalamazoo, Heather Carlson refrained from urging, in no uncertain terms, that everyone should go home. They were there already.

***

Could Al Baumann claim intervening world events fell heavy on his shoulders? After all, here in Worcester, Massachusetts his audience was entranced, caught in a snare of his making. But they didn't want to hear anything too off the beaten track or spontaneous. A prepared script was enough to meet all expectations.

For this next part of his speech he could not help but be animated. 'Lest we forget,' he said, 'it was an angel that came to Jennifer Coutinho to tell her of her and her baby's fate. She was told that Death would take her, but in return she was given a gift. It was to be her Last Day, but in return she could do whatever she wanted. She could do as she pleased.'

'It was a statement from God. That He would stand by us no matter. We are His children. The Church of the Last Day is as legitimate as any of the traditional churches. But where they serve the spiritual needs of every other day, our Church exists for one day only.'

He lowered his head and breathed out. It was a pause which heralded an explosion of noise from the people of Worcester. He waved, adjusted his stance, stood and took in the clatter, the vibrations, the resonances; the rolling, thunderous coming together of mudslides. It felt like something was trying to break out of his chest, and for a moment the pain threatened to envelop and take over the whole of his body. The pills were having increasingly less effect. Part of him wanted to say a little more, spend more time with the faithful, say things differently, give a little more insight, perhaps be a little more truthful. But the crowd got to hear what they wanted, and it was by far the most sensible option to quit while he was ahead.

This was as close to his last will and testament he was going to get. At least in his own lifetime. As he left the stage he looked up and surveyed the crowd once more, more out of routine, out of habit than expectation.

He exited stage left having already made clear with regret that he would not be attending the official Church luncheon due to be held later that day. Once back in the limo, the talk had already receded from his mind. His focus switched to the next item on the agenda. He had faced so many obstacles, placed for so many years in the way of progress, he could no longer think any differently. And now in the car there was only him and his driver, and even then the back of the limo was soundproofed. He was expecting an important phone call.

Surprisingly, when it came it was in the form of a crackly line. A male voice nonetheless informed him that it was a secure one which Baumann, blissfully unaware of the man's credentials, accepted. There was a click followed by a tinny female voice that seemed trapped inside a box.

'The President will speak to you now,' she said.

'Where the hell are you?' the President's voice boomed. Not for the first time today, tumultuous sound pummelled Baumann's senses.

'Worcester, Massachusetts,' he replied.

'Good, good,' the President said, 'the good people of

Massachusetts. They don't bite off your head in Massachusetts. Don't fuck you over. You have a lot of your people there in Massachusetts?'

'A few.'

'No need for figures. I have a breakdown in front of me, Church membership across every state, every county. You know me, I like a good set of figures and what I'm looking at now, these are a good set of figures. You're everywhere, all around the world. I like that. You're one of our chief exporters, you know that?'

Baumann was at a loss for words. He wasn't the only one to find the forty-fifth (or was it forty-fourth) President of the United States mystifying. One moment he'd be complaining about the complexity of Israeli-Palestine relations, the next claiming he still masturbated on a daily basis. Although Baumann was sure the effect, in time, would be mitigated if he only got to know the guy.

'Going to cut to the chase,' the President said. 'There's been another incursion in Yemen and I need to decide whether the United States is going to support or condemn this time. I'm going to chew the fat over this one. I'm going to eat a burger with my initials on it. Rest assured one hundred per cent American beef.' Over the line came a rattle of cutlery and ceramics to announce the setting of the table, presumably with an all-American burger so embroidered occupying centre stage. 'Mr Al Baumann, you given any thought to my offer?'

'I have Mr President, sir,' he said. He enunciated well-rehearsed words, perhaps delivered a little too briskly, but it was not every day that one turned down the President of the United States. 'After much deliberation I'm afraid, with regret, I can't be your running mate for your next term of office. Magnificent as your offer is, humbling as it is, the timing isn't right.'

'I suppose you have your reasons,' the President said, allowing himself a moment's pause, a tinge of disappointment the lifecycle of a firefly, before quickly moving on, returning to his default setting of ebullient and brash. This was the facet of personality that fascinated Baumann most. The way certain things didn't appear to affect him at the time, only to then rear up subsequently, to bear a grudge to an explosive degree weeks, months, and especially years later.

'Tell me,' he said, 'you know I've been thinking. If those jokers in the Kremlin were about to drop the bomb, we could already have predicted it, we'd already know, yes, because of the *Light*. The figures in advance for that day would back this up already. It would make the First Day look like a picnic. I'd be obliged to retaliate. It would be a mess. Hundreds of thousands dead, hell, millions. You could say, now that would be a helluva Last Day.' Baumann couldn't work out if the President was being flippant here. He decided to just go with the flow. 'What would happen if we changed our minds—I changed my mind, my counterpart in Russia changed his mind, and we didn't push the button? If all those folks were earmarked for destruction anyhow? Now, you gotta ask, gotta think, was it ever my mind to change in the first place?'

Baumann was given those kinds of hypotheticals all the time. The response was always the *school bus* theory. Some guy is shot at; he's a goner. At the last moment he dodges the bullet and next thing he knows, he rolls out onto the road and is hit by a school bus. So the bullet didn't kill him, but the school bus did. Death will get you in the end. Even if you miss all the messy and noisy deaths, it'll come for you in some form. It'll creep up on you.

Or there was the marathon runner who discovered it was his Last Day. He makes the decision to run the race because he's going to die in any case. He reaches the finishing line with no complications. In fact, he feels like a million dollars. He fists the air, feeling joy on so many levels. He's invincible. He's so thrilled he keeps on running—running past the race perimeter—only to be hit by a school bus (another one) seconds later.

Baumann wasn't for biting. The President remained on the line but was no longer properly engaged in the conversation. Instead, he was toying with an idea. Pinging around his brain, there were always potential business deals to be pursued for when he was no longer in office. Baumann wondered why, out of the blue, he was considered Vice Presidential material and now he believed he had his answer. He was pretty sure the President wanted to secure a place on the board for him or a member of his family. But no matter how things might pan out, Al Baumann knew one thing for certain: he wouldn't be around to see how it worked out.

'One thing, you guys will need to build a lot more Churches.'

There was a click and the line went dead. Baumann reflected on his lower status, the fact he no longer warranted a Presidential goodbye. He smiled to himself, had to stifle a chuckle, but that was fine by him. It was a good place to be. He thought of the last Vice President of the United States, who hadn't quite dodged a bullet or been hit by a speeding bus, but might as well have been.

7

Church Of The Last Day

Events. Landmarks. The spirit of revolution. With the advent of time, such things inevitably must merge, shapelessly, like an ink blotter, a Rorschach test, to form unseemly clumps of memory. You could no longer see the join.

The events of 1998, however, remained crystal clear. That year, Al Baumann answered the call. As the governments of the world legislated to prevent 'Last Day' runs on the banks and general end-of-the-world-styled panic, he started buying up plots of land. He acquired an interest in Hospitality Franchise Systems with its networks of hotels, which he would eventually take over years later. He and his growing band of associates scooped up buildings both public and private, clinics, hospitals, disused town halls, and churches. For a time he really wanted the church in Kalamazoo where it all started, but that particular venture was to prove elusive, forever tantalisingly beyond his grasp. Even so, it was a case of creating a foothold in every community. It was about establishing in every town and city the Church of the Last Day.

There was resistance from the traditional churches and organisations. That was to be expected, but Baumann never lost sight of the f-word; that being *focus*. It was all about the individual's Last Day. How to cope? How to deal with it? Over and above saving its own skin, no other organisation had an answer to this. They couldn't offer an alternative vision, nothing remotely comparable. Baumann was genuine when he said he was all about preserving the status quo; normalising the establishment; shoring up the great and the good. But nor, he insisted, could all interested parties bury their heads in the sand. The day that was someone's Last Day, momentous as it was, had to be set aside and granted privileged status. The Church of the Last Day would exist outside the traditional institutions, supplying a need that did not exist previously.

He took her under his wing and pushed a reluctant Heather Carlson forward as the face of the Church. In truth she was never truly sold on the idea, but in presenting herself as someone on the outside she fitted the profile perfectly. She in turn was given free rein to challenge certain aspects of the Church. Some Last Dayer excesses did not sit well with her, convinced as she was that this was only the start; that the floodgates were still to open. But the greater the levels of dissent and soul searching within, the more debate it generated, the more the Church was accepted by society as a whole. It was a revolution; one of sweat, construction, and conviction; the emergence of a pocket universe; a necessary reaction to a new and bewildering, uplifting and terrifying development in human affairs. Death had changed and it was only right that people would change with it. It was an unsophisticated argument which grew simpler as the Church took hold. It was on the map.

The way Heather Carlson saw it, she wanted to continue Jennifer Coutinho's work. This is what she believed in. She wanted to help the dying; wanted them to realise that even then, at this point in their life, they could be everything they wanted to be. And he was of the opinion that she should want for nothing and be given everything that she required.

It became obvious that the Church as a business concern was proving lucrative. No different from the rest of society that it was the wealthy who could pick and choose. Tax loopholes subject to Federal law allowed budgets in excess of half a million dollars to be paid in advance. It was common for billionaires to have a number of death funds spread over the length and breadth of the country, around the world if need be. When it was their time, they would call on the location closest to them. Time was precious and no more so than at the end. The option to plan in advance was the last preserve of the rich. For everyone else, for anything else, it was a case of turning up on the day. It was a case of strictly 'cash only.'

Encroaching, expanding, multi-tentacled, infectious. A train of thought made real; entering the public consciousness. Invited through the front door, never then to make its excuses and leave. But to offer something so tantalising and then raise the threat of it being taken away was a sure-fire way to unsettle a populace. And Al Baumann found the less settled the population, the better to drive home the point.

'We've won the right to our Last Day, but what are we prepared to do in order to keep it?' He would ask this in the manner of arguing with himself, which was his style at the time. 'In return for the potentially unlimited freedoms of a Last Day,' he continued, 'maybe we all have to pay the price a little? Give things back on those other days in terms of checks and balances?'

He was of course referring to the role of Big Government. He wanted to be seen as an ally to it, happy for it to become an even bigger part of people's lives—except for one day.

There were howls of protest from neo-conservatives, from libertarians. Baumann was never swayed by dissident voices because when it came down to it, the purity, certainty, and finality of the Last Day was absolute. Inextricably linked to this, the Church was more than iron pyrite; a fool's errand. It was a genuine game changer.

For the ordinary person, there was nothing ordinary about his or her Last Day. Let them have their tiny slice of freedom. Let them have their mattress fund (to spend in due course on Church activities). Let them be crazy right up to the end when, let's be honest, none of it mattered anymore.

Let them.

People wanted what the Church had to offer. They'd find a way. You couldn't underestimate the appeal. It was written into prenup agreements. Some Last Dayers would just appear on the doorstep without spouse or family knowledge (although official Church policy stressed the importance of all loved ones being in agreement). They would fail the *Light*; they would be flagged up in the system; in perfunctory fashion, they would turn up with whatever money they had and the Church gave them what they wanted, what they could afford.

It was a predominantly male clientele at first, but the gap between males and females grew less as time went by. Age limits varied from state to state, but an age range of twelve to one hundred was not unheard of.

There were departure rooms set aside, for a limited time only, for the soon to be deceased to say their final goodbyes. Medical staff and porters were in situ for those unable to walk unaided. The organisation took a financial hit on this, but Baumann always resisted cutting back. There was a duty of care, he argued. It was a church. It wasn't always about making money, not all of the time.

Various services were offered dependant on the size of the church. In theory the choices were endless, within the confines of what a room and augmented reality would allow. For the most part, though, Last Dayers would ask for the same deal. Men and women, but mostly men, wanted a room where they could whore, take drugs, and drink their last few hours away.

Others only wanted someone to hold, to feel the warmth of another human being lying next to them, to see them over the worse of it; that was the best of it.

Then there were the cottage industries built around a burgeoning institution. For a premium, insurance companies offered logistical support to get you to the

Church on time. Taxi services offered special rates. Cities introduced priority lanes. There were numerous apps to call upon. The whole process had its own *Uber* stamp of approval.

Some died in transit. Many more experienced a new lease of life. Invariably, people got to where they wanted to be, or at least were headed in the right direction.

There were teething problems—or for a less diplomatic, more accurate way of putting it, a myriad of snafus to circumnavigate. There was always the chance of waiting times at busy periods. You might be asked if you were prepared to share a room (an experience in itself). There was the Church guarantee to keep you alive long enough to experience value for money, although if it came to it, who'd still be around in the morning to complain about the service?

Euthanasia was written into the small print. Proof if proof was needed that the landscape had shifted, that normal laws on this day no longer applied. In some states the Church was legally obliged to carry this out on completion of its Last Day services. Official Church policy was to euthanize only in the most extreme of circumstances, bringing an end to unbearable pain and chronic suffering. That, and cutting down waiting times. There were media reports of corpses in body bags spilling out onto the streets invoking a flurry of threats of fines from the Department of Public Health.

The traditional churches continued to protest. There were demonstrations against jumped up whorehouses, crack houses, charnel houses; what was seen as Sodom and Gomorrah returned. Protests would likely turn violent. There would be 'Last Day' fatalities.

Lutherans raised a legal challenge, demanding one room in every Church in every major US population centre to be set aside for its teachings.

It fell to Baumann and other trusted advisors to respond to all issues and questions—and more besides from politicians, pressure groups, lobbyists, the media, government departments, and all the other grand institutions.

'*Some call it the death of society.*'

'What functional use is society for the dead?' he'd respond. 'That surely is the domain of the living.'

'*It is wicked and immoral.*'

'All Church activities are consensual,' he'd say. 'There is no suggestion of compulsion, and yes, to give a more appropriate answer to a more appropriate question, I think the worst can bring out the best in what it is to be human.'

'*When will it end?*'

'You know when it will end. That's the point.'

Baumann wasn't slow in pointing out that he himself was a born-again Christian. How many times did he have to say it? He did not wish to challenge the US as a Christian country. In fact, he wanted to bolster it.

The US Senate and House pushed through a bill passing into law a Last Day transfer of wealth from individual to state. A Last Day amnesty—guaranteeing immunity from prosecution for consenting adults on their final day (protections were put in place for minors)—was written into the Constitution. Spreading the word, global expansion soon followed. The whole of Europe succumbed; only Scandinavia resisting for a time. North and South America, Australasia, most of Africa and

Asia. There were even plans to establish a Church in Antarctica.

And slowly the world recalibrated and adjusted and returned to normal again. Death was normalised. It was put in a box and tucked away under the bed.

As the organisation grew into multinational status, an army of managers and executives were hired worldwide to roll out the model that was the Church of the Last Day; to make sense of global expansion, economies of scale, the building of infrastructure. Which was fine by Baumann, who was now CEO, no longer involved in the day to day. No longer having to do the heavy lifting.

He filled his time with lecture tours around the world, but was never shy on intervening if he thought the Church had overstepped itself, strayed too much from the original vision. It was all about the checks, the balances; this continued to be important to him. It was all about the Last Day.

Heather Carlson, while never especially outgoing, became increasingly inward-looking. The Church had become so vast, so powerful, it felt like she, along with everyone else, was caught in its gravitational pull; going through the motions, all fulfilling a role. She would be the first within the organisation predictably to voice her concerns. But hers was a lone voice; a tired voice. She was aware in other people's eyes she'd been reduced to caricature, saying no to everything; naysayer for the sake of it. She had lost her grip. She was a non-believer.

It wasn't always the case. She was one of the first to have a *Light* device installed in her home. She'd extol the virtues of a piece of kit which forecast a Last Day outcome with a probability of success of 99.9999%. The remaining 0.0001% was there for theoretical convenience, a legal and statistical throwback. And yet she was also the first to query the necessity and morality of testing babies. What price was society willing to pay, she lamented. Where had it got us, our even greater levels of fascination with death? She'd ask this, even though she numbered herself as among those enthralled.

She knew her time was up. Their final conversation began like this:

'After all these years you've been part of it, you're saying this now?' he said.

'Why does it have to be a church?' she said well after the fact, but something that had gnawed away at her all this time. 'It is absurd. Why call it that?'

'Didn't you see the cracks? Do we have to go through all this again? The world was about to tear itself apart and I couldn't stand aside and let that happen. You couldn't. None of us could.'

'It's not for everyone, Alan,' she said. 'It's not for me. It's not a question of me being grateful to you for all you've done, what you helped make possible, but I feel like I'm envying the dying. Not the dead, but those who possess those last few precious moments, the twilight hours. I am just so tired of myself, of the person I am, and I want that kind of meaning for myself so much. I don't know, I just want to go away and find a quiet place somewhere and bide my time and wait for it to happen.'

Baumann was stunned initially. At the time he'd swear he did not see it coming. As her parting words sunk in, his cheeks were flushed. He was disorientated, didn't know where to look, but he knew the feeling would pass. Heather Carlson leaned forward. She gave him a little smile, a glancing touch of the hand. Simply put, she was the most complete human being he had ever known. He just wished she thought the same of him.

'The world isn't going to tear itself apart,' she said, 'despite the provocation, despite the terrible things we do as individuals, as a group, as a species. In fact, the opposite will come about. The more we try to understand death, the more we understand ourselves. Alan, you're living testament to that.'

Al Baumann motioned to speak, but didn't get as far as enunciating actual words.

'It doesn't matter,' she said. 'I could be by your side or not, no one notices me anymore. No one will care when I'm gone.'

She left that day. He swore to himself that he would never try to track her down and through the years was too stubborn and proud to deviate from his vow. But he hoped she might of her own volition come back to him one day. And over the successive years, all fifteen of them, she was like a ghost to him, haunting his dreams, clinging onto his clothing. Never a physical one, to reach out and touch, but an ethereal presence nevertheless by his side.

***

Al Baumann entered the doors of the former Hampton Inn & Suites on Prescott Street; now renamed Church of the Last Day on Prescott Street.

He was expected.

A quick scan of his palm at the desk confirmed both his identity and the inevitability of his impending demise. The penalties for impersonating a Last Dayer were severe, including and up to losing all Last Dayer privileges, which was unconscionable to the point of universally unheard of.

As receptions go, it was intentionally low key. He was aware of the thrum adjacent to the counting machines.

Behind closed doors, the best part of two years ago, on the day of his seventy-fifth birthday, he announced to the board his last wishes. All said, he had done well to get this far. The warning signs were there and it was unlikely in terms of age he would reach a further milestone. The board members listened to him in silence as he related exactly what he wanted, trusting and expecting them to make it so. There was always the chance, but realistically, he supposed, nothing would happen in the interim to persuade him to change his mind. And so it was done. It was prepared for.

The Church of the Last Day wasn't for everyone. It wasn't for anyone with no money.

He had taken it as far as he could. It was a different beast now having evolved into something he had no control over, or wish to have control over. Age had stripped him of that type of empathy.

And now the day had come. That morning he took the *Light*, which shone sangria, in his hotel room. He was confronted by an 'X' on the screen and decided in this instance he could trust his fading eyesight. He could see but could not feel the touch of his hand on the screen. To compensate, he felt the hairs on the back of his arm stand on end like they were recipients of tiny, perfectly formed kisses. He closed his eyes and imagined that it might be her.

Despite the *Light* he saw no reason to cancel the talk

at Worcester Memorial Auditorium, although the irony of the prospect of him keeling over during his speech was not lost on him. In any case it didn't happen. At Prescott Street he was greeted by Church staff in quick-fire fashion. As specifically requested there were no airs and graces. He was ushered into a first room where he was met by a doctor in a grey suit joined by a nurse in a white uniform. He underwent a quick medical. Two puffs of glyceryl trinitrate were applied under the tongue—treatment for chest pain, relieving the strain on his heart—followed by the medical instruction, 'do not swallow'. While never prepared to go as far as welcoming it like Heather Carlson, he wasn't afraid of death, nor was he especially interested in prolonging the day, but equally didn't see the need to cause a fuss. His attitude was to let the medical staff have their twenty minutes. He was monosyllabic in his responses; bar on one occasion when he asked both doctor and nurse to stop smiling.

Among the pitiless, undercooked thuds that came with each tap the doctor made on his chest, Baumann's thoughts strayed. He considered, probably for the last time, the empire he was so instrumental in building. The media liked to portray Last Dayers as sex mad, nonagenarians included, wasted on drugs. Grudgingly, he'd have to admit to some truth in this, but that wasn't the whole picture. This wasn't the way he chose to visualise it. A Last Day was a bare room with a bed, IV drip, and a solitary cigar. It was a hospital room with surgical table set up to carry out gender reassignment surgery. It was a room of projections, made to look and feel like a fish tank, its occupant swimming in oxycodone. It was a luxury suite tailored and primed to administer several cats with lethal injection, allowing an owner to die the exact same time as her beloved pets.

But he had to come clean and admit that his favourite instance of a room was a pre-arranged one, set aside for hedge fund billionaire Harold Deeds. Deeds wanted a bank heist, having put up the five hundred grand needed to transform interconnecting rooms to stage it. He then used the ill-gotten proceeds of the 'theft' to fund several hours of post-heist luxury class debauchery, and in the process take a stubbornly long time to die. Baumann liked his style, but suggested in the future, should some wealthy entrepreneur request something similar, the mock bank shouldn't hold cash but gold bullion, which wasn't acceptable Church currency. Or else, as down payment, they'd be accepting gold fillings from the back of people's teeth.

No religious themes. (They'd held the Lutherans at bay on that score, at least so far.) There were the traditional churches for that. One could join the Church of the Last Day at any time to lend his or her support.

When the day came, members could hope to be given priority status. No cast-iron guarantee, though, especially at busy times.

Al Baumann was a priority lane all of his own. He did not enquire, but it seemed to him that he had the full run of the hotel. Examination completed, he was escorted to a second room, which he walked into alone. What greeted him was perfectly above board. A single item of note to mark it out of the ordinary; a line of cocaine on the dresser. He had stopped taking coke two decades previously when the paranoia which followed threatened to get the better of him. This also coincided with the decision to enter therapy. Not that any of this mattered anymore.

He undressed, dropping his suit and undergarments on top of each other so they formed a pile. Using his foot—intuition, in the absence of feeling, informing him that he was pressing down—he guided the pile of clothes next to the bed before urinating on them. He hadn't planned on this. He revelled instead in the spontaneity of it all. He changed into a cotton Kimono robe. Once done, Baumann tried his best to convince himself he felt like a new person, although not to the touch.

He was so close to it he could taste it.

Sitting down at the dresser, he stuck the straw provided without ceremony up his right nostril. With a bold snort, he made short work of the coke. The effect of the drug was as he remembered; instantaneous. His chest tightened, he couldn't breathe and was sweating profusely. His heart felt ripe to burst, threatening to undo any benefit from the medical treatment of before. If this was the thing that killed him, then so be it. So it began, and possibly might bring to an end, the rite of passage that was his Last Day.

One thing he had learned from all those interviews with Last Dayers, no matter how many years of dilapidation and lack of movement through chronic illness endured, a Last Day coincided with a surge; a much vaunted, newfound lease of life. It wasn't for everyone, but still a minor miracle; a final hurrah of the human spirit.

He was still alive. He was animated. Grabbing and twisting the collar of the robe as he muttered to himself. He could feel the knotted tension against his neck, which contrasted with the lack of feeling in the fingers doing the twisting. Inside him it was like his organs had rearranged, having swapped places with each other. He sweated with so much force it was unbearable, but suddenly the fever broke and he could breathe again. His robe was soaking wet, so he changed into another one. There was pressure around his bowels, but this time he decided to walk to the bathroom. Barefoot, his steps seemed weightless, like they were nothing at all. He experienced strange tingling from the calves of his legs upwards, like a set of tripped alarms, each the size of nerve endings.

He sat slumped on the toilet seat, not wanting to push or hurry things along. And then he was feeling serene, on the margins, like he didn't have a care to call his own. He thought about the *Light* from that morning, the last one he would ever take, and how it confirmed a fate he not only suspected but had been actively waiting for. Did such a frame of mind really bring him closer to Heather Carlson, who left him a decade and a half ago on a wing and a prayer and a death wish?

He was in his seventies, took cocaine up until his fifties, smoked up until his sixties, and was known to drink heavily even now when the occasion demanded. He had neither thought himself immortal nor particularly looked after himself. He had an inner drive that kept him going; didn't need much sleep, hated the idea of vacations or taking time off. If he tried to relax he picked up every illness going, his immune system collapsing like a house of cards. He had patches of painfully thin skin. He was surprised body and soul he had got this far, but wasn't asking for a recount.

When he moved, every muscle complained bitterly. Even so he was restless, not overly thankful for his life. Only history would decide if he had done any good—and only once he was no longer around. It was only natural to hope his achievements would be viewed as important and worthwhile. All woven into the one great tapestry. The history books when written might not see it that way, but he believed he had saved the world, at least temporarily, from itself.

With that, Al Baumann had his last shit. He wished it had been a solid one.

Feeling a little underwhelmed, he left the room. It only confirmed what it took him all those years to decide, that coke was overrated. He walked out into an empty corridor. Shoulder up against the wall, he experienced a crisis of faith; no longer sure if he wanted his last two wishes to come to pass. He was suddenly afraid of what might lie ahead. Had he intended to be taken quite so literally? He was giddy, which might have been another effect of the cocaine. He smiled as he reminded himself that this situation was ongoing. It was an experience, not essentially an enjoyable one. He didn't need to prove himself to anyone, but equally this was not a time for looking back. His resolve sufficiently stiffened, he opened the door to the next room.

What greeted him was a broad table which took up half the room. On top of the table was a platter; sixty inches across and forty inches wide, the size of a monster truck tyre. On top of the platter was a leatherback turtle in excess of one hundred and fifty years old. Or so it was, until boiled in an industrial pot about to be served to Baumann as his last meal. He stood for a moment to take in the size of the shell; the sheer magnificence of the creature. The turtle was killed in its prime and he wondered how many centuries of life he had deprived it. There was one he knew of in captivity at the Guangzhou Aquarium in China that was four hundred years old. In all probability, there were others swimming in the oceans older than this.

But not this one. He wanted to do something cruel and unnecessary so he could compare it against all the things he had done in the past. In his detached way, he had always thought himself to be a heartless man. If he lived a less fortunate life, or was born in the Middle Ages, or brought up in a city or country that attached less value to human life, he wondered if he would have adjusted, do what was required to get ahead, if indeed he would have prospered? He liked to think he might have.

The head of the turtle had been removed. Baumann nodded to the chef who took this as his cue. Underneath the chef's jacket was a well-built physique, Baumann noted, which wouldn't look out of place on a calendar somewhere. Noiselessly and efficiently, the chef's toned arms flexed and arched and made surprisingly short work of turning the turtle on its back. There followed a series of hefty crunches as, using a cooking pry bar, he removed the creature's backbone. He swapped the pry bar for a twenty-four centimetre chef's knife, which he used to prise out a chunk of meat from the tail. Expertly done, impaled on the knife, the meat was a near perfect square.

Baumann stepped forward in his robe and motioned to take the knife, meat and all. Chef showed no sign of hesitation as he handed it over.

Baumann scooped the meat into his mouth carefully,

mindful of the sharp blade. He chewed once and reflected that it tasted like beef. Chewing twice, it tasted like veal. He continued to chew, reluctant, almost afraid to swallow. It tasted like everything he had ever tasted before. There was nothing new here. Nothing to titillate or excite the palate. He spat the masticated contents of his mouth onto the floor, and avoiding eye contact with the chef, turned and walked out of the room with a grunt.

He returned to the corridor and couldn't stop his body shaking. He was convinced in a way now he wasn't fully before that this was his time. He was ready to submit, finally, and be done with it. There was pain. For a long time—for as long as he could remember, probably longer—there had been pain. He clutched at his chest, his body hunched protectively, which seemed to him a pointless act. There was nothing external to protect. It was all happening inside. On his Last Day he hoped for a deeper understanding. He hoped for meaning, enlightenment, but there was nothing of the sort, only muddled thinking and confusion.

His clutching hand was up at his face now. He saw it was so by the crooked shape of his fingers, which he supposed was progress of a kind. He wasn't going to die, at least not right this minute. He was still himself, still possessive of his faculties. He wasn't the kind of man to stand still. It didn't matter if this turned out to be a journey of adventure or misadventure. It didn't matter to him at all. It hurt to breathe, but breathe is what he did, elevating it into an act of defiance. So resigned, he took the next door along, to face head-on what remained of his day.

She wanted to die, or so she claimed; or so, when

they last spoke all those years ago, she had him believe. She disappeared and the more he fought against the need to try and find her, the more abrasive and painful the obsession it became. There were rumours that she was starving to death somewhere in Eastern Europe. That she was participating in drug trials in South Africa. That wherever she was, in some godforsaken part of the world, she bated death at every turn. He wondered if she ever contemplated ending it all, drinking a cup of acid or throwing herself in front of a speeding train. But that would have meant suicide and that was never her style. And in any case, she knew very well since the advent of the *Light*, suicide levels were broadly unchanged. Suicide did not come before the *Light*. It did not take precedence.

Still, over the years he did his best to keep rumours of her various death wish dalliances out of the media. He made it known she was the opposite. Wherever she went, she was all about safety first: the blunting of knives, the closing of fire doors, the halving of grapes. He claimed he did so to protect the reputation of the Church, but his motivations cut deeper. Some days he woke, glad of the growing distance between them both; the fact she was nowhere near him. Other days an intense longing surrounded him like an outer layer of skin. An overwhelming, cascading desire to see her again that could not be explained, not least by him.

And it occurred to him that up until now they'd been clean out of his thoughts, First Mother and Child: Jennifer and Daniel Coutinho. Never to get a look in, it was them and God. Forgotten, swallowed up by the banality of it all, the triteness of familiarity, the daily running of things.

He walked into the next room knowing that this would be the last one he would ever walk into. Deep within him, burrowed so far down—even if it could be found it would be impossible to remove—was a profound tiredness. He was done with life and done with fighting for it.

Waiting inside was a woman roughly about Heather Carlson's size, from what he could remember. She wore an ill-fitting wig, more silver, more platinum than blonde. In her mid-to-late forties, perhaps. A little on the young side, certainly. She didn't fit comfortably in her own skin. He had to cut her some slack, though; whoever she was, the board would have acquired her services at very late notice.

Her hand went up to her mouth and she coughed. It was a violent cough, an upheaval, things shifting inside. When she took away her hand, there was a trace of blood on her fingers. Visibly flustered, hand withdrawn, she did her best to hide the bloody discharge from the watching Baumann.

'You recognise me,' he said. 'You know who I am?'

'Yes,' she said, but her voice carried little in the way of conviction. 'You are Alan.'

'You're a Last Dayer?' he said.

'Yes,' she said. This time her response was more assured.

'You have family?'

'Two children.'

'They'll be well looked after. You have my guarantee.'

She nodded. Baumann nodded too. This was her price. His personal guarantee after today wouldn't mean a thing, but he knew the board would ensure all was in hand. They'd fast-track the paperwork; cross the t's and dot the i's. This was why she was here, why she was part of this. It came down to ensuring the future welfare of her children when she was gone.

Baumann had his children as well. They numbered in the millions.

She glanced down and saw there was a knife in his hand. A twenty-four centimetre chef's knife to be precise.

He lunged forward and stabbed her in the throat. He tried with limited success to twist the blade one way and then the other. There was hardly any give on the knife and he couldn't put it all down to the lack of sensation in his hands. Even so, where it entered, the blade was sharp and unrepentant, and before he knew it blood was everywhere.

Her hands convulsed, taking on the shape of ever decreasing circles. For a second she was up on her tiptoes. It was over in a blink of an eye and Al Baumann was thankful for this. Believing he had done enough, he let go of the blade's handle. She fell back onto the bed as gracefully as someone fatally wounded could be expected to; knife still stuck in her throat, body shuddering ever so slightly, until even those understated movements came to a stop. Surprisingly, through all the violence, her wig had stayed on.

For one last time he examined the woman, now lying dead on a hotel bed. She was supposed to look like Heather Carlson—that's what he had asked for—but this unfortunate creature barely mustered pass marks. Heather Carlson often called him Alan, so at least her substitute, the short time he'd spent in her company, seemed adequately briefed. And she had to be another Last Dayer. She had to die that day, or else what would have been the point? It was confirmation, if confirmation was required, that the Church—his Church—was in capable hands.

How much further could it go? The world was its oyster. They were inextricably linked; one synonymous with the other. Where there was the *Light*, there was the Church of the Last Day.

He had been so close. He wanted to see what it would be like; to feel something, but at the end of it there was only numbness towards what he had done. There was no revulsion or guilt. Perhaps these emotions would come later; so late in the day that they may never in fact arise. It was never a question of self-gratification. What satisfaction was there to be gained from extinguishing a life? Something so determined and written in the stars, it was death that brought them together. They were kindred spirits. They were the same. Time was borrowed, no longer their own. And yet, here he was still standing, breathing, covered in another person's blood while she bled out in the same room missing a pulse.

Could there be such a thing as a concord with death? Nearly two years ago, Baumann had decided there was no going back, that he wanted to take a life. And it would be death in turn that selected his victim. Was this to be his payoff, his reward for helping to bring death so much more into the fold?

But it wasn't death, it was its emissary which did all of these things. It was its herald; its envoy. It was the *Light*.

Except that this wasn't enough. She had to be held up as a reflection. She had to be someone very much from the past.

131

He sat slumped at the bottom of the bed. Depressingly, too many questions were rolling and bouncing around in his head. At this stage in his long life of three quarters of a century even a single question was one too many. The world around him, the walls of the room, were fading, now barely worthy of an outline. Or was it him who was fading slowly from view? He was not a murderer. He had never killed anyone in his life up until today. And today did not count.

Al Baumann's first memory, as first memories invariably go, was a traumatic one. He must have been two or three years old. He had no recollection of his surroundings, but he guessed he must have been outdoors. Who knows what he was thinking of? No doubt they were blissful, infantile, incomplete thoughts, effortlessly at ease with a world he was only at the cusp of beginning to understand. A yellow hornet appeared buzzing around him, occupying more than one position at any one time, evading his flapping hands. It toyed with him the way hornets were prone to do. Then he felt it, like something had grabbed his mouth really hard and twisted. The twisting soon turned to burning. He stood for a few moments as his brain tried to decipher what was happening to him—the sting like a miniature lance protruded from his bottom lip—before a reaction at last kicked in and he ran howling for his mother.

He felt stupid and broken without her, but on he went. He was still that child; still feeling his way. Still howling. Nothing had changed. He had only grown old.

He had long expected that the only days which mattered would be the First Day back in 1998 and the Last Day, which in his case was today. Everything that fell between would seem meaningless in comparison, trivial and wasteful. It was only now looking down that he registered his blood-splattered robe. He thought about changing into a fresh one, but decided against it.

It was all about laying a ghost to rest, but he couldn't even lay himself to rest.

'You can get up now,' he said. His voice, at least to his ears, was surprisingly fresh and strident. 'It's OK. We can do anything we want. This is our day and no one can take that away from us.'

With this, he waited for his own demise, but not before a variation had come to him, a twist if you will on one of his most famous lines. At least it was something he could still enjoy now it was just him on his own.

If Death didn't do irony, then tell me what else would it do?

8

Gossamer

The house was spacious, bereft of furniture as it was, but freezing cold. Si could have sworn it was colder inside than out. One thing for sure, if he needed any encouragement to wear a dead man's coat then this was it.

She took him to a room on the first floor. Before leaving, she issued strict instructions not to go wandering off. 'Some of the people here can get a teensy bit proprietary,' she said. 'They don't take well to trespassers.'

Si was again left to his own thoughts, despite having proved earlier that this was a lot like playing Russian roulette. He had no idea if anything of any note would occur to him. He had a tight social circle of family and friends. He only spent time with people he didn't know and trust when he had to (a work night out, basically).

Although he hadn't a clue where his current arrangements would fit in (this was no work night out).

He never took himself to be vacuous and empty-headed, though, that was a new one on him. He was particularly proud of the time he lost half his friends on Facebook thanks to a post enquiring whether there should be a name for the social media fad for putting up regular selfies of yourself losing weight, but neglecting to post anything when you piled it all back on again. But that was last year. It all blew over and he got all his 'friends' back (and more besides). Now he was thinking, trying to remember the last time he had something to say that came across as actually something to say.

The room was a fair size, more so while empty. Laid out on the floor were a couple of bare mattresses a couple of feet apart. Both had seen better days. Si was doing all he could to avoid staring at them, and therefore establishing just how grim the whole set up was. The only other thing of note was a bookshelf packed with books up against the far wall. The closest thing to a splash of colour on offer on an otherwise blank and utterly miserable canvas.

Just like waiting for the number 442 bus—you wait for hours for a single thought to enter your brain for hours only for twenty to arrive all at once. Evidence of thinking now rushed through his head like a flash flood; one that threatened to carry off his brain. *These guys are squatters; what have they got to be proprietary about? They don't work, spend most of their time skulking on street corners and staring down grandmas and shouting insults at dog walkers; they've surely got the time to brighten things up, some painting and decorating maybe? They're going to murder me, not today because the Light gave me the okay, but that doesn't mean they won't bide their time and knock me unconscious, take me hostage, and lay me out on one of those mattresses and eviscerate me like Jack the Ripper. They'll steal my organs, hide my limbs. Bury my body parts under the floorboards.*

He wondered how much more internal dialogue it would take before he drove himself mad. Grateful for the distraction, he nudged his overheated mind towards the bookshelf. He checked out the spines of the numerous books there.

There was *The Escaped Cock* by DH Lawrence, which stood out for reasons he hoped weren't too immature. *Trainspotting*—appropriate enough considering the grimness of the surroundings—by Irvine Welsh. *The Master and Margarita* by Mikhail Bulgakov. *Time's Arrow: or The Nature of the Offence* by Martin Amis. So far, along this hard and paperback landscape, it was an eclectic list. He spotted one that piqued his interest, or at least one he thought he recognised. He placed his finger on the top of the book and felt a connection to the outside world.

'*I Am Legend*. Richard Matheson,' a voice rang out. 'Greatest last line ever.'

He turned to see that Ollie had returned. In her hand was a 70 cl bottle of whisky, three-quarters full.

'I've seen the movie,' he said.

'Which one?' she said.

'You mean there's more than one?' He was thinking of the Will Smith-starring feature. From what he could ascertain, having never read the book, they stayed true to the source material. He knew the novel was written in the 1950s and book and movie were set during a vampire/zombie apocalypse. So there was no *Light*, but that didn't stop Smith's character from knowing he was going to die anyway. Si felt incredibly sad at this, consumed by unhappiness, sinking as he did into a well of misery. But instead of Will Smith, perhaps he was really thinking about the dog from the movie.

She was thinking too. She shifted the whisky bottle from one hand to the next, careful not to froth up the liquid. She joined him in appraising the bookshelf. They stood in silence but hadn't known each other for long enough—hadn't grown comfortable in each other's company—for the tranquillity to last.

'Old Charlie, he didn't want to burn books,' she said. 'He may have been many things, but the one thing he went to great lengths to point out—he wasn't a fucking Nazi.'

'Was that before you burned him alive, then?' Si turned to look at Ollie. He hoped she was taking him seriously. He wanted her to know he wasn't afraid of her.

She shook her head slowly, despairingly. 'Oh, for god's sake,' she said.

She crouched and eased out with her finger a thin book from the bottom shelf. She held it out to him. The book had an illustrated cover of three children sat high up on a tree on a large twisting branch. Two girls either side and in the middle a white-haired boy. They had a look of freedom about them, the kind only children could truly express.

Si made a funny face but took the book from her anyway. He leafed through the pages. 'It's got pictures inside,' he said.

'It's a children's book. *The Magic Faraway Tree*,' she said, making a face. 'You don't know it? Maybe you're too old. Yes, that's probably it.'

'It's about a boy called Dick,' she said, taking care to place a little too much emphasis on the boy's name. 'He joins his cousins on lots of secret adventures in magical lands on top of the Faraway Tree,' she continued. There's a different land each time they visit. *The Land of Toys*—more dangerous than you'd think—*Topsy-Turvy Land, The Land of Tempers* …'

'There's *The Land of Do-As-You-Please*. I suppose this strikes a chord with the *Light* generation that's helped spark a revival, made it popular again. I just love the book, always have.'

'The one you're holding, that's the UK version, not one of the horrible sanitised American versions you see around where Dick becomes fucking Rick.' She smiled, then sniffed, then breathed through her nose. 'Enid Blyton wrote it in the 1940s, but if she was alive now she'd probably call it *The Land of Do-What-You-Want.*'

'I know what you're thinking? ' she said.

'You do?'

'Enid Blyton was a product of her time. If she was with me now, we'd have a sit down, a cup of tea, and I'd have a quiet word.'

Si wasn't sure how to react to this. He wondered if she'd still be having this conversation even if he wasn't in the room.

'Maybe one day I might get the chance,' she said.

She was smiling at him. What he wanted most at this time was to clear his head, but none of this was helping.

He handed the book back to her. 'I was thinking, the 1940s,' he said, 'she wouldn't have known it was going to happen. No foreknowledge. The day she was going to die, I mean.'

'She was in a nursing home by then, in her seventies,' she said. 'She might have had an inkling.'

'Don't know why I said that,' he said. 'Don't want to come across as one of those people who dismiss out of hand anything that happened before 1998.'

'Who cares what happened five minutes ago?' She waggled the bottle in front of him, no longer averse to whipping up a little froth. 'Come on, sit your arse down and let's get anaesthetised.'

It couldn't last forever. None of this could last forever. Even forever couldn't last forever. Now that he'd kick-started that part of his brain, he couldn't figure out how to shut it down. The thinking wouldn't stop and there was the further realisation that this was still the same day. It was still light outside. How could this be, after all that had happened? After all he had seen? The smell of smoke was still about him, on his clothes. How could this still be the same day?

He didn't relish the prospect of parking his arse, or any other part of him, on the most terrifying mattress in the world, but boy was she the bossy one. He had a threshold where if it got too much—if someone got too overbearing—he'd simply walk away, but she hadn't pushed him to that point, at least not yet. He couldn't remember the last time he saw a bare mattress for any more than five seconds, but this one rendered him pathologically squeamish. But he was 'resigned to his fate,' he'd have that on his gravestone. The carpet showed signs of recently being hoovered, which was something at least.

As soon as he plonked himself down, she passed him the bottle, cap removed. He'd always avoided whisky. His spirit of choice was vodka, or at a stretch gin. He'd never felt the need to change. But he was thinking after the day he'd had, nothing could make it any worse, could it? He was thinking that he'd already taken up too much time thinking.

He took a slug and swished it around his mouth before swallowing. An explosion of heat burst out across his nose and throat. There was the pressure to retch. He had never drunk disinfectant but had just discovered mankind had reinvented and repackaged it in the belief it could be somehow mistaken as fit for public consumption. He withdrew the bottle from his mouth, holding it askew, casting over it an inquisitorial half-crazed eye. On the bottle was a black label moving up forming a diagonal. A forward slash of treacherous possibilities.

For a second, he was back in his hall, Geoff's fingers tight around his neck.

All he could say was, 'Why?'

'You never had whisky straight before?' she said.

He hurriedly passed the bottle back to Ollie. It was literally too hot to handle. His fingers slid down from his chin to his throat, circling and massaging his Adam's apple. Eventually, thankfully, gloriously, the heat abated.

'You know what, I don't remember,' he answered. 'If I did, it probably killed those sets of brain cells that did remember.'

They sat on separate mattresses. She took off her cardigan and exposed her arms, which showed signs of scarring. Long splintering lines, making their starting point the bend of her arm. She stared at him long and hard; waited until he was sure he had noticed. He was a difficult one to work out, but then again, so was she.

'You still gay?' she said.

'I don't have some switch,' he said. 'How do you think it works? Wait, I don't care, please don't answer that. Look, I'm just some dude. My fuck-ups are no different from any other guy. I hope for the same things. I like what I like. I mean, in this day and age, does it matter? Please for your sake, not mine, don't tell me it matters.'

She made another face. 'Christ, keep your hair on. Didn't realise you were my big gay dad.' She stuck out her bottom lip. 'You ever been with a girl?'

It was his turn to suck up air, noisily and greedily, through his nose. 'Once,' he said, 'it didn't work out.'

'Obviously,' she said and broke into a broad smile. 'Hey, hot stuff, I'm only shitting with you.'

'Why not try telling me about yourself?' he said. He looked around him, if only to serve as a reminder that there wasn't much of anything to look at. 'This some kind of squat?'

She looked away from him, her eyes instead settling on the bookshelf, which from where she was sitting, like any self-respecting oasis, seemed pretty far away.

'I don't believe in the past,' she said. 'I'm no great fan of the present either, and I think the future might be overrated. But I'll make an exception for you, dear, always for you. Charlie was an angry old man. He spent most of his time in bed, but for an hour every day it was like he summoned his energy, gathered his strength, and he'd swear like a trooper and bang on the walls and threaten the neighbours with murder and rape. All kinds of demented behaviour.'

'Didn't the neighbours call the police?'

'The police again.' She turned momentarily to flash Si a half-smile. 'It was us—*we* turned up. That's what we do: me, Mo, and Elijah. You've met Mo; he punched you in the face and gave you a coat. Elijah is a little more understated, one of the world's duckers and divers who likes to keep in the background. He does like his hashish, though. Mo's dad knew Charlie from the Merchant Navy. So, like I said, we turned up and started living here and we went round the neighbourhood and assured everyone that we'd look after him. We'd keep a close watch. We'd be no trouble. We'd keep ourselves to ourselves.'

She took a swig of whisky then handed the bottle back to Si. For a moment, time stood still; Ollie with outstretched arm, Si not sure, not wanting to move, not even to make the simplest of gestures. But it was clear she wasn't going to continue talking until he'd taken a drink. She wanted her pound of flesh.

The whisky went down his oesophagus, but not without a fight, not without leaving a stain. He thought he might spew, but the sensation thankfully passed to be replaced not so thankfully with a tightness around the belly. He would have loved to have remarked that this was a more bearable experience than the first one, but hand on fluttering heart he could not. He was in Hell.

'We'd push Charlie on his chair and he'd take the *Light* at the flat end of the street. He didn't trust us to climb the hill. He thought we'd let him go and the fall would kill him. As it turned out, something else inside him was doing just that. He knew he was going to die, insisted we make preparations, and he made us promise. He'd set his heart on a Viking funeral, or at least his version of it. The bastard had planned it all along, one last finger up at the neighbours. Pretty fucking twisted.' She held out the bottle in brisk fashion once more. 'He was so out of it on whisky and co-codamol he wouldn't have felt a thing. In fact, before the fire, he was probably dead already.'

'And before you ask, I gave him the co-codamol, so I would have killed him that way as well.'

On this occasion Si took the bottle without persuasion. It was vile stuff, but so was the world. 'It's horrible,' he said. 'It goes against everything that is civilised.' He took stock before deciding he wasn't done judging it. 'It's not … normal.'

'There were children watching,' he said. 'Why didn't anyone stop it?'

'Fear,' she said. 'Isn't that the answer to why we do—or don't do—anything? It's always fear. And on the day we die, the government automatically owns everything. Someone's whole estate handed over to the state, excuse the fucking wordplay. This is serious. How did we allow this to happen?'

She was smiling now, but there was no light behind her eyes.

'We just did,' she said. 'All we have of ourselves—to call our own—are our deaths, as fucked up as that sounds. Everyone is so shit scared their Last Day will be taken from them, they're not going to take it from anyone else—even from Charlie, even if they despised the old fart and he hated them back with a vengeance. They were never going to interfere.'

143

She hunched her shoulders. 'And kids, they love the idea of fires, yeah,' she said. 'They don't much care what's in them.'

Her shoulders remained hunched. She released a long sigh, tucking one leg underneath her other leg, her knee pointing at him. 'And whatever you're thinking, you're wrong. I tried to persuade him against it. I tried my best and I lost.'

'Now there's nothing left of him,' he said, suddenly feeling emotional, more than he ever would have expected.

Maybe the firewater was having an effect. It wasn't just that, it was everything. He was in such an utterly hopeless situation. He felt he could cry.

'It's what he wanted,' she said.

'I've no idea why I came back to the pub,' he said. 'I realised, I don't really have any friends. And I've let down my best friend and I can't stop feeling angry when I think about what he did. I wanted to be with people who weren't anybody. I thought I was worthless. I should be with people I deserve to be with, if that makes any sense.' Si's eyes widened. It was Ollie who filled his vision. 'Sorry. I didn't mean…'

'No offence taken,' she said. She leaned forward, suddenly quite excitable. 'I don't take the *Light*.'

'You don't…'

'I don't take the *Light*. I refuse to die.' She brought her wrists together, twisting them so at angles to each other. She did so subconsciously, or so it seemed to Si. 'I won't play the government's game. Think about it, who benefits from all this Last Day shit? Death equals massive business. *What* benefits?'

As it happened, he wasn't in the mood to say anything and she wasn't in the mood to pause for breath.

'What about the charities, why don't they complain? The good citizens can no longer donate their life savings in the event of their deaths to their favourite charitable trusts. It all goes to Big Brother. Every registered charity gets their share of the pot. They receive their percentage. They're not complaining because they've all been bought off.'

'Even Barnardo's?' he said.

Si was thinking again. He was thinking it was time to thank the person in front of him for her hospitality and insight, make his excuses, and go home. He would make peace with Sofi, grovel if he had to—would have to. He'd take the blame for everything.

And then he didn't feel anything like that. He was seated on a mattress drinking whisky straight out of the bottle in the company of a lunatic. He didn't feel threatened.

Part of him was curious, devilishly so, to see where all this would lead him. He was on two weeks' compassionate leave, this was true, but compassion was the last thing on his mind. In his younger days he was fiercely compulsive, which made for some great nights and some horrendous days. Then he settled down and he'd stop himself from thinking about those times by counting from a thousand backwards. By hook or by crook he'd force his mind onto other things. Now he was feeling differently, now there was an itch he could not ignore. He wanted to put it to the test, did he miss them or not, the *good old days*?

He had everything he wanted—Sofi, the kids—but that

in itself could never match up to the exquisitely excruciating sensation of wanting something else.

There was a creak from the outside the door. Sticking his head through the door was the man who punched Si and gave him a dead man's coat.

'We got a screamer, right,' Mo said. 'We're all meeting downstairs. Ten minutes.'

Si sat, face crumpled, feeling his whole body sag. Understandably, he was wary of this man. He looked at Ollie, who he didn't know at all—but not for the first time he had this need for immediate emotional support and she would have to do.

'It's okay. I promised, didn't I?' she said. Half a smile became three-quarters. 'He's okay, you two just got off on the wrong foot. He likes you really, I think, or why would he have given you the coat? Like I said, his name is Mo. Sometimes it's Moses, other times it's Mohammed, easier just to call him Mo. Honestly, he's a sweetie pie, you'll see.'

Everything seemed to come back to the coat, but for Si he wasn't convinced. He was a million miles away from calling him sweetie pie.

The whisky was in Ollie's possession and she took another drink. 'He likes you, honest. You know, I was fond of Charlie, more than I should have been. I wanted away from the Viking funeral first opportunity I got. I was knotted inside.' And she held her stomach in a way to suggest the knot was still there tying up her insides. 'And you turned up and you were the excuse I needed to up sticks and vamoose. Mo saw that; saw beyond the rashness of his actions. I mean it was just him being stupid, lamebrained, whatever.'

She could see Si had become withdrawn. As words of comfort went, hers were proving flatter than a pancake. 'You came back,' she said. 'You remember what you said to me when you walked through the door a second time, tail between your legs? Even more bitter and disillusioned with life than before if this was possible? "You promise no one's going to hurt me again?" That's what you said. That's what you asked me.'

'And you promised,' he said meekly. He knew what he was asking for. No more punches from Mo or from anyone else. He was miserable; the saddest wretch in Christendom. 'I'm messed up, there's no point denying it. Things have … happened. Things I need to deal with. And my head's still messed up. I just wanted to be somewhere, anywhere, where a promise might mean something. Or not mean something, I don't know.'

He looked sick. He was sick. Too sick to be in the company of dead people. 'Screamer?' he asked, voice just audible enough to be heard in an empty room.

'Just an expression.' She handed over the bottle. 'Here, one last mouthful for courage before we go check it out.'

They ventured outside as a group; Ollie, Mo, Elijah, and Si. Si was the one who stuck out; didn't fit in; didn't walk like them; didn't smell like them (apart from the old man's coat he picked up when he returned to the pub). The others walked at pace, bodies tensed, coiled, ready for anything lurking around any corner should it decide to jump out at them.

Lining the street, the blackened husks of Charlie and his belongings still remained. It was like an urban version of a killing field, too cold for there to be residual heat. Monuments of residual ash atop an asphalt lake of

147

hardened tar. Someone had put a blanket over what little was left of Charlie and his favourite chair.

All four of them played the part, kept their heads down as if in supplication. As they shuffled past, an ambulance attendant and someone official wearing council overalls gesticulated at each other while they argued. Still no sign of the police, though.

Once they'd left the street, they took a route the shape of a lightning bolt. Si moved along with the others, but if his legs sought an explanation for the erratic, alternatively flat-footed then fleet-footed movement, his brain was unable to offer them one. Then, as he approached another street which could have been any street in the whole wide world as long as it was situated in London, he could hear where it began and ended, the outer shell of a roar. A fearful combination of shouting and screaming which seemed to come from one source, one voice. For a second, just a moment, Si was disorientated. He was spinning and had to reassure his legs, and every other aspect of himself, that it wasn't him. He wasn't the one screaming.

They were in another street. On each side was a mishmash of flats. Council flats. Ex-council flats. Terraced flats. Rabbit hutches; door upon door; indented slabs of wood and plaster and glass. Si was comforted by the presence of streetlights, a recently painted red pillar box, and a small compact convenience store. Things he could accept without question as real.

There was another crowd; another set of people with apparently nothing better to do than stand outside in the bitter cold. There was shouting, 'Jesus Christ! Jesus Christ! I don't fucking believe it. It's not right. Not right!'

In another life, a short time ago, these could have been Si's words.

The group joined the crowd, assimilating perfectly. They weren't there to interact, only spectate like the others. They were watching a man in jeans and loose dressing gown. No shoes; he was only wearing socks. He had the look of a deranged person, baring jagged yellowing teeth, which absolutely added to the effect. Occasionally, he dropped down to his knees to pound the pavement with his bare fists. Si had to make sense of it somehow. The guy, the focus of everyone's attention, was Charlton Heston on the beach at the end of the movie *Planet of the Apes* (the original one). He had been shouting and screaming at the top of his voice for hours. Si could hear it in his vocal chords; raspy and breathy, raw and taut. Amongst the relentless ranting, Si thought he heard an utterance of: 'God damn you all to Hell,' but this was probably wishful thinking on his part.

Si observed the faces around him. Ollie's impenetrable stare, Mo's busy, bouncing eyes, Elijah's dreadlocks dividing up a sallow face and heavy eyelids. He didn't know these people and yet he felt he already knew them more than he would ever have wanted to.

There weren't any children this time around, but the watching crowd seemed to have regressed to that of a childlike state. Mouths open, mawkish, childish in every aspect. They were in the thrall of every involuntary jerk played out by the shouty Charlton Heston man, for here was the Last Dayer they were all there to see.

Si was trying to join dots that were not on the same page. In order, he supposed, to go quietly, we needed to make a noise. You didn't have to experience burning to know how awful it was, to realise how much it would hurt. But that didn't stop you, either, finding out the hard way.

So what was the point of life? To exist? To sample what you could? Experience everything the world had to offer? To love and be loved in return?

'I'm going to die today! Going to meet my maker! The *Light* says so, but there's nothing wrong with me!' Charlton Heston was now on his back, flat out on the ground, bloodied hands not so much flailing as paddling. He remonstrated through a mouth so contorted it hardly qualified as human. 'I'm not ill. I'm only forty-nine! I want to see a doctor! Why won't they send me a doctor?'

Si found he was largely unsympathetic. In coming to this conclusion, he had surprised himself. He wasn't used to this, being a man of surprises. How many hours had the guy sat in his flat, disbelieving, before finally snapping and marching outside to make an exhibition of himself? Where was his family, did they even want to know? Did they care? Did he live alone? He'd never known a place like London for so many people to live alone. No one knew anybody anymore. It was bad enough for the living needing to deal with the aftermath of death without having to cope with the day leading up to it as well. Where you could reach out and touch and embrace the ones you love, only to hold hands and wrap arms around shoulders already dead to you.

Si was searching; grappling for context he hoped was not in vain. He didn't want to be a stranger in this city he had come to call home. He turned to gaze at the other side of the street. The sun was setting and as it dipped, reflected on many windows. It was done with them—Charlton Heston, him, the rest of the sorry bunch—happy to see the back of yet another day.

He thought about his children, Alex and Julia. He wasn't with them; they weren't with him. If there was a connection it wasn't a strong one; not as strong as it could and should have been. Back before they made the decision to adopt, if Si was being honest, he wasn't too crazy about the prospect of having kids. But Sofi wanted children and Si loved Sofi. He wanted to give him what he wanted. The children were actual brother and sister, aged a couple of years apart with Alex the elder having turned five at the start of the adoption process; at the point Si and Sofi first showed an interest. Their parents were drug addicts, or this was as much as Si could ascertain. At least one of them was dead or in prison. The upshot of it was that the children were taken into care.

So many hoops to jump through, a process without end, but every obstacle brought Si and Sofi closer together to the point they were inseparable. They were a unit. Behind closed doors, there were tears. So much in the way of intrusion into their own lives from so many faceless bureaucrats and social workers. But they played to the rules; the more the professionals peered through the looking glass, the more transparent they both became. Significantly, it helped their case the fact they wanted to adopt both siblings together. Many couples, they were informed (at least anecdotally), would push for the youngest only. It would appear including a six-year-old as part of the package (time was moving on) was a deal breaker for many. And then one day—a blessed day, a different day, one with a radically different outcome—they were successful. They took them on and rebranded them; showing little interest in knowing, never mind retaining, the children's original names.

His first memory of them was of their tiny eyes, terrified and alert. They were two tiny aliens having beamed down to a planet they found incomprehensible. That was typical of Si. He always looked at the eyes, maybe not at first but he'd get round to it as inevitable as rain in Manchester and smog in London. And he wondered what sights they'd seen living with their junky malfunctioning, hopelessly biological parents. In the beginning, Alex was overly protective of his younger sister. And to be fair to Si and Sofi, no amount of courses and meetings could have prepared them for the levels of violence from someone so diminutive and fierce and young. But Sofi was tenacious in terms of patience; the determination to turn things around and make it work. And Sofi won out; he brought normality where before there was only upset and fear, and now two years on they were just the brightest, kindest kids, tremendous potential, great company, full of life. It was all in the eyes.

As Si got to know them, laugh and cry with them, he began to love them. He saw them as his own, but with this came a nagging doubt. He had always found love the easiest emotion to acquire. How simply it came to him and how cheapened in turn this would eventually make him feel. All those relationships in the past ruined, sullied, crashed on the rocks. He could have made them work if only he had tried hard enough. If only the initial part hadn't come so easy. And yet—if Si was honest with himself, or with Sofi or with anyone, with these kids—despite the unbelievable levels of hard work, the threat hanging over them of an emotional and physical battering, the stranger and more alien the children were at the start was the time he felt closest to them. For a long time Si was a child himself, let loose on an adult world, lacking the incentive or means to properly grow up. So it was the early days, the embryonic ones, it was the baby steps which made the most sense to him, where it all felt that much more real.

And now danger seemed everywhere, especially to Sofi, having sent the kids off to stay with his sister. For how long, who knows? To be fair, they had been threatened in their own home. By a man Si had more or less invited in.

And he could count on one hand his friends on Facebook that weren't Sofi's as well. The ties that bind now seemed like threads.

It felt like he was in a cage, one of his own making; one he had walked into voluntarily, locking himself in and throwing away the key. It was only hours since he had last set eyes on his husband and already this seemed like the longest day.

How was he feeling today? It wasn't the first time Si had asked himself the question, but this perhaps was the first time when he was afraid of the answer. Earlier that morning he'd wanted time to think and now see where that had got him. His thoughts grew darker, devoid of light; darker than the dark side of the moon.

And now day was turning to dusk and he could feel the freeze moving surreptitiously into everyone's pockets. The Last Dayer remained kneeling, sobbing, interspersed with exaggerated heaves of the chest. Some of the crowd, sensing the show was petering-out, began to peel away.

Ollie walked towards the man and with a flourish

presented the bottle of whisky from inside the front of her coat. 'Come on, get up,' she told him.

The best the man could offer was a shake of the head. Otherwise he was a spent force, strictly not for moving.

She rolled her eyes and decided against offering her hand. 'Okay just stay there,' she sighed. She unscrewed the top of the bottle.

She handed the kneeling man the whisky, of which he took a sizable gulp, swallowing vehemently, his Adam's apple bobbing.

'Tell you what, I know what you'll be dying of,' she said. 'Alcohol poisoning.'

He looked up at her looming over him like a Mother Theresa dressed in combat trousers and duffle coat. He began to chuckle; the very beginnings of a belly laugh so low it could have started at the knees.

'Funny,' he said before switching his attention to the bottle, lips already apart, ready for the next almighty swig.

There was a crack in the air. Something sliced through the man's neck. The projectile followed a precise trajectory carving up the femoral artery, obliterating several cervical vessels. Instantly, the man dropped the bottle, which smashed as if part of some ceremonial launch, except this was no ship's bow, only pavement. Almost as an afterthought, the man placed his hand on his neck, but it was so much window dressing. He couldn't halt the blood spurts pushing through the gaps in his fingers, only altering the direction of dispersal. The man still on his knees leaned back, stretched like the back end of a catapult.

Ollie eyed the flats on the opposite street. Up on high

she detected an open window and there, sticking out, was the barrel of an air pistol.

It was an air gun pellet that did the damage. It could just as easily have hit kneeling Charlton Heston in the shoulder, resulting in nothing more than a flesh wound. Normally the chances of causing anything approaching this extent of damage were miniscule, but on this day of all days, perhaps less so.

She turned her head to take in her side of the street. From a long, perhaps never-ending line of flats she sought a telltale sign and found, situated on the second storey, one in particular with front door left ajar. 'Is that your place?' she asked absent-mindedly, not expectant of a reply.

She turned to Elijah.

Elijah got out his phone and jabbed in a single digit three times. When he spoke into it, it was little more than a hiss. 'Ambulance,' he said.

In the attendant shock, Si couldn't help but stare at the phone and think of home and of zipped fleece pockets.

Blood was pumping out of Charlton Heston at an alarming rate. It was as if the blood had never wanted to be there in the first place, had been previously held inside his body against its will, not sparing the horses as it seized the chance to escape. Ollie urged the man to keep applying pressure on the wound. All the while she could see his fingers twitch, slowly relinquishing their grip. The blood was finding other escape routes. Crimson bubbles lined his mouth.

Elijah was on the phone talking to the call handler. He was raising his voice, which volume-wise, where anyone else would be concerned, came across as speaking at normal levels. 'Yes, yes, he's a Last Dayer, but you're not listening to me—he's been shot. He's bleeding. He's out in the street. What? What other priorities? Come on, man, that's mental, that can't be right.'

There were more shots; this time pinging around Ollie's feet. She turned to run.

'Fuck it!' Elijah hung up and followed her lead. Si and Mo weren't far behind.

By the time they reached the far end of the street, a strange metamorphosis had occurred. Where before there was only fear and flight, they now experienced something different.

Si and Mo ran side by side. Si was aware of Mo's wheezing mixed with laughter. Si was smiling, too. Perhaps this was the only way for Si to deal with this new world uncovered before him. Here he was scurrying alongside and sharing a moment with the man who punched him. The man who put him down on his back for deigning to protest at the monstrous spectacle of another man set on fire. Si realised right then that he was on the same alien planet Alex and Julia first landed on. Back then, it was him and Sofi who stopped them from running; put themselves up as emotional and physical shields, but in the here and now there was no one to block Si, not in the same way.

Si angled his run slightly so he was closer to Mo. He jutted out his arm, landing a hand square on Mo's chest and gave it a push. Not a strong push, but enough to upset the big man's balance, causing him to take a tiny, baby stumble.

Mo's initial reaction was quizzical and furious, but this quickly changed, feeding on Si's playful expression. Arms thrust out, so he resembled at least from the waist up Boris Karloff as The Mummy, Mo tried to return the favour. But Si was too quick and nimble for him.

Si was running not from something or anything, but from everything. And he would keep on running, he was sure of it, up until the point he reached *The Land of Do-As-You-Please*.

Sprinting, scampering, breathing out, breathing in, he was having the time of his life.

9

Panda Panda

When he went to bed, the last thing on his mind was pandas. When he awoke, his first thought was of pandas too.

It wasn't always that way. Professor Arnold Freemantle, Arnie to his associates (he wouldn't go as far as to claim he had any friends), was a radical thinker, and you don't become a radical thinker without putting challenging theories out there along with the stats, projections, and sheer bloody-minded conviction to back them up. In the early seventies, he was, among others, a proponent of the worldwide population sterilisation programme. This proposed all families should be restricted to a maximum of one child, with financial inducements to be made to parents in return for their consent to be sterilised. Freemantle argued that only having one child wasn't the end of the world; in fact it would go a long way to ensure the opposite. He also pointed out, rather superfluously all things considered, that he was an only child and he turned out all right.

His and his ilk's theories were generally discredited, but India did adopt a sterilisation program in the mid-seventies where men who volunteered to be sterilised received the gift of a transistor radio. In 1979, China also introduced a one-child policy and Freemantle was quick to take credit for this. When confronted by the assertion families desperate for a boy were abandoning female babies to die in ditches as a result of the directive, he was unrepentant. He was typically apocalyptic and apoplectic when interviewed in 1982 by the flagship BBC current affairs TV programme *Panorama*.

'If it's up to me to think the unpalatable thoughts so you don't have to, then fine—that's what I have to do. If it's up to me to constantly question and explore and debate antiquated ideas of morality for all our betterment so that you don't need to, then equally I'm fine with this also. Collectively we have buried our heads in the sand. Overpopulation, over-mining of our natural resources, the pumping of unmatched levels of noxious gasses into our atmosphere. What people don't understand, and this doesn't appear to be changing no matter how much they hear it repeatedly, is that we are slowly but surely wiping out the planet—and without the planet where do we live? What do we live on? If left unabated, we will continue to procreate and eat. We will never stop. We shall not only eat each other, but ultimately in one last, despicable, desperate act of self-immolation, we shall eat ourselves.'

He was Professor of Geomicrobiology and Earth Science loosely affiliated to the UCL, though he hadn't taken a class for several years. Students protested on a semi-regular basis, or at a stretch biannually, to have this most controversial and divisive of figures—with his 'human-baiting' and 'human-hating' views—removed. But the university was built on the foundation of radical thinking, so argued the Academic Board, and you didn't get much more in the way of radical thinking than a Professor of Geomicrobiology and Earth Science who insisted on people calling him Arnie.

He was characteristically outspoken as a champion of alternative foodstuffs and campaigned energetically for people to go back to eating pigeons. He urged the general populace to broaden their minds and as a consequence their palates. On a discussion on eating horsemeat, he summed up helpfully: 'In this respect, your pet dog eats far better than you.'

He cast his inscrutable gaze long and wide. Gram and millet as substitutes for wheat; whiting as substitute for cod; ostrich meat instead of beef. Ironically enough, considering he was a committed anti-vegetarian. He attributed several nasty allergies to the consumption of Quorn. It got to the point he claimed that the mere mention of the phrase 'meat free' brought him out in a rash. Considered otherworldly by a nation brought up on steak pie and fish and chips, in the mid-eighties he famously ate a kangaroo burger on daytime TV (along with a side salad and serving of onion rings). He claimed the experience was a wholly satisfactory one, adding that it tasted 'a little like chicken.'

He personally invested in a pasta sauce made from beetles and other insects and suggested Ringo Starr should head the promotional campaign. All well and good until Starr's manager pointed out that *beetles* and *Beatles* were in fact not the same thing. Freemantle held his hand up and admitted to the faux pas, claiming in his defence that he'd always been a Creedence Clearwater Revival fan.

Most people thought he was a nut, an eccentric, but basically harmless. He went everywhere dressed in a waxed Barbour jacket and cap, brown moleskin trousers, and a thick cotton checked shirt. He was always unshaven. He owned multiple versions of the same outfit, taking the idea from world renowned theoretical physicist Albert Einstein, so never had to waste valuable thinking time on deciding what to wear. He was never sure if he he'd heard this in passing from the great man himself, as appeared in some grainy black and white documentary footage, or from the mouth of Seth Brundle. In any case, Freemantle's appearance in terms of clothing, unlike Einstein, was more man of the country than man of science.

He was also known in interviews, especially when seeking to force a point home, to take off his shoe and bang it repeatedly on the table. Again evoking echoes from the past, smatterings of Russian leader Nikita Khrushchev who back in Soviet times banged his shoe in order to make his displeasure known to the United Nations. Professor Freemantle, Arnie to some, was the sum of his parts; a whirlwind of elemental forces who on one occasion went further than Khrushchev when throwing his shoe at a defenceless if, in his honest opinion, hapless interviewer. The interviewer would later describe the Professor as demonically possessed.

What did the future hold for Professor Arnold

Freemantle, what might he amount to? Up till now, he was little more than a footnote in a little read and unloved reference book. This changed nothing. It was up to him to keep pushing the envelope, to keep grasping the nettle. It was his views on the panda bear—one of the most famous, most endearing animals in the world, with distinct black patches around big, twinkling cat's eyes, and over adorable ears and across a magnificently rotund body—which would earn him true notoriety.

Freemantle deemed the facts irrefutable. 'Do I really have to repeat them?' he would protest.

But repeat them he would. In captivity, it was near impossible for pandas to breed. In the wild, births did happen, of course, but they were difficult, problematic, and if more than one cub resulted from the birth, the mother would abandon the weakest one at birth. (If there were similarities to previous statements made on *human* population control, he didn't appear to make the connection.) Their diet was based exclusively on bamboo, disappearing naturally from the wild. Millions were spent on keeping pandas in zoos with the certain knowledge they could never be reintroduced into their natural habitat. Surely all that money and resources would be better channelled elsewhere on the thousands of other species at risk due to climate change and destruction of habitat. Where a fraction of the panda budget could make a real difference to their chances of survival. Not only a matter of life and death, but value for money also!

'Where's the logic?' he asked in a tone of voice that suggested logic was important to him.

In conclusion: 'Pandas are a species not only destined,

I would argue, but intent on dying out. Here we have nature's version of a suicide note. Despite all our good intentions, at bamboozling expense, the best he could do is only delay the inevitable. And why?'

This was a rhetorical question. 'These animals are unbearably cute. We've been suckered in. They make for a good sticker.'

In some ways, Freemantle maintained, he wanted to give the pandas back their dignity. Basically, he believed pandas should be left to their own devices, which was another way of saying should be allowed to do the right thing and die out. In this way, the Professor cast off his 'human-baiting' label to be replaced with something many claimed was far worse.

Among the human population, all hell broke loose. There were death threats, excrement sent through the mail, his front lawn was firebombed. The latter action prompted a period of police protection. Such were the levels of verbal abuse, Freemantle had to go ex-directory. Not that he ever answered the phone, but the savagery of the comments upset his housekeeper Joan. If it confirmed in Freemantle's mind one thing, forget the other ones, it was that he'd finally met his calling. It was clear to him now; as clear as glass, as clear as anything could be. It was muddled sentimental thinking. It was excruciating. It was human emotion. The uproar, passion, and sheer befuddled devotion pandas brought out in people represented everything that was wrong with the planet.

So he would tell them, try to reason with them, ad verbum, ad infinitum. So it came to pass in a Radio 5 Live interview, an early morning slot with Victoria Derbyshire. The Professor's solution to rising at the crack of dawn for such an early start, a tremendous struggle at the best of times, was not to go to bed in the first place.

'I'm joined by Professor Arnold Freeman,' Derbyshire began. 'Inventor of Creedence Clearwater Revival sauce, who has some controversial things to say on the conservation of the giant panda.'

'The panda bear, much loved,' she continued, 'in everyone's top three favourite animals. I know that's true in my case. The symbol of the World Wildlife Fund. If Sweetie and Sunshine, current panda residents and stars of Edinburgh Zoo, were here for this interview today, what would you say to both of them, Professor Freemantle?'

'I'd say in the first instance,' he answered, 'call me Arnie.'

'Very well, Arnie. The pandas aren't here so I'll have to speak on their behalf. You'd rather the panda was extinct?'

'It's nothing to do with what I want or desire or need, Ms Derbyshire, you'll find the facts are irrefutable...'

As the words, the reasoning, the undeniably flow of logic, filed out in orderly fashion, his mind waded through a sea of black slick. There wasn't much in the way of resistance, he could move freely enough, but all the same he found the process deeply monotonous. For as far as the eye could see, floating before him, was an ocean of shit and mediocrity. His scalp itched but he refused to scratch it. Something was blocking out the sky. It was like a mighty, mountainous shadow had fallen on him, but he chose not to look up and identify the source. The shade in a psychological sense pressed heavily on him. He was certain if he kept moving forward he would shake free of it, eventually. He would reach a point, somewhere else, a different set of circumstances, he'd be clear of the shade. He hoped at this point he would have his reward.

Back in the real world, or as real as he could make it, he finished relating the facts. He wasn't expecting a standing ovation, but surely a nod from Ms Derbyshire would not be out of the question. She wasn't even giving him her full attention. She had a finger placed on her earpiece.

'We have some listener's calls,' she said. 'Arnie, are you ready?'

'Ready for anything,' he said; which he was. He was already recipient of every brickbat conceivable to date. His head swam slightly as lack of sleep finally caught up with him.

'Dad,' the voice came from the speaker. 'Dad, is that you?'

'Sheila,' he said. He was certain it was her voice even though it was weak and broken. It wasn't strong at all. That, and the fact it was several years since the last time he'd heard it. And he was so terribly sleepy.

'Dad, there's something I need to tell you. You're not taking my calls. I've been ill. Oh God, I … I had it confirmed an hour ago. It was the *Light*.' Her voice trailed off. There was silence over the radio waves, dead space. Usually in terms of broadcasting this was a big no-no, but on this occasion it seemed poignant. As an afterthought the voice said, 'You don't seriously want to kill off the pandas, do you?'

***

In the end, he never attended his daughter's funeral;

would have considered it hypocritical if he did so. He never showed much interest in her when she was alive. Not in her or his three other children—or his ex-wife, for that matter, who left him thirty years ago when in his late thirties. Nor could he name any of his grandchildren. The truth was that he was ashamed. He was mortified by the fact he was responsible for bringing so many resource-guzzling, poison-spreading human apes into the world. Once, when stuck in a traffic jam, he lamented he had four children, with families of their own, and all with family cars. He had effectively—echoing the words of comic and poet Spike Milligan—created a traffic jam all of his own.

***

In the plush bungalow in Wiltshire he called home, having negotiated a particularly heavy one-man drinking session the night before, Professor Freemantle arose in the wee hours of the afternoon. He took and passed the *Light*. Too late in the day to prevent his accounts from being locked, but not too late, he hoped, to have them unlocked. This the *Light* could do, but could do nothing for his crushing hangover. He would live for another day, which was as it should be. He had too much to live for. He had one thing to live for.

He believed that this would be the year, that the tide was turning. Prominent right-wing politicians were moved to highlight the wastefulness and futility of panda conservation. The millions spent could be better used elsewhere. The US President even Tweeted about it.

A dying boy on his Last Day was prevented from

seeing the pandas at ZooParc de Beauval in Saint-Aignan. It transpired that this part of the zoo was in lockdown following death threats made against—irony of ironies—the pandas, but this fact was reported latterly, and not before images of a devastated young French boy, his final day on this planet, head bowed, hit home around the world. The report from *Reuters* said it best: 'Panda backlash as boy turned away on Last Day!'

More worldwide reports followed of a man in a panda suit boarding the NYC Subway J train, taking out a hunting knife and indiscriminately slashing passengers. Some animal charities deemed it necessary to make it clear that no part of any donation would go towards the preservation of the giant panda. The next instalment in the hugely popular animated feature film franchise *Kung Fu Panda* had the main protagonist Po, voiced by Jack Black, turn bad, requiring The Furious Five (a tiger, crane, snake, monkey, and mantis; anthropized warriors all) to battle and defeat him. Bloggers, vloggers, punters, and social networkers commented on the dark patches over a panda's eyes, implying this to be something insidious and sinister.

The Professor dressed, head aching. He started moving in slow, exaggerated movements, like a silent movie villain, in the hope of navigating towards the dining table without drawing undue attention to him. He even went as far as removing his slippers to negate any telltale shuffling. It didn't work. Joan was already in the dining room dusting. At the sight of him, she fired an incriminating, laser, bottle-and-a-half stare, which he attributed to the empty bottle of Speyside Cragganmore left on the kitchen worktop plus the half-empty one unceremoniously pushed into the cereal cupboard, squashing a box of cornflakes.

Things hadn't changed. The world was still in flux. There were experiments on dogs, rats, and monkeys—a study into whether animals experienced the Last Day phenomenon, but surely this was missing the point. There was a part of being human at a crucial point in their lives, at the time of their deaths, where all logic and control was lost. What would happen if the President of the US or of the Russian Federation or the British Prime Minister woke to discover that this was their Last Day? What checks and balances were in place?

Whether the experiments bore fruit, confirmed one way or the other that animals had Last Day awareness, what would it matter? The stark reality was even if they had the knowledge they could do zilch with it. The survival instincts, the will to live, eat, and sleep would continue unaffected. They would go on as if nothing had changed, blighted by the symptoms of fatality, but not bound by them. They wouldn't start World War III—and this was where they had an advantage over us.

It didn't take a genius to grasp when an old dog knew his time was up he found some quiet place to die. No, the sheer pointlessness of such research maddened him. Rendered him apoplectic. Why didn't they just listen to him instead?

If he could get the most powerful people in the world to change their thinking about the panda…

The Professor waited for the verbal tuts and hard stares from his housekeeper of many years to subside before sitting down at the dining table. There, already set out, was everything he required; cutlery, napkin, and remote control for the TV. He sat shoulders stooped and eyes half-closed. He licked his dried lips. In his head, he counted out various transcendental numbers to twenty digits—pi, Feigenbaum numbers, Chaitin's constant—in the attempt to wait out his hangover.

It wasn't long before, mercifully, Joan appeared from the kitchen carrying a tray. He was presented with baked pork chops coated with bread crumbs and served with rice. Poured over the chops was a tangy mushroom sauce (in truth, he never much cared for his insect alternate). Joan's closing act was to thump down a tall glass of water on the table with sufficient force some of the liquid jumped out. He had a penchant for lime cordial, but decided given her frostiness, and his bedraggled state, it would be best to settle for what was on offer.

'My eternal gratitude,' he said.

'Sure,' she said. Most days a brief verbal exchange at the dining table was as close to a conversation as they got.

It wasn't that he hated the panda; the panda bear; the giant panda, call it what you will. It was never a vendetta, never anything like that. He was born-again; realisation having dawned on him in the third trimester of life. It was just that he now considered the alternative of hating mankind, of despising his own species, to be the coward's way out. Self-loathing was too much the easy option.

As a rule every day, having tended to the necessary ablutions and evacuations, he would sit down to his only meal of the day. He had no time for this breakfast/lunch/dinner malarkey. His philosophy was simple. On your single visit to the table, you stocked up, rather like filling up your car at a petrol station; sufficient to propel you forward like a whirling, pointing, flapping, pontificating evangelist through the rest of the day. Although for his supper, it wasn't unheard of to indulge in a croissant and mug of hot milk.

Taking no time at all, he cut up the non-rice part of his meal into bite-sized chunks. He used his fork to pierce a piece of chop, then, diverting his attention momentarily from his meal, grabbed the remote and switched on the flat-screen TV mounted on the wall facing him. With this, the outside world—or a version of it—was summoned into his home. Mission accomplished, he grabbed the fork and scooped the meat into his mouth. He chewed slowly and expansively, like a horse champing grass in the field.

When eating, his jaw would click, but there was no associative pain or tenderness. He was advised to alleviate the effects, he should cut back on the jaw clenching, but for the life of him he couldn't imagine a life without jaw clenching. If symptoms worsened he promised himself he would assess things and look at it again, but for now quite simply it wasn't a price worth paying. His jaw clicked decades ago when he appeared in front of a live TV audience while eating a Kangaroo burger. There was rarely a time when any kind of clicking didn't give him pause for thought, sending his mind back, reliving the day of that burger. The one and only time he ate for the benefit of TV.

Now he ate in front of the TV. He chewed the pork long and hard, wistful, wishful that it was something else.

He was greeted by the reassuringly plummy tones of the BBC News channel, *Live from Parliament*. Dominating proceedings was the rising diplomatic tensions between the UK and Argentina, but this wasn't the main event at least where the Professor was concerned. There was still parliamentary scope; time put aside to debate other issues.

An online petition to remove protected status from the panda had received over seven hundred thousand signatures. Another petition for the retention of all aspects of panda conservation received over a million signatures, but that was by the by. If a petition secured more than one hundred thousand signatures it could be considered by MPs for debate in the House of Commons. The unthinkable was now being thought; the unpalatable now served on a plate. The future status of the panda was being debated, dissected, and deliberated upon by the lawmakers.

The debate, which took place over a couple of hours, was a lively one, reasonably well-attended, veering towards the emotive; the facts for much of the time kept at an arm's length. It was decided not to hold a vote at the end, but this was a start. The beginning perhaps of something very significant indeed. Satisfied, the Professor grabbed the remote and waved it around like a magic wand and turned off the TV.

Yes, the tide was turning.

Like the Sirens of Greek mythology luring sailors with their beguiling songs of enchantment, from the cereal cupboard calling for the Professor was a half-finished bottle of Speyside Cragganmore.

'Arnie … Arnie…'

If he could get the most powerful people in the world to change their thinking about the panda, what else could he get them to do? He could save the world.

That night he slept like a baby, although to be fair this

was the case most nights. He dreamed that he was naked, dancing a jig on a pile of old skeletons. Some of the bones had jagged edges which nipped at his feet, but he didn't seem to care about that. Nor did he feel the inclination at any time to take a look down.

When he went to bed, the last thing on his mind was pandas. When he awoke, his first thought was of pandas too. And at times, less frequently than one would expect and never in plain sight, you would find them if you looked hard enough in the place in-between.

10

Eighty Per Cent Water

It was night-time, near enough bedtime. They were back at old Charlie's house which, without trying, looked like it belonged to one of those old black and white haunted mansion movies.

Despite Ollie strenuously advising against it, the notion was not for shifting; a little worm squirming, burrowing inside his head. It was never a question of him not giving into it, only delaying it, but never indefinitely, so Si went for a shower. On making his approach across the hall towards the bathroom, taking care, not wishing to disturb the fellow occupants, his every step was betrayed by loose floorboards under a criminally emaciated carpet. Creaky old house, he thought, lots of places to hide secrets in. Plenty of loose floorboards, plenty of opportunities to stash shoeboxes. The trick was to hide so many guilty little secrets that adding another wouldn't then stick out. He compared the threadbare carpet to his current state of mind. Each creak of a floorboard was so treacherous, resounding and thunderous, he worried if one misstep might bring the whole house crashing down. Still, he could feel it imprinted on his skin, lodged into every pore: the smog-laden, petroleum-laced city sweat that was East London air. There was nothing else for it, he needed a shower.

There was no hot water. For quite some time, apparently, Charlie was content to do without. And now a naked Si was faced with an unholy waterfall, full of pitfalls and broken dreams, an icy cold fist trying to grab and hammer the life out of his bones. Freezing, the water—if you could even call it that—was too cold to stand under for any amount of time. Keeping a safe distance, clutching onto the shower curtain for dear life, he used his free hand to flap pitifully at the stream and splash some water onto random bits of him above the waistline. It was torture. No further interrogation techniques required. He would have admitted to anything; to knowing the whereabouts of every shoebox hidden across the land. Under his breath, through gritted teeth, his brain on fire, he invoked the names of gods past and present—Yahweh, Odin, Zeus, Lady Gaga.

Shoebox, shoebox, shoebox; he had grown obsessed by the word. He knew what it meant; what he meant by it. If he could have devised some way of deceiving himself, blocking out its meaning like an angry cloud obscuring the sun, then surely he would have done.

A freezing cold shower only brought the bad thoughts back into focus. Sure, these days, cold showers were considered healthy in terms of anti-ageing, helping weight loss, curing baldness, you name it; but for Si, a hot blistering dousing was the highlight of the day. Was nothing sacred? Must everything have the enjoyment sapped out of it? Was the only healthy option to recover from a freezing shower while sitting in a darkened room, starving you half to death with only cucumber to munch on, washed down by blended wheatgrass and battery acid? Actually, come to think of it, take away the cucumber and wheatgrass and he was already there; he was already in that place. Giving in to the inevitable, Si eventually withdrew from the shower, recoiling from the sheer unalloyed misery of it all.

What a day it had been. What a fucking day.

There wasn't a towel, so he used the last of the toilet paper to dab himself dry. Wincing at regular intervals, he reverted into the clothes he had been wearing all day, including old Charlie's old coat. He breathed out, which on its own volition turned into a sigh. His eyes widened at the escaping vapours such was the iciness of his breath. Any minute now he expected the White Witch of Narnia to walk on by.

With the newfound grace of a hypothermic elephant, he bounded across the hall and back into the room. There he used the faint light shining in through the window to navigate his way around. The reality remained of two single mattresses but only one duvet, which Si had insisted Ollie should take. This left him with the only option of hitting the sack wearing as many layers as he first arrived with. Si reflected dolefully that normally he slept naked. *The Twilight Zone* episode he was now part of—the one having taken him hostage—had taken on another twist. He was determined come hell or high (freezing) water not to feel sorry for himself. He wanted to somehow magically split and become two people, so Si#1 could stand next to Si#2 and point at him and laugh. And in turn, Si#2 could then laugh back.

The shittiness of his present arrangements—the void that was the complete absence of creature comforts—had already put distance between him and the horror and exhilaration of the day just gone. There was no better word to describe how Si was feeling but glum. The epitome of glum. Just glum.

Tentatively, sluggishly, like a felled tree at the very beginning of its descent, still grappling with gravity, still harbouring a hope, a chance forever forlorn, it may not succumb to such forces, slowly he lay himself down on the mattress. He was on his back with a difference. He wanted to be brave, so he took his hands out of his coat pockets. He crossed his arms on his chest, imagining he was a Pharaoh of ancient times, finally laid to rest after doing something really useful like spreading civilisation to half the world. His body inexorably sank into the mattress like he was in quicksand. The mattress grabbed him, entrapped and restrained him, a cage of coiled metal springs. It taunted him. It amplified all his aches and pains, ramming the message home. He felt a spasm of unpleasant, dull heat around his left shoulder, which moved to his arm, then the small of his back and finally that part of his leg around the knee. Pain knew all of his weak spots and showed no mercy using this knowledge against him. He was on compassionate leave, he found him reminding himself. The mattress, seemingly in response, strengthened its grip. A loose spring gone rogue pressed against Si's right thigh, piercing the epidermis. He was too dispirited, body too much in bits to move or adjust. A night in old Charlie's house, this equalled torture without end.

His head was buzzing. Sleep seemed an impossibility; so he resigned himself to indulging his mind, allowing it to roam, running through the long grass and scaling the most rudimentary of mountains. But such thoughts were not made to last.

Images turned to those of violence. He imagined a knife in his back and how it must feel. In the face of such an onslaught, the aches and strains of modern living could only go one way and shrink into insignificance. Modern living, which included being punched in the street and shot at by an air gun, wasn't much of a life at all, but at least it was still living. The fact that people died along the way would have to go down as incidental. People died all the time.

It was the pain that stayed, the idea of it. Thoughts of the knife, sharp, extreme beyond belief, such a small wound relatively speaking, but sufficient to take absolute control of the body. He imagined being on fire, pain dwarfing meaning; darting, excruciating, every nerve end screaming in unrelenting unison. The pain knew only how to take and keep on taking, shutting the body down piece by piece, pigment by pigment, cell by cell. At what point could he no longer express love or friendship—the love that previously came so easy to him—eaten up, made useless and dysfunctional. The pain would be so bad, so unbelievably intense, that you would welcome the transition to another state. The process that leads to death would begin, irreversible; a fantastic, fatalistic version of *save the date*.

There would be the *Light*…

There would be *a* light…

He imagined himself shuffling off this mortal coil with aching, bendy legs. He was Old Father Time, next stop the pearly gates. He thought of his own pearly whites, a near perfect set of teeth, and so unearthed an epiphany. Dental hygiene was the key to getting into heaven. How could Saint Peter answer a knock on the door and turn away a dazzling set of gnashers?

Shuffle. Gnashers. He thought of Sofi who often teased him on his choice of words. He used old man's words. True, there was a generation between them. Si often wondered if Sofi was just another passing phase, but if so, one he'd steadfastly clung to. The fact was the more he got to know Sofi, the more he watched him grow and develop as a person, the more he loved him. And it wasn't effortless love; it was the type of love that you had to work at; the type that yearned to be reciprocated.

He thought of a different time and a different kind of pain, an exquisite one. He remembered Sofi biting hard into his shoulder and wishing he could grow more arms, become a multi-armed deity, a Kali, a Vishnu. He couldn't get enough of him. In truth, they hadn't been that close to intimate for quite some time. It was strange to think of such things, such vivid evocative memories, trussed up as he was so much in the way of clothing. No more stranger, he supposed, than to imagine being stabbed to death or burned alive. For a second, back in real time, he opened his eyes, and then he closed them again.

The more he wanted to push them away, the more he realised he needed to be with them. He was the kind of person who had to drive himself to one extreme in order to fully comprehend what he really wanted was the opposite.

He'd had his fun, if he wanted to call it that. He would go back to Sofi he decided—again. He was sorry, so sorry for his behaviour, sorry for running away and leaving Sofi to deal with everything. He would turn his back on the idea of a mattress fund. Recently, the word *mattress* had lost its appeal. If you pronounced the word in a certain way, went heavy on the *ess*, it came across as quite sinister. And here he was on an actual mattress that had seen better times, probably in the nineties. Nothing to be found underneath it, except possibly a label which read 'Property of Guantanamo Bay.'

Nothing but tangents. His brain was going off in all directions and he was doing his best to fight it, to regain focus, and so set him on a single path to never look back. Sofi was right to burn the shoebox, contents and all. It was time for a new start.

He just wanted Sofi to take him back, to get the kids back, and start living like a proper family again. He was invigorated. If it came to it, he'd climb up onto the roof and shout and profess the extent and depth of his re-energised devotion. If it meant leaving London, looking for another job, then he'd do it; whatever it took. A new day, a new beginning. He wanted to spend the night in this house of despair and disrepair so it would make him even more certain in the morning that this was the way forward. It would be in his head, his heart, under his skin. He'd get it done. He'd make amends. He would do this and so much more first thing, just as soon as he prised himself out of this fucking mattress.

There was a voice. It wasn't in his head. On the lines of a murmur, the odd shout, some moaning. He looked across at the other mattress a couple of feet away and saw Ollie tossing and turning in her sleep. Things quickly escalated, her head twisting, pummelling her pillow into submission. She talked in her sleep; enunciating incoherent thoughts, annoying the air around her. She perspired profusely, beads of sweat sliding down her brow, joining together and making criss-cross patterns on her face.

Her head stopped moving, but she couldn't stop shivering or prevent her teeth from chattering. Her face was deathly pale. The sight of this—where the shower previously had tried, came close, but ultimately failed—froze Si's blood. Normal blood. No more or less than eighty per cent water. He sat up, feeling on the way every mattress spring leave its mark like a sinister lover's kiss.

He moved, was crouching over her. He placed a hand on her fevered brow.

'You're burning up,' he said.

'So cold,' she said, her lips barely moving. 'Cold.'

Si wasn't sure what more to say or do. He tried to shape his mouth into something reassuring, but it felt wrong, more Peeping Tom than Doctor Finlay. He was useless. If it came to it, he was thinking, could he even take her to hospital if she hadn't taken the *Light*. Surely they'd take a look at her, but how could he be sure?

'Tell me what to do,' he said.

Perhaps seeking divine inspiration, perhaps for the want of something to do, he looked towards the bookcase. Positioned there in front of it was old Charlie, sitting on his favourite chair. He was on fire, enveloped in flames; skin blackened, organs cooking, eyes liquefied, hair and nails crackling.

'Cold,' she said. Her lips were turning blue.

'Come on, get up', he said, helping her to her feet, making sure the duvet was still wrapped around her.

She stood wearing a vest and jogging bottoms, arms exposed, feeling pain in the joints when she moved. The room had never seemed as vast. He stood next to her, tried his best to support her; at least he was doing something. Her arm was wrapped around his back; his hand resting on the shoulder furthest away from him. He gently nudged her forward and together they hobbled in the direction of the bookcase. Hand on heart, he could not deny that he'd be grateful for some heat as well.

'Can you see him?' he said.

She laid her head on his shoulder. 'Yes,' she said, 'it's his house after all.'

All that was left for them to do was put out their hands and warm themselves on the fire.

11

Cry For Me Argentina

The cry went up that war was obsolete. Countries baulked at the prospect of sending in troops who knew before going into battle that they were going to die. It muddied the waters. War for centuries, the argument would go, was integral to the development of Homo sapiens. It built empires; it established borders. Now, war was plagued by uncertainty caused by the certainty of knowing who the fatalities would be in advance. Before a shot was fired, a living human face was already attached to every human casualty. Truly, they were the dead before the dying. After much in the way of legal wrangling, of process, of flexing of international law, the United Nations rebranded war as voluntary genocide. Which didn't make sense, only for you to think about it some more and for it to eventually make sense after all. Which may have been the point.

The cry went up that war was obsolete, more or less.

There remained hotspots of activity in Africa and the Middle East, but even here things were in flux. In Nigeria it was official policy to intercept victims of terrorism before they became victims of alleged terrorism and turn them into alleged victims of something else. So it was the world over, how death was now managed. It got so convoluted that some individuals—they knew who they were—pined for a return in terms of war and death to the simpler times of Hitler, Churchill, Roosevelt, and Napoleon.

This meant that the rules of engagement were up for grabs; they were there for the changing. Warfare, what it had become; now that was the thing. In such emergent times, which country was prepared to stick its head out first above the parapet? Argentina had long laid claim on Islas Malvinas, aka the Falkland Islands. A remote South American island lying within Argentine maritime territory, but over which, for the last two hundred years, Britain held sovereignty. Matters had come to a head in 1982 with *Guerra del Atlántico Sur*, where British forces went to war to liberate the islands from the invading Argentine army. After seventy-four days of fierce fighting, the statistics of war returned losses across all sides of short of a thousand souls.

But that was then.

Now, with tensions on the rise once more, the UK government, having withdrawn the smattering of Royal Marines deployed on the island, had put down a marker demonstrating zero appetite for war. Instead, it issued a commitment to contest any Argentinian incursion on purely diplomatic grounds. In response, the Falkland

Islands Government claimed it would resist any advance, but betrayed and bereft as it was, it did so in a state of shock. It knew very well it had been served up on a plate.

The President of Argentina shrugged and commented that this was not war. This was not voluntary genocide. This was an invitation.

It rained as several amphibious landings, carrying a brigade of Argentinian soldiers, set symbolic foot on East Falkland, principal island in the archipelago—as prelude to marching unopposed on the capital Stanley. Final figures were totted up as it emerged that two soldiers and four islanders had failed the *Light*. One could only speculate as to how they were going to die, but it was decided soldier fatalities would be attributed to military exercises. Two islanders were bedridden, their deaths put down to natural old age. The remaining two active islanders were credited as resisting the invasion, as stipulated by the Falklands government, one of its terms of surrender.

Both Argentinian dead were privates: Joaquin Herrera, nineteen, and Santino Pérez, twenty. As for their current whereabouts, they both stood at the bottom of a hill looking out at the boggy terrain. Beyond this was the incoming tide, constituting a tiny part of the South Atlantic Ocean.

'Why?' Santino said.

'Why this piece of shitty godforsaken land?' he continued. 'The asshole at the end of the world? I don't know. Politics, you think?' He looked at his comrade with an almighty grimace, having previously directed his face towards the biting wind. 'Revenge, you think? National pride? Because we could? You think, you think, you think? Like anyone with a brain in his fucking skull would want to come to this fucking place. It's all fucked up.'

It was the island's westerly wind that took hold and slapped you and demanded to know why you were here—and before you had a chance to reply told you in no uncertain terms that you did not belong. It was a motherless wind. Nothing could grow here unless it was tough and ugly, old beyond its years. The lie of the land was exacting and brutal and promised nothing in return. A place where life had to be earned, and at times more than earned.

The soldiers were dressed in their combat uniforms, but the camouflage design was too elegant a thing for the ruggedness of present surroundings. Both were issued with standard service pistols, limited to two rounds of live ammo each. Even if they wanted to, there was nothing, except for some rogue sheep, to take a potshot at. The sheep were big dirt-orange-white round shapes some distance away. They appeared to float on the boggy terrain.

'Look at those fucking animals,' Santino said, pointing an accusing finger at a sheep far away. 'You can't even see their tiny heads for all that fur. It's all fucked up.'

Joaquin didn't want to spend his last few hours correcting Santino on the lines of, to give a current example, using the word wool instead of fur. He didn't fancy, full stop, spending much more of what precious time he had left with his boorish companion. On the other hand, it was understandable; Santino was right to be so angry. Their combined age was less than his father's.

'We should get to the café,' Joaquin said. 'They'll be expecting us.'

'Why?' Santino said. 'Because *they* say so? What do they tell you at school? It's the victors that write the history books, huh, but all of a sudden it's the English fuckers on this island who get to dictate terms. It's all fucked up.'

Joaquin could see that Santino's nose was bleeding and his eyes were puffy. One of his eyes was half-closed already.

'You think there's a Church of the Last Day around?' Santino said. 'At least tell me there's a place where I can buy a packet of cigarettes.'

Joaquin shrugged. 'I don't know. Wasn't in the debriefing.'

Santino pointed another crooked finger at the sheep. 'Then I think I'll take my chances with one of those furry fuckers over there.' Without further ado, he tossed Joaquin his gun and started wading through the bog in their direction. As way of farewell, he lifted his arm, clenching his fist as way of victory and hollered, 'Islas Malvinas!'

'Islas Malvinas,' Joaquin responded. But such was the strength of the wind, which nipped at the seams of his uniform, itself a little on the baggy side, he doubted his departed comrade would have heard his words.

He watched Santino, now also in the distance, take a further step forward. Next step, by degrees, proved more difficult than the last, his legs slowly sinking into the mud. It wasn't until he was down to knee level that he stopped moving. Instead, he stretched out his arms, circling his hands at the wrists. Beguiling, curling, flexing fingers, like a twitchy warlock, seeking to charm the creatures still some way away. Further on as backdrop was the tide, which gained in urgency, waves twisting, wrathful, turned to foam as it crashed against the beach.

Santino had never left their sight. The sheep, action smooth like they were rolling on curtain rails, appeared to float ever assuredly towards him.

With this, Joaquin looked away and left his viewpoint at the bottom of the hill. Originally he wanted to catch some of the island, but was now of the opinion he'd seen more than enough.

He walked towards signs of municipality, around half a kilometre away, which was the outskirts of the capital Stanley. He saw buildings, however modest, evidence of construction and life. In terms of scale it reminded him of his hometown of Pinamar, but not so in terms of climate or the colour green. Here the vegetation was anything but green. At least, he thought, the ground was firm underfoot.

Initial thought on failing the *Light* was that he wasn't happy about it—who would be—but he was philosophical. Better to die for something he reasoned than, say, be murdered and left lying in a ditch. But something tugged at him, something new and unexpected. It wasn't only the image in his head of his dying comrade sinking in the mud, or of floating sheep, pulling at him in many directions; it wasn't only the wind.

Two of the 'dead' islanders met him halfway. They greeted him with a 'beunas tardes,' which set the scene from them for more standard pigeon Spanish. Joaquin smiled gracefully. He was conscious of a missing canine tooth which revealed itself when he smiled too wide. He was also hiding, given the continent they were on, how appalled he was at their lack of fluency in Spanish—while choosing to ignore that he himself had always wanted to learn English, but had never got round to it.

The elder one was male, in his fifties or sixties. Joaquin started to count the lines on the man's face but gave up after a few seconds. From what Joaquin could ascertain his name was Peter. The woman was younger, but not by a great deal. Her name sounded very much like Helena.

With an exaggerated movement, Joaquin arched his arm and pointed at his puffed out chest. 'Private Joaquin Herrera,' he said, taking his time to enunciate every syllable.

His mind drifted back to that morning where he was briefed personally by his commanding officer. This having occurred not long after both him and Santino had taken—and failed—the *Light*. They were ordered to board the landing craft, chain of command having decided symbolically that the soldiers should die on the island. Joaquin was ashamed to think at the time he sobbed into a handkerchief like a kid, but his officer's words rang clear.

'News just in, private,' the officer said, 'they're claiming four dead. Four! During the whole of the last war there were only three civilian casualties. Three! You could call that a result.'

And now, moving on, seeing with his own eyes how ancient the islanders Peter and Helena were, this left a bitter taste in his mouth. Add this to the realisation sinking in that the other two *official* civilian casualties were so frail they couldn't get out of their beds. He was afraid he did not agree with his commanding officer. He did not think this was any kind of result. It hardly seemed fair to Joaquin, not an equitable trade at all.

Helena had a confused expression on her face. She pointed at Joaquin. 'Dos,' she said.

'Dos?' she repeated, pointing again.

It was pretty clear that she was expecting two of them, but Joaquin was not confident they would see Santino anytime soon, if ever.

Joaquin hunched his shoulders and after a moment Peter and Helena hunched theirs too. It had quickly come down to communication by aping the other person's actions. There wasn't much else for the dead to do but resume walking, and with every trod on alien turf they'd find themselves one step closer to Stanley.

The café didn't prove to be too much of a jaunt at all. It had an outdoor sign, a faded print of a king penguin. At the sight of this, Joaquin didn't know if he should laugh or cry. He certainly couldn't have had a conversation about it.

Except for this intrepid, unlikeliest of trios, the café interior was empty; no staff; no one; the rest of the island population clearly elsewhere. Not to worry, Helena and Peter knew their way about the place. They emerged from the kitchen with cups of tea and scones and it wasn't long before the act of setting the table was complete. The flower-patterned plastic table cover had a puckered sucking motion which stuck to Joaquin's elbows.

Helena smiled and for all Joaquin knew it seemed genuine. 'Buen provecho,' she said unconvincingly.

'Muchísimas gracias,' Joaquin said, deliberately parroting the stilted staccato delivery.

He drank the tea, which was gritty to the taste but he'd drunk far worse. The bread/cake concoction on the other hand was far too dry. And what was that dotted around and inside it—was this some kind of dried fruit? Sweetened rabbit droppings? Accompanying it on the side plate was a portion of butter still in its wrapper, which he prodded at with his finger. The butter was so soft, he was amused to see his finger had left an indentation in the wrapper.

Islander Peter was first to tuck into the scone. He made grunting noises. One modest, tentative bite followed another and it took an eternity of chewing before mustering the confidence to swallow. Joaquin guessed he had false teeth.

Helena noticed Joaquin had hardly touched tea or scone, and leaning forward, was about to say something when there was a resounding crack from close by. It was enough to give each of them a start. Instantly they all knew what it was. The rifle shots came from the waterfront next to the Liberation Monument a kilometre away, signalling the ceremonial swapping of flags as the Governor of the Falklands surrendered to the Argentine army.

In advance of the invasion, the Falklands had communicated *unofficially* through official channels a number of terms and conditions. It didn't take a genius to work out once the British withdrew military support that the writing would be on the wall. The British themselves seemed less concerned with relinquishing their rights to the Falklands and more on retaining their rights—linked to its acquiring of the Falklands—to the Antarctic a mere three thousand odd miles away. Both Argentine

President and Congressional Palace were receptive to all requests. All Argentina wanted to do was invade.

A Falkland Islands stipulation was that casualties from either side would not attend the ceremony. When informed of this, Joaquin had simply hunched his shoulders, which was his default response to many things. It was more Santino's style to get angry and throw a hissy fit and claim that it was all fucked up. In stark contrast, the life of Private Joaquin Herrera could be reduced to a series of shrugs, confined to barracks and little else of note; nothing to write home about. (And it was true that he had never written home, not even as much as sent a text.) And now…

He was a statistic, nothing less, nothing more. Something to be kept out of the way; snuggled into a local café and trotted out—in a ceremonial coffin no doubt—when someone official had something to say. What pitiful amount of life he had left was an inconvenience and best for all concerned if he could please just hurry it along.

The reality of the situation was the company of dear Peter and Helena was doing exactly that, sucking the life out of him. To liven up proceedings he lowered his head to the side, stuck his tongue downwards out the side of his mouth, and positioned a clenched hand so it hovered suspended in the air just above the neck. Repeatedly he moved the hand in an upwards direction, neck following likewise in a succession of jerky movements.

Initially, Peter and Helena were rather stunned by such (admittedly bizarre) behaviour. Was he miming hanging himself? Peter and Helena looked at each other, one with eyes wide open and the other blinking, uncertain how to react beyond this. Joaquin was sure that they knew each other from before. It was a small community of course, and there were no significant rings on their fingers, but he liked to think perhaps they were lovers. Perhaps there was only one person they wanted to say goodbye to, and in turn by happy and unhappy coincidence, it was each other. Peter gave Helena a little nod and in unison they returned their full attention to Joaquin, careful to come across as laughing with, rather than at, him.

Joaquin made to eat the scone, then dropped it and grabbed his throat. Pushing back in his chair, clear of the table, legs thrashing, he made out as if poisoned. More laughter.

Spurred on, he leapt to his feet and simulated impaling himself with a sword. There followed the anguished silent cry of a mime artist, revealing a not quite full set of teeth. More laughter, a little more strained this time.

He copied a mime he saw performed by David Bowie in footage from the early seventies. Caught in grainy black and white film; a response to a first meeting between him and pop art pioneer Andy Warhol which hadn't gone as well as Bowie hoped. Employing shuffling hands, he pretended to disembowel himself; merrily pulling out in elongated fashion imaginary colon and scooping out make-believe guts. Back in Pinamar, Joaquin was a street performer for a short time before realising, first, this only made it harder to get a girlfriend, and secondly that there was no money in it. So he joined the army not long after his eighteenth birthday, much to the disgust of one of his uncles who wasn't much older than him. Revulsion happily not shared by his newfound sweetheart, Agnes, who stuck her tongue down his throat and promised him a proper hero's welcome when he returned home from his first posting.

He would get his hero's welcome on his return, this was true, but not the one he might have wished for. He hoped that in death his family could be proud of him in a way that they were not always when he was alive.

The laughter stopped. Joaquin pulled out his pistol and shot Peter and Helena. She died from her wounds instantly. From Peter, some laboured breathing and grinding of borrowed teeth alerted Joaquin to the need for a second bullet. Joaquin then placed the gun in his mouth. The heat from the barrel burned his lips. He used the pain to focus, closed his eyes, tears stinging his cheeks, a final shrug of the shoulders, before he blew his brains out.

And with this, Islas Malvinas now belonged to Argentina.

12

The Goodish Samaritan

It was another day and decisions were made, unmade, and then made again. And yet his eyes were closed. None of this amounted to being part of the waking world. There emerged a pinprick of light. It was behind him but he went about his normal business, steadfast in ignoring it. The whole of his attention span, no exceptions, was taken up by an egg on a stove in a pan of boiling water. It was the simple things, the things you could do at any time, the first casualties of modern living. The downgrading of darning a sock or making pasta as things best left undone. The modern way would be to buy a new pair of socks or purchase pasta out of a plastic packet from just about anywhere.

The light was no longer a pinprick; grown to the size of a ten pence piece. The heated water around the egg for its part began to eddy and spit; egg seemingly unmoved by the increasing volatility of its surroundings. Bubbling molecules knocking together, rubbing themselves up the wrong way, turning to steam. The egg looked the same on the outside, but Si knew, watching on, that the swirly, topsy-turvy, ping-pong environment was having an effect. The egg was hardening inside. The light had grown to the point he couldn't do anything else but be aware of it. He could feel it, a tugging sensation at the nape of his neck. Knowing he would need to address the issue soon, for the time being he parked it. He threw a blanket over it, assured himself he would get back to it later at some unspecified time. The act of putting something off; another symptom of modern living. He concentrated instead on the boiling egg, one of those simple things in life, which up until now he'd never quite got around to.

Boiling an egg, who the fuck had the time for that?

***

It was another day and by opening his eyes, Si had made it official. He was lying on his side, body curved like the Mariana Trench. The bone of his hip, through his layers of clothing, was embedded deep into the mattress. As uncomfortable as it was, he was reluctant to get up. For a fearful, sickening moment, he was thinking, what were the chances this present arrangement, as horrific and painful and uncomfortable as it was, would turn out to be the highlight of his day?

That everything was downhill after this? Not for the first time, he needed to remind himself that this wasn't just about him. With a long, tuneless grunt, he fought against the gravitational forces pressed down against him and up he got.

Like a mother hen, he hovered over Ollie who, given the state she was in the night before, was now a surprising picture of health. Lying back sleeping, she looked angelic, untroubled. It would be a crying shame to wake her.

Her eyelids flickered.

Si was still at a loss for actual words. There was the beginning of something, whatever it was, but it died at the back of his throat. He turned his head to glance at the door. It made sense that this would be a good time to leave.

'Thank you,' she said.

Her voice caught him in mid-thought. He would have preferred if she'd stayed sleeping. He wouldn't have had to say goodbye. They could have left the events of yesterday and of last night's malady behind them, not spoken of it. Not wasted any more time.

'It was nothing,' he said, still eyeing the door, still going through the motions, still hoping he was being discreet about it.

'Malaria,' she said.

'Huh?'

She had made some decisions too. 'I think I was twelve.' She was clear in her own mind he deserved to know more about her, whether he wanted to or not. He had earned that much. 'Egypt. Family holiday, me, my mum, Dad, we were in Luxor. Mum and Dad were only interested in the main tourist attractions. Valley of Kings, tombs, and then even more tombs. Back then I wasn't the shrinking violet you know of now. I was wild and full of adventure. I wandered off the beaten path at every opportunity. You could say maybe, I suppose, I wanted to lose myself.'

'I sneaked off with an Egyptian boy called Ako who took me to a village nearby where I drank sweet tea. Sweetest thing I ever tasted, nothing has come close since. I had a ride on a really old donkey. Ako showed me the temple where there'd been a terrorist massacre a year before I was born. The victims knew they were all going to die before they went to the temple, but their thinking was where else would you go if you knew you were going to die anyway, but to the temple?'

Si was aware of something buzzing behind his eyes. He blinked furiously until the sensation passed.

'It's a headfuck,' she said. 'You could say they had seen the light.' Her expression was neutral. There was a pause, a natural one, before continuing. 'Suddenly there was this shout and Ako was slapping my arm. I reacted. I screamed. I saw a squashed mosquito in his hand. I'd taken anti-malaria tablets on the lead up to the holiday, maybe not the full dose, but my folks were pissed off with me for my disappearing act, so I couldn't tell them, could I, what had happened with the mosquito. I covered up the bite mark with a plaster and claimed it was a graze or something. I fell ill during the flight back and was diagnosed with malaria by a doctor with freezing cold hands back home in Shuddersfield. It's not fatal or anything, but sometimes I have bad nights. You saw that already, I have a fever. I just need to sweat it out.'

'Illness doesn't bother me,' she said, smiling, trying to lighten the tone. 'Really it doesn't. I can't die remember?'

Si handed in his better judgement to the cloakroom,

mindful to put the ticket as way of receipt in safekeeping. He would be calling back for it later. He sat back down on the mattress. Unsure what to do with his legs, he decided to cross them. 'Shuddersfield?' he said.

'Just my name for Huddersfield,' she said. 'If you've been brought up there, you'll know what I mean.'

'You don't have a Yorkshire accent.'

'Private school.'

By opening herself up to him, she had opened Pandora's box and he couldn't resist one last question. One more question, he promised himself, and that was it. One more question, more out of concern, and he'd be out of here. He was gone. 'Tell me about the marks on your arms.'

Head still on the pillow, she raised one of her arms to better examine it. Her eyes flicked from one scar to another, like she was reading runes; that there was knowledge to be divined; a story to be told. 'I could explain,' she said. 'It's not as simple as the mosquito one.'

He visibly bristled. Again, it was never far, the prevailing thought process demanding to know what he was doing. Why was he still here?

'But I can tell you,' she said, her head moving to the side so she could look at him the same way she did her arm. Then she changed to staring at the ceiling.

'It was five years ago, maybe a little later, but not much later. Anyway, I must have been fourteen and it had taken my parents two years to get over Egypt and begin to trust me again. It must have killed them not to go on holiday the year before, to put up a united front, to be so fucking strict; they were so incredibly liberal at heart. They loved their trips away did Mum and Dad.'

'So we went to New York. The Big Apple. They weren't joking; it's big, big! I'd seen the city in the movies and on TV, but nothing can prepare you for the first time you set eyes on Downtown Manhattan. The buildings are gigantic. Not just the Empire State, but all kinds of office buildings, they just go on and on. I never realised people could be so small.'

'The scale of it all, this contributed to my generally good behaviour throughout the trip. That surprised me as much as it did Mum and Dad. Then there came the time they planned to spend the day in Brooklyn. I couldn't bear the thought of setting one foot outside Manhattan, so I pleaded to be left behind. I took the *Light*, which was good for something, told everyone I wasn't going to die that day. Mum had misgivings, Dad less so. But Mum had developed a bad, constant cough. She was forever complaining of tiredness and couldn't put up much of a fight. I mean, I promised I would be good.'

'I looked older for my age—fourteen isn't that young anyway. Still not quite sure how I managed it, though; maybe they wanted so much to keep the peace we'd worked so hard for, but they left me in the hotel, my many promises still ringing in their ears; that I wouldn't leave the room and if I had to, I wouldn't stray too far. And I would be back before five, when they were due back too.'

'And they left with an air of agitation that told me they were already behind schedule. I gave it twenty minutes before mouthing the word "suckers." The plan was to go the memorial site of the World Trade Center. I was only a baby when the planes hit the Twin Towers. Many of the dead never went to work that day; chose to die at home or find themselves a Church. But it wasn't enough—didn't come early enough—for the authorities to piece together what was about to happen. The city was in enough of a panic anyway. It didn't make it any less symbolic, less an act of terrorism, less what it is. Don't believe any of those conspiracy theories you hear.'

'I was in New York and I changed into a t-shirt, arms cut off at the shoulders, and my short skirt. I would have walked down the sidewalks of giants in my underwear if I thought I could get away with it. I felt that free. It was the last time I'd feel that way. Did I say how fucking tall the buildings were?'

There was a shuffling and scraping sound and she looked again in his direction, only to glimpse his back as he was walked out of the room. She sighed and then smiled, flip-flopping between each response. Eventually she took out a cigarette, lit it, and sharply inhaled.

He was outside. He had asked a question, but did not wait for the answer.

As soon as he'd left there was a trace of regret. It wasn't that he wasn't interested in hearing how Ollie's tale turned out. It was just that he was overcome by another need. A yearning so intense it made his teeth hurt. It thumped his chest and threatened to take away his breath. He marched towards the end of the street, every twitchy step bringing merciful release, joints in the grip of lactic acid slowly unwinding, free of the twin tyrannies of discomfort and pain. His focus was not for wavering. He was hell-bent. The object of his desire, his desperation shining through, he could hear it whispering in his ear, the promise of blessed relief. A new start. No old beginnings. It might not have been the tallest structure in the world, but nevertheless, the streetlight ahead of him loomed larger than life. There was the *Light*, only the *Light*; iris, magenta, all the purples. It took hold of him, led him by the hand, pulling at him by the eyebrows. His penance—the one he had to endure—was to exist in normal time. It made every step at normal pace seem all the more sluggish and cruel. He was a drowning man, bobbing, adrift, seconds from salvation; if only he was able to walk on water. To be kissed on the forehead and suddenly all the bad stuff would go away. To be transported back to two days ago—to a time before a portentous knock on the door—when life was uncomplicated and predictable and oh so good (that's how he was feeling; that's how he chose to remember it). But for now, he had to settle for each torturous step. It came down to the need to stay alive. To feel alive. It was the need to know.

He didn't know why, but if he was sure of one thing in an otherwise vacuous and hollow life, it was that the *Light* held the answers to questions he couldn't even think to ask in the first place; couldn't start to piece together in his mind. It would cocoon and insulate him. It would lift him, fix him, and fill him up. Without the *Light*, how else could he exist in any other fitting or defined way?

It was within reach and Si wanted to reach out, stretch his arm, extend the tips of his fingers to the point they threatened to disengage from the rest of his hand. He felt something irresistible, exhilarating, a tingling that shot through his arm down to his wrist. He swore if they could bottle it, it would be the ultimate drug. And maybe they already had; maybe we were all already addicted, and had been for such a very long time.

It was in that instant, the moment of anticipation, that everything was turned on its head, and how he hated himself for being so weak, so fallible and predictable. But it was so close and he was so committed. He was ready for the *Light*.

All of his senses, so devoted, predicated to the act of moving forward and nothing else. All the more shocking then when his body, in a fit of flailing convulsions, was unceremoniously yanked bank.

It was Mo who was doing the yanking.

'For fuck's sake, right,' Mo said. 'What in the name of fuck do you think you're doing?'

Si was a mass of flapping, wriggling limbs, which did the job, enabling him to squirm away from Mo's clutches.

'What does it look like I'm doing?' Si said. His voice was surprisingly calm given the circumstances, but such a condition was not built to last. 'Just stop touching me. What is wrong with you?' Si stood his ground. He wanted to know the answer to the question. He *seriously* wanted to know.

'Isn't it fucking obvious?' Mo seemed surprised he had to explain himself. 'We don't take the *Light*. We've opted out.'

'That's just crazy,' Si said. 'That's just…' He took a second to think about it before deciding to go with the flow, '…fucking crazy. Do you people make it your life's work to fuck everything up?' He counted out on two fingers. 'First, you fuck yourself up. Second, you fuck up every poor sod you come in contact with.'

Mo's granite features appeared to melt in front of Si's eyes. He was genuinely perplexed this time round. 'You see ghosts, right?'

'I…' It seemed pointless for Si to accept or deny this. Up until now, he hadn't given it serious thought. Geoff from the office. Old Charlie popping up in the middle of the night, turning once more to cinder and ash. He hadn't questioned it and it was obvious to him now why this was the case. He was as crazy, loop-de-loop as the rest of them.

A van screeched to a halt outside the house; the police markings giving the game away. Police officers spilled out of the back of the van, shouting, forming grunts, not words, like they were Carthaginian barbarians. It was one of the things they taught them as police cadets, to make as much noise as possible, to be threatening, to be big, to disorientate and discombobulate and so gain the upper hand. Some methods were immutable, tried and trusted, and never to be changed.

Si thought for a moment that they were coming to rescue him, but in so doing they'd only be rescuing him from himself, and he wasn't aware it was up to the police to do that sort of thing.

'Come on, then,' Mo hollered as he rushed off back to the house.

Si stood for a moment. He realised that in all the toing and froing, and some twisting and turning, the *Light* was now behind him. A light shining on his back; a version of 'X marks the spot.' He hated the fact he had turned his back on it. But recently, hadn't he turned his back on everything? While the police intervention wasn't quite a dawn raid, it was still early. Surely now was the time to vamoose and kick old Charlie's dust from under his shoes. The whole day was in front of him. There was time to get things done.

He didn't want anyone to get hurt. He was thinking maybe he could intervene and calm everyone down, try not to get arrested, and be home in time for brunch. He didn't feel he owed these people anything, but if he wasn't going to do it for them, he decided he would have to do it for himself. He would reinvent himself not so much as a Good Samaritan; more on the lines of Good*ish* Samaritan. The small of his back was sodden and his hands were clammy. Taking a gulp of chilly early morning air, he rolled his shoulders forward and marched in the direction of old Charlie's old house.

Reinvigorated limbs, rejuvenated joints; bouncing on adrenaline, and grateful for small, large, and any other size of mercies.

It was about to kick off outside the front of the residence. Mo was squaring up to a policeman. He was actually growling.

'Don't touch me,' the policeman said.

'What are you going to do about it?' Mo said.

Elijah took out his phone, only for another police officer to slap it out of his hand. It hit the ground and shattered into three pieces.

Ollie was in the process of being bundled out of the front door by the shortest of the coterie of Viking policeman. Seemingly trapped in a loop, with no hope ever of escape, they too were telling each other to shut up.

It wasn't what Si was expecting in truth, but the major players in all of this seemed to be going through the motions. Placing the empty posturing to one side, it was like they had been there before and what's more sometime in the future they'd be there again. To reinforce the point, the police removed from the house a couple of rucksacks which carried more than the whiff of suggestion of being pre-packed.

'You shut up.'

'You shut up first.'

It was all too much for Si, who in pure exasperation, arms out to either side, roundly proclaimed: 'Can everyone just chill?'

This had an immediate effect on the main players. Each of them turned towards him as if to say *who the hell are you?* Ollie and company included.

Si had the floor and he was on a roll, at least in his own mind. He took it upon himself to make the moment count. 'Why can't we all get along?' he said.

Mo snorted. He grabbed one of the rucksacks, and before Si could start quoting from Mahatma Gandhi or Martin Luther King Jr., had already stomped halfway down the street.

Elijah shoved his pieces of phone diligently into his jeans pockets. He scooped up the remaining bag before following Mo's lead, taking lengthier, leggier strides.

Si open-mouthed held the sallying Mo and Elijah in his sights. At a different time of year his mouth would be catching flies.

It seemed to do the trick, though. Calm was restored.

Ollie was standing next to him. 'They're off to the pub,' she said.

'It's not even nine o'clock,' Si said.

'They know a side door.'

The police had disappeared into the house. From what Si could discern from the shouting, one of the officers seemed to have found a kettle.

Still outside, Ollie was rolling her eyes. 'C'mon, let's put some space between them and us.'

Ollie and Si, like the pair of chickens they were, crossed to the other side of the road. There, she sat on the kerb. He remained standing.

'You left me,' she said.

'I'm sorry,' he said.

'No you're fucking not. There I was pouring my heart out to you. There you were planning on making a sharp exit.'

He didn't know how to reply, which was fine because she wasn't expecting one. She peered up at him and broke into a wide grin. He found himself smiling back.

He wasn't sure which one of them had won a reprieve; spending more time in each other's company. He was seized by a determination to enjoy what little time the voice inside his head insisted they had left together. The role of Good*ish* Samaritan was strictly for a limited time only. He was already thinking about the stories he'd tell Sofi when he got back home.

She was smoking a cigarette. 'Quick turnaround on this one, PC Plods turn up Johnny-on-the-spot,' she said. 'Not surprising really, it's an empty big house occupying a prime spot in London. Old Charlie's choice of exit was hardly inconspicuous. Neighbours will be keen to see the back of us.'

At this, she gave a small wave in the direction of an incriminating twitch of a curtain, two doors up, which came from a lower window.

'The police. No sign of them yesterday, but here they are now.' Si wasn't sure what to make of it. 'Why didn't they ask us any questions?' Ollie was silent in return, nonchalant even. It occurred to Si that he was asking a question that applied to his world, not hers. 'You ask me, I'd say you're used to this sort of thing,' he said, finally.

'Eviction?' she said. 'You think?

'Yes,' she said. A single word to answer a brace of rhetorical questions. 'We use our eyes and ears and when we're not going anywhere we're at the pub waiting for word to come through. When people find out they're dying, they like to make a song and dance of it. We're under no illusions, it's a short-lived relationship, in more ways than one, but basically, they die and we take over the house until the police turn up and turf us out. With old Charlie it was different, Mo's dad knowing him and all that, but we knew he didn't have much time left.' She took one last defiant puff, smoke exiting her nostrils. 'And there we have it, friends, countrymen, *your ears*, as surely as anything good happens it will surely turn sour. It's done, it's dusted. Old Charlie's estate now held officially in trust by the state.'

'Trust,' she repeated before a grunt brought up some phlegm from her throat. She spat onto the road.

The house now across the street descended into silence, and so did Ollie and Si. It felt like they were approaching a natural end to an unnatural twenty-four hours.

'I did make the memorial site,' she said.

Si, eyebrow arched, looked at her inquisitorially before another dollop of realisation dawned on him. 'New York,' he said. 'The World Trade Center.'

He sat down on the kerb next to her.

'It was terribly moving. Raw, beautiful, heart breaking, mystical; I don't know how to describe it. All those messages of condolences, handwritten, so incredibly sincere. What the living have to go through. What the dead leave behind. Normally I think people are such arseholes, but not that day. There were boxes of hankies at various points positioned around the site and I never thought I'd have the need for anything like that, but I cried my eyes out. The buildings made me feel tiny, but this, the memorial site, I was just humble. Apart from such childish, morbid fascination, the temple in Egypt meant nothing to me, but New York was so different. I thought to myself, yeah, I had grown up a little after all.'

She took out her cigarette packet, and holding it up to her ear, gave it a quick shake. Her seemingly inexhaustible supply of a nicotine fix was close to being exhausted. She stuck out her bottom lip and tipped out from the packet, as it happened, her third last cigarette.

'One last grab of a hanky, a blow of the nose, and I decided I was done. To stay any longer wouldn't have felt right, so I started the long interweaving route back to the hotel. On the way back, there was this little quaint boutique shop. The buildings are so tall, but the tourist shops are so tiny. It was a little thing in the window that caught my eye. A little figure shaped like a Hindu goddess. It had four arms, as beautifully painted as anything I had ever seen. Brown skin. Wore an outfit all the colours, red, orange; they caught the light just right. The colours shimmered. I hunched over to take a better look. It was perfect. I was captivated. I think I even made a cooing noise. Next thing I know an old guy, older than my dad, stepped out of the shop and started making conversation. He had a really broad New Yorker accent. "First time in *New Yawk?*" he asked me. It took me a moment to catch his meaning, but as it turned out the only conversation he was interested in was the one-way kind. The way he talked; it was like forcing words out of an insincere smile. He had read my mind, though. "Beautiful piece. Beautiful, beautiful," he said. "Pure ivory. Give me a price and I'll see what we can do. You look like a nice girl. Such a stunning piece. Maybe I can do you some good here. Don't worry I won't be offended. You make me an offer."'

'That was the point I noticed there weren't any prices displayed in the shop window. His voice grew quieter. The more he talked the more he sounded like an old man. I think I might have felt sorry for him. Part of me thought he was trying to snare me and no matter how I answered, I'd be walking into a trap. Just like the poor animal that probably died, hunted and slaughtered, to supply the ivory. But I'm saying that with the benefit of hindsight. At the time it never occurred to me that ivory was bad or unethical. It just sounded expensive and I liked the colours. "Fifty dollars," I said. I don't think I even had that much money on me.'

'The whole shape of his face turned and changed. It was a slow fuse, but he exploded soon enough; hostage to emotions that were anything but good. "Fifty dollars! A disgrace. You think I'm old? Senile? You take me for a fool? A chump?" He lifted the back of his hand as if he was about to lash out. Instinctively, I took a step back, and then I took some more. I recoiled from him and his ugly face and uglier words. And then, somehow, I lost my footing and I was falling backwards. I know it's a gigantic cliché, but it's true, everything was in slow motion. I remember thinking how unfair a world it was. And when I think back and try to remember how it was, I experience these strange insights. I don't know if I saw it at the time or if it's my memory playing tricks, but I saw the Hindu goddess standing in front of me, the centre of the universe; the reflection of divinity. Her likeness carved out of tusk, of horn, at the expense of a great living beast, an elephant, a rhino. An affront to everything a goddess would stand for. Is anything truly sacred? Is there nothing on earth the human race is prepared to stand side by side with? Share the planet with?'

'Then everything got fast. I was thrown up in the air and came down really hard. There was really bad pain. It took hold of the whole of my body—and then there was—I don't know what it was.'

'There was nothing.'

Outside the house, as she spoke, the police van was joined by a larger white van. This one was unmarked, and out popped two removal men wearing dark blue tops and baseball caps. The removal men ghosted into the front door and returned minutes later, wrestling out the bookcase, holding it an angle to stop the books from tipping out.

They took a moment, called a timeout, resting the bookcase down. One of them removed his cap and wiped down his brow.

Si didn't know what to focus on. The shocking nature of Ollie's story or the situation of an evicted bookcase playing out in front of him. He couldn't concentrate on both.

Ollie passed him a cigarette and applying absolutely no thought to the matter he took it. She leaned towards him brandishing a lit cigarette lighter. Thinking only a little, cigarette in mouth letting it take hold, he gravitated towards the flame.

'It was a yellow taxi,' she said. 'I'd fallen back onto the road and it hit me. I was in a coma for four weeks. I needed as much time more in rehabilitation. The medical bill was enormous. There was talk about a police investigation, abandonment of a minor or some such, but that never amounted to anything. My mum went home, my dad stayed.'

'After all that, it's still with me. Sometimes I don't have feeling in my hands. There's nothing there. I could fail the *Light* and still see out the end of the day.' She held out her hands so Si could see, but to the naked eye they looked normal enough. He wasn't sure what he was looking for. His mind reverted to the lines he knew existed underneath her sleeves.

'The scars on my arms came from the accident,' she said. 'Or from that period of time after the accident, I can't really remember. I like to think they show on the outside what I feel on the inside. And they're never going to fade, not completely, until they're ready to. Deciding you're never going to die, that doesn't guarantee a life of happiness.'

'That's terrible,' Si said. He wasn't sure if this was the right thing to say. He had grown weary of asking questions.

No matter the extent of the enigma tied up in knots in front of him, he was determined to draw a line—and understand.

She gave him a look; tightening her eyes to the point he thought she might be some kind of mind reader. But she wasn't a mind reader, not really. 'Maybe one day you'll understand,' she said, 'but for now, it's good you want to try.'

He dropped his head. 'Shouldn't you have it checked out?'

'No more doctors,' she said. 'No more tests. Nothing more to do with the *Light*.' She looked down and slid the sides of her trainers together. 'Done with all that shit.'

'Look at those wankers,' she said, rising up to gesture towards the house. 'They've apprehended a bookcase. They're told to clear the house and they know how to clear a house all right. Jawoll, mein Führer!' She gave what Si assumed was a half-hearted Nazi salute.

Si took a draw of his cigarette. Inhaled smoke took him by surprise, garrotting him. Intense, piercing; it was like he'd breathed in a warm, slaloming, fast-acting sickness.

'Jesus,' he said, before dropping the offending item onto the road. His backside was still planted on the kerb. He was too low down and the oxygen had disappeared around him. In response he got back up on his feet. He walked towards the house.

'Quite right,' Ollie commented, choosing to stay put. 'That stuff is poison.'

She lit her last one, holding it for inspection betwixt finger and thumb before guiding it to her lips and taking one quick puff.

Si needed to get away from it, the latest reminder with a jolt—a natural aversion to smoke. Not for the first time, he saw the world through a nightmarish lens. What was he thinking? Why so squeamish? Self-righteous? He'd taken worse substances in his time. He coughed, stifled a cough, coughed some more. He must have been thinking of something.

His trajectory took him towards the removal men, who didn't appear to be in much of a hurry, one arm apiece rested on the bookcase. Si raised his hand in greeting.

'Morning boys,' he said. 'You don't mind if…'

Both men bristled, swift to establish no matter how Si planned to finish his sentence that they would mind.

Unfazed, Si reached into the bookcase and took from it the illustrated book with the three children on the cover, *The Magic Faraway Tree*.

'Oi, put that back,' one of them said.

'That's government property,' the other piped up.

It wouldn't be long, Si thought, for the posturing to really begin. He rather fancied that he would stand his ground.

'It's all right,' another voice emerged from the house. It belonged to one of the police officers.

The officer in question, poker-faced, walked forward. Without the distraction of the kerfuffle from before, Si now noticed the officer had a cleft chin. Very prominent, like a bullet hole.

It reminded him of Hollywood actor Michael Douglas' dad, another actor, Kirk Douglas, the man who played *Spartacus* in the movie from the sixties of the same name. Boy was Si a sucker for big Hollywood movies—and chins—from the sixties.

PC Spartacus held out his hand expectantly and Si, suddenly feeling less bullish, handed the book over. PC Spartacus briefly examined both front and back covers before handing it back.

'Good book. Unusual, a bit off the wall,' the officer said approvingly, his voice sounding older than his appearance, which put him in his thirties. 'I remember liking *The Saucepan Man*,' he continued. 'Read it to my kid.'

They exchanged the briefest of glances, blink and you'd miss it, but it said everything. There was a tinge of sadness to be found, mourning for both what the world could have been and for what it had in fact become. Even *The Land of Do-As-You-Please* had to have some kind of ending.

'It is yours, isn't it?' PC Spartacus enquired.

Si nodded. To reinforce the point, he pinned the book to his chest with both hands.

PC Spartacus turned and barked at the removal men. 'It's his. Just get on with your job.'

Putting the lunacy of recent events to one side, even now there was a sliver of sanity to be had. Now the hullaballoo had receded, there was little else to anyone's repertoire. They were only doing what had to be done, Si reflected. Lovable squat-evicting, bookshelf-bothering ponies. Who was he to take offence? Mad times. Dangerous times. *I am Spartacus.*

He returned to her. The cold had descended, although nothing as bitter as yesterday. There was no wind, lending his surroundings an unearthly calm. With the bookcase gone, there would be no trace left of old Charlie. He would be written out of the street, erased from the tapestry, washed out of the tarmac. It would be left to his ghost to decide whether to follow suit.

How could he know how much time any of them had left? There wasn't a calendar somewhere with the date circled, however far in the future, marking out emphatically your last day on earth. Or maybe it did exist, but was residing plain out of sight. To find it only required the minimum amount of investigation or effort. If there was such a calendar in existence—an almanac of death, call it what you will—what purpose would it serve to go off and look for it? What would this achieve? They say knowledge is power, but too much power can prove the opposite. It can be a distorting force, destroying and tearing things apart. Wouldn't the ideal scenario be just not to know? For the overwhelming majority of your life you were in a state of suspense, so why should today or any other day feel differently? If we didn't have it, would we have need of it? Would we desire it, covet it? Would we then search for something like the *Light*?

On walking back to her, Si took tiny steps, resigned to the fact that after all he had seen, tiny steps was the only way to go. A strange resolve took hold of him to take a thousand steps and then a million and to keep going after that. But there were flights and there were flights of fancy. In full view of Ollie, still a couple of feet away, he settled for something entirely in his control and slipped the book inside the front of his coat.

'You have your memento,' she said, smiling. 'Maybe you'll get the chance to read it to your kids.'

'Yup,' he said.

'You enjoy your time as a rebel? A spaceman? On the margins, outside of things?'

'I'd need to think about it, but not particularly. You?'

'I get to meet interesting people.'

He still hadn't reached her side of the road. How much of a chasm this represented *he* hadn't decided yet.

'This goodbye, then?' she said.

He put his hands in his pockets. He had an air of resignation about him. Ready for whatever life chose to throw at him. 'I doubt I'll be much use to anybody. My wallet has taken a pummelling and chances are it's been too long since I last took the *Light*. Can't risk my cards and can't get hold of money until I sort myself out. I'm not streetwise; don't have the wherewithal to support myself otherwise. Never put it to the test to be fair, but pretty sure I can't live on fresh air. And I'm sure you'll tire of me soon enough.'

'You not going to take the *Light*, then?' she said.

'Not in front of you,' he said. He thought he could feel the world spinning on its axis underneath his feet. 'It can wait. I've waited long enough. It can wait until home.'

She laughed at this, although as laughter went it was remarkably brief. It was difficult to work out where she hoped to go with this, the most ephemeral of chuckles, but for Si, this summed her up perfectly. She had spoken a lot about herself, it was true; a series of unreal and dramatic events with none of it really explaining anything about her. Egypt? New York? London? He couldn't place her in any kind of context. He couldn't spend the rest of his life attributing even more questions to each of her answers.

'How much money do you actually have?' she said.

'Enough for a taxi,' he said. 'Someone with *The Knowledge*, so I don't need any.'

'Enough for one last round, then?' she said.

13

A Very Russian Hacking

It was minus six degrees in Moscow's red light district, which ran uphill on a slight incline off the North End of Red Square. It was so cold it trapped the smell of sex in the air. You could taste it in what little moisture there was. It made your eyes water. There was a lot of fucking. At minus six, it was one of the few things that kept you warm.

It was here that Mikhail lived on the top floor of an old Georgian whorehouse which went by the name of дом Павлова, or Pavlov's House for the tourists. He was a cousin to one of the proprietors and his residence was only supposed to be a temporary one, but seven years had already come and gone with no end to his occupancy in sight. They were not the best of fits. The best of bedfellows. How he would curse and swear and stamp his feet when the room below his was being used. With unrivalled venom and clockwork regularity, he would invoke the names of Lenin and Trotsky. He would yelp and scream of betrayed revolution, lost to soiled sheets. Of dreams smashed and tattered like an escort's pelvis. He wished an ice pick to the patron's cock. For some of the clientele he was part of the package, taking pleasure and not too little excitement from the racket he created from the room above—this whirling dervish. This foul-mouthed upholder of the revolution, emboldened by a febrile mind and a pair of sturdy Muscovite boots.

Plus, Mikhail paid his way intermittently from the not insubstantial sums earned from the odd job picked up here and there. Otherwise, he lived a frugal existence, generally treating money with disdain. The devil's daughter.

He had the same meal normally three times a day—bread, crackers, cheese, and vodka. Some borscht maybe. Some sweet and sour cabbage.

He did not indulge in what Pavlov's had to offer. It wasn't that he was vehemently against the idea of shitting on your own doorstep, more on the lines of fucking on your own doorstep. He was certain Lenin would agree, but less sure Trotsky would. For much of the day, in his head, he would play them out, engaged in endless discourse on this and that, usually building up to a frightful froth, debating the choppy, ferocious ocean that was the current state, political or otherwise, of the Russian Federation. 'The Motherland' as Lenin would call it, careful to direct as much scorn as polemically possible towards his old comrade. Trotsky would respond by decrying Lenin as a revolutionary peacock before exiting stage left, appropriately enough with a slam of a door. Trotsky's lover Frida Kahlo waited for him on the other side of that door, but Mikhail's mind dared not to venture so far.

Mikhail wore a bandana and was fluent in English and German, although not conversationally so. As a rule he left his room only once a day. He needed to walk in order to loosen his insides and uncoil his bowels. If he neglected to do so, not to put too fine a point on it, he would be unable to defecate. When gone, one of the ladies, sometimes one of the men, would sneak into his room to perform some basic domestic chores.

It never seemed to get old, but they would report back the same thing. Strewn across the floor of Mikhail's room were all manner of books, magazines, periodicals, and newspapers all opened without fail at page numbers ending with six and seven. Some of the pages were ripped away; a page twenty-six on the left-hand side could be followed by, say, page forty-seven on the right. When challenged on this, Mikhail would respond on the lines only that there were secret messages to be deciphered; conspiracies to be unravelled. The room was in permanent tumult.

They'd confirm that his laptop, without fail, was locked away in its case. Not only this, but was surrounded by actual barbed wire. One time, one of the girls, Elise—silly cat, curiosity got the best of her—ventured too close, only to get her hair tangled up in it, resulting in some of the others needing to fetch the big pair of scissors in order to cut her free.

She'd gotten close, but not too close, which for her was just as well as Mikhail didn't consider barbed wire alone to be sufficient deterrent. Various pieces of metal were greased and fed through the wire; a hacksaw, utility knife, razor blades, and a number of rusty iron nails.

As for Mikhail, he would venture outdoors. In the winter it was too cold for snow. He was conscious of having to control his breathing. The air, cloaked in ice, would threaten to lacerate his larynx. Often he would walk to Red Square, and while there, he would stare in silent contemplation at the statues of Kuzma Minin and Dmitry Pozharsky, careful not to wander too close for fear of being torn apart by their power; the sheer forces of nature invested in each of these bronzed effigies. He would feel the pull of Lenin's mausoleum as it exerted pressure around his face. He would stand until he could cope with the vigour of insurrection and antiquity no longer, and so take his leave of Red Square to return to his room where it was a simple enough matter to then empty his bowels.

Having returned, he would see evidence of cleaning and general tidying; the repositioning of magazines on the floor. He would see a clump of hair stuck to the barbed wire and would explode into an apoplectic rage at such violations of privacy. He could shout and scream through the walls and floorboards and call the occupants every name under a reluctant Moscow sun. 'Rats! Vermin! Cocksuckers! If I had my way, I'd have your backs against the wall! Crack open your skulls and feed your eyes to the crows! Fill your empty eye-sockets with worms!'

Eventually he would tire. His wracked body would collapse onto the bed as he waited for the last embers of his fury to subside. Slowly, his heart would cease thumping, his head would stop circling. He increased the rhythm of his breathing; tried to take in more air. Somewhere in the back of his head a tiny, distant voice told him that it was okay now he was indoors; that his vocal chords were safe; that oxygen was his friend. In the forefront of his mind there emerged the usual suspects.

'Freedom in capitalist society remains the same as it was in ancient Greek republics: Freedom for slave owners,' Lenin said.

'The end may justify the means as long as there is something that justifies the end,' Trotsky said.

'Oh, go set your hair on fire,' Lenin would tell him.

'Stick your finger in your ear,' Trotsky would counter.

This, Mikhail considered good advice. In fact he would often stick a finger in both ears. It was all he could do to block out the outside world. Radio waves, electrical pulses, white noise. Sometimes he returned from his sojourn to Red Square less empty-handed than when setting off. He would be passed an encrypted flash drive by a man or woman—it was difficult to tell under so much heavy clothing—with whom he would never make eye contact. Glove on glove, the most furtive of transactions, a sleight of hand; so formed a contract, the sketchiest of terms of employment. He was a hacker. He hacked on behalf of individuals or corporations identity unknown, but was under no illusion he did so on behalf of the state. Everything eventually led one way or another back to the state.

It had been more than a month since his last assignment, but in that time he could not escape from the world. Every day it followed him into his room and poked at his eyes, stabbed at every orifice. It tortured the life out of him. His face was constantly contorted to the point it was the manifestation of *The Scream* by Edvard Munch. Matters came to a head when he decided the air was no longer his friend. He pressed his lips together with all his might and willed his lungs dormant. His face, like his insides, turned a dull purple. He was still, deathly still. He couldn't command his body to move even if he wanted or needed it to.

Inevitably he gasped. He noisily and rapidly inhaled pockets of oxygen. Keep your friends close, he decided between every frantic breath, but keep your enemies closer.

He then slept for thirty-six hours straight and dreamed of bears.

When he awoke he found he was no wiser or happier. He'd been too long away from the *Light*. There would be the pain of having to reactivate his many bank accounts. At this rate he'd never have the means for long enough to move out of Pavlov's. But some colour had at least returned to his cheeks. On reflection he dismissed such a thing from his mind, going as it did against his idea of haunted self-image.

He was chameleonic. One time he was Cozy Bear, the other Fancy Bear, and the other Guccifer 3.0. He counted himself among a number of like-minded souls dotted across the country. All with specific instructions and all unaware of the identity of the others, of what any of them were doing at any one time, which contributed weightily to the random element of the attacks, making it more difficult for others to detect or trace back.

They were cyber-drones. Chaos breeding chaos. He would break down cyber defences and steal data and seed wildly malicious malware and ransomware. He would navigate financial portals to facilitate the laundering of money and strategically implant fake news as it was delivered to him, wrapped up in words of truth and certainty (although they could have taken more time on spelling and grammar).

Targeting businesses of all shapes and sizes, political machines, banks, men of influence of weak morality, mostly USA-based, but some to be found in Germany and the UK. He would do all of these things, hitting keys on his keyboard with ferocious purpose, navigating through the Dark Web, swallowing whole firewalls while sweeping clean his tracks. Although none of this would be possible, not before the physical act of putting on gardening gloves and meticulously liberating his laptop by carefully guiding it through the barbed wire.

Only he knew the pattern to weave and twist and cajole the wire in order to gain safe access. Failing to follow a specific path—gloves or no gloves—you risked losing a finger or worse.

All that time, two great Soviet behemoths would bicker and roar in his ear.

'A lie told often enough becomes the truth,' Lenin said.

'You think?' Trotsky said.

Mikhail admonished himself constantly. The state was all-serving and in his small way he was helping perpetuate this. The state even had *death* on its side.

The establishment was attempting to bring back the trappings of the Old Russian Empire—and of the Roman Empire before that. Behind White House doors—he was sure of it, it was happening right now—orgies were taking place. Across all the palaces, vineyards, and duck shelters. Across the Caucasus an early warning system was in place that covered an age group no older than twenty and as young as … he shuddered to think how young. A system where Last Dayers were bussed to government buildings and forced in their last hours to be sex slaves to the elite. Displays of opulence and decadence, the new Russia ushering in the old, but this version was much crueller, and in terms of reach, more extensive than anything devised by a Caesar or Czar. In this Russia he was surrounded by a world of Dmitry's and Vladimir's.

Only the young were dying; and only the dying were abused. The old and debauched were left unscathed. For Mikhail, here was conclusive proof that the Last Day was a state conspiracy. The government was in cahoots, inextricably bound to the Russian Orthodox Church, and together the fate of the motherland was decided. There could be no other kind of feasible explanation.

Out of the blue there was a recurring, violent thumping. It took him some moments to realise that the furore wasn't down to the crashing and whumping going on inside his head, but rather originated from the room below.

'Degenerates!' he screamed. 'Muck spreaders, plague carriers!'

It was no use, he knew he would need to toilet soon or risk exploding within as well as without.

'When there is state there can be no freedom, but when there is freedom there will be no state.'

'If we had had more time for discussion we should probably have made a great many more mistakes.'

Even though he had slept for thirty-six hours, even

though they originated from inside his head, he was too tired to distinguish the voices. From downstairs there came a wolf-like howl, intimation that the carnal act, if not spent, was on the wane. It grew quiet; as quiet as a whorehouse during working hours could realistically be expected to be.

Like a somnambulist, a lifeless automaton, a subject of the state, Mikhail proceeded to dress himself without thinking in sheepskin coat, scarf, gloves, and ushanka hat.

He was out and walking smartly, his head hurting. His mind was a snow globe, shaken roughly, a blizzard of busy, easily spooked white particles. He had come to hate the country of his birth. Or more specifically, he hated what the world had become and the role his country had played in this. Russia was complicit in the changing nature of death; although for Mikhail any change was purely cosmetic. It was the same final result for all after all, everyone was still perishable. But it meant, without any real prompting or fight, that the proletariat had rolled up the white flag and peddled themselves lock, stock, and barrel to the tyranny of the state. Democracy was going out of fashion, but in Russia it had never been too much in fashion.

At one point, assignments came his way that enquired into the machinations of the Church of the Last Day. They came in the form of security assessments, server injection attacks, a harras of Trojan Horses; the works. Not that any of the attacks appeared to get through the Church walls, but this was by the by. All such activity, all interest, at least as far as Mikhail's sponsors were concerned, came to a halt nearly a year ago. However, that didn't stop him stumbling over something noteworthy, perhaps even crucial. If it was anything, he decided to keep it to himself. A blip in the spaghetti code; the beta software, an app in development not entirely ring-fenced, intended to be rolled out to the global village mobile network. He couldn't be sure, not one hundred per cent, but if he was right, he had in his grip the means to bring down the whole cathedral architecture. Not with a crash, but with a tap.

There wasn't much of a crowd. He held his arms out straight either side. He was aware that he was spinning, plainly, resolutely. He was on the hallowed grounds of Red Square. Saint Basil's Cathedral, the GUM department store, the Iberian Gate, a litany of pastel shapes, everything was a blur as he continued circling round and round. Not quite entering, but knocking on the door of an altered state, knowing if he should stop, giddiness would make him its bitch.

A hand was placed on his shoulder. At this Mikhail stopped rotating, and after a pause that promised to last as long as the lifetime of a cathedral, his legs gave way beneath him. Someone, the owner of the hand on his shoulder no doubt, caught him, so preventing him from falling, at least physically. Spiritually Mikhail had fallen from grace a long time ago. But this was the least of his worries.

'Thank you,' Mikhail said in croaky fashion, not realising until he spoke that his throat was so dry.

The comrade who caught him was male, not much older than himself but younger around the eyes. Mikhail normally avoided the eyes, so the fact he noticed those of his rescuer was proof that he wasn't himself. The comrade was certainly handsome and rugged in the revolutionary sense. But such an impression may have had more to do with the comrade's pointy moustache on full display and Van Dyke beard.

Not to disappoint, his knight in shining armour was moved to speak, 'But every little difference may become a big one if it is insisted on.'

Despite the utter worthiness of what was said, Mikhail still experienced a disconnect. His words were delivered with the conviction of a deflated balloon; the result of a blocked nasal passage. Bunged up. Mikhail broke a second rule by looking at the comrade's nose, which was as red as *90377 Sedna*, the reddest planet in the universe, to be found in the outer reaches of the Solar System. You didn't have to be a brain surgeon to correctly diagnose that the comrade had a cold.

Any lingering doubt was dispelled by an almighty sneeze and subsequent sliver of snot in the shape of Italy hanging from his nose.

Mikhail rummaged around his pocket and handed over a handkerchief. It was only at the moment the grateful recipient sneezed into the hankie that Mikhail realised with horror it was unlaundered. He had only days previously masturbated into it.

They stood for a moment, not sure what to say. Not sure, if anywhere, to take things from here. The comrade, blessedly unaware of anything being amiss, handed back the handkerchief which a flushed Mikhail—who tried to play it cool but ended up snatching it back anyway—returned briskly to his pocket. There followed a discrete, quick rummage of the pocket which confirmed there was no memory stick under the cover of a soiled, sticky handkerchief. No assignment, nothing in the way of orders having come back to him. Perhaps the individual in front of him wasn't a handler but a normal citizen—or at least as normal a citizen as Mikhail had the wherewithal to distinguish from the abnormal ones.

'Call me Vlad,' he said while offering a glove in greeting.

'Comrade Vlad, I don't live far from here at all,' Mikhail said. The briefest of moments was all he took to shake gloved hands. He didn't feel a thing. 'Let me take you in from the cold.'

It was such a bold thing to say. Where did it come from?

He could have retracted, but this would have required another equivalent amount of brazenness and he had already reached his limit.

They both set off in silence, each occupying a space in reasonably close proximity to each other, but never what you'd call walking side by side. Never to show in terms of body language that one was even aware of the other. It was the way. It was the Russian way. To employ stealth; to be secretive to the end; to not fully trust anyone, including oneself.

On reaching their destination, comrade Vlad was greeted by the old Georgian façade of Pavlov's House. The construction had its own particular scent and he needed a moment to take it in. It was understandable, facing such a monument to sin and decadence, Vlad took stock, he hesitated. Sensing his trepidation, Mikhail, a picture of spontaneity, reached across and pinched Vlad on the shoulder. Such an action, the rashness of it, took Vlad by surprise, but for Mikhail there were no regrets. Regret was never an emotion he had cause to ever familiarise himself with. Anyway, the pinch seemed to do the trick as Vlad, feet shuffling, began to move forward.

Together, they moved inside and climbed the stairs. From behind the various florid rooms there came a cacophony of moans, groans, and bangs. It left nothing to the imagination.

The building itself was officially sanctioned. The Russian way was to take a potential problem and build a solution around it. In this fashion Pavlov's House was affiliated to the Church of the Last Day.

With all kinds of hubbub kicking off around them, the idea of sneaking in hardly seemed necessary, but intrepid revolutionaries to the last, they sneaked in any case into Mikhail's room.

As soon as he entered, Vlad took one glance at the barbed wire around the laptop and made to leave. Mikhail, deciding not to let this happen, jerked like a jack-in-the-box and bounded towards his quarry. He placed both gloved hands with menace around comrade Vlad's throat. His hands were arranged, set in place, as if cradling a mug or tankard of ale. Thumbs circling before taking hold of something solid. There was nothing in the way of sensation. His body had been taken over—a strange and compelling and violent metamorphosis—no longer his own. Mikhail did his best to strangle him.

'Not believing in force is the same as not believing in gravity,' Trotsky's voice bellowed, easily the loudest utterance to emerge from the entire house. Surely everyone could hear it?

In Red Square, it was an error of judgement on Vlad's part to quote from Lenin. In the end, Lenin was Trotsky's ideological nemesis. When Lenin died, Stalin filled the 'mortal enemy' vacuum created by Lenin's passing, and Stalin had Trotsky killed.

It was clear to Mikhail now, who had chosen Trotsky—who was channelling him, becoming him—that this was a case to kill or be killed.

'Ideas that enter the mind under fire remain there securely and for ever.' The words so deafening and true, causing the very fabric of the building to shake. Surely it would cause each of the occupants of the house to freeze; to stop cold in the act?

More young than old were dying, and the rich no longer died young. But the stakes were much higher than mere self-preservation. Mikhail could not accept the certitude of the Last Day. There had to be a glitch, he reasoned, a random element. He was certain of his destiny and that he'd be the man naturally to prove it. He imagined how he would take someone, the recipient of verification at the beginning of the day, having passed the *Light*, and chopping him into pieces. There would be no surviving this. Even if it was not his time, diced into a hundred segments, how could it possibly be anything other than his time?

It would keep Mikhail awake; would make him ill if he let it. It was obvious to him that the Verification Light network, next to the World Wide Web, was the most extensive globally. He had broken the latter many times and now he set his sights on the former.

Even here there were national boundaries. There were many firewalls to navigate, which was the why, how, and where that surrounded the flaw, the blip. It was where the code stalled after the trillionth or so passes of self-interrogation. It may have been a one-off; it may already have been identified and rectified. He may have sat on it for too long and missed his chance, but he had embedded a script. A simple enough batch file, but the trick was how deep he had buried it. If activated, it would wait patiently, furtively, for the glitch to reappear. More an idea than a theory. A logic bomb entombed in the vastness of cyberspace. That it could switch off everything, it was capable.

It was capable of what bombs were capable of.

He wanted to know. He had a point to make. The *Light*, the rights and wrongs, that's what we should all be focussing on. He would push a button on his laptop. He would write comrade Vlad out of the equation. It was simple really, except to come to a decision between the two of them of what to do first.

Perhaps he was looking too far ahead. He was still in the middle of trying to choke his unfortunate victim to death. Vlad was pushing back, which caused both of them to shift their feet. The floor was moving like it was alive. Vlad lost his footing, slipping and sliding on some opened glossy magazines pages. He stumbled forward as if his legs had been chopped from under him. On the way down he cracked his nose against Mikhail's knee. He fell back unconscious, out like a light.

'In a serious struggle there is no worse cruelty than to be magnanimous at an inopportune time.'

These were Trotsky's words, but it was Mikhail who was saying them. As his victim lay out sprawled before him, still breathing, he experienced a moment of clarity. Previously, he had a choice to make: where exactly did he see him slotting into the pages of history? Was he the new Lenin or new Trotsky? He was the latter, he decided, or had allowed recent events to take shape and make the decision for him. He was the man of action. The man the authorities chose to exile and kill because they considered him too great a threat. The man who was refused a seat at the table alongside those monstrous ideologues he once called comrades. The mere thought of this, the injustice, the unfairness of it all, made Mikhail's ears burn.

Upper body quaking, he took tentative steps, growing bolder by the second, moving closer to the box that contained his laptop. In the correct manner, he removed it gingerly from the barbed wire. Too much shaking—in the throes of spent adrenalin, hands not up to scratch—he was less than his usual scrupulous self. In the course of being shifted, some barbed wire enhancements fell to the floor. He could hear the sound of several iron nails make their escape, rolling away to different parts of the room. But there wasn't much he could do about that for the moment. He could only focus on one thing at a time.

Much to his surprise, mixed in with a little shock and horror, he saw he'd left the key in the lock of the box. This was at odds with the whole barbed wire defensive set up he had going on, but could not deny at this particular time the convenience factor.

He opened the box and lifted out his laptop as carefully and diligently as he could. He was no brain surgeon lifting up a bone flap, ready to delve into the soft tissue underneath, but this was his version of a craniotomy. He flipped the laptop open. The screen saver—consisting of a giant panda as happy as Khrushchev eating a bamboo stick—burst into life. There wasn't much charge left, the laptop had been asleep for several days, but there'd be enough. A tap of a finger revealed a command line, which flashed expectantly: blip, blip, blip. There was a translucent square enveloping a winking solitary 'Y' which awaited the press of the return key. Ominous as well as expectant, a tap was all it would take.

In his other hand was a hacksaw, which he had also retrieved from the barbed wire farrago. The question *'What came next, the chicken or the egg?'* would obsess and torment him at times. It was a question of waiting and pondering and allowing the question to flow over and nestle in the pores of his skin and under his eyelids until he felt strongly enough that it was one thing or the other.

'Wait, it's what came first, isn't it? The chicken or the egg.'

And in this way, in full view of his present predicament, he had to decide what came next, what came first. Return key or comrade Vlad, comrade Vlad or return key?

'Hurry up,' a voice, probably his own, lashed out at him. 'Hurry up, hurry up.'

Next thing he knew, or was aware of, he was hunched over comrade Vlad who was still out for the count.

With the hacksaw, he began sawing through dark green corduroy trousers into Vlad's leg just below the knee. It wasn't that he wasn't putting the effort in, but after a minute of sawing he'd achieved little more than a flesh wound. There was more grease from the hacksaw in evidence than actual blood. The predominant colour was a murky dark green.

He thought this particular course of action was too hard. Too arduous. Removing his victim's boot, he was now thinking maybe he should start on something easier and *kick* on from there. Carefully, he took off Vlad's sock, and using his forefinger, separated the big toe from the rest and twisting it away from the others. He hunched over the toe with the hacksaw and could feel the strain the change of position was already exerting on his shoulders. No time like the present, he surmised, as he resumed sawing with real vigour, demonstrating a refreshed, revitalised level of enthusiasm.

At this, Vlad awoke. With a swinging motion, he instantly sat up, wriggling and withdrawing his foot from Mikhail's clutches. He pointed an accusatory, Shakespearean finger at his oppressor and screamed. It was a blood-curdling scream. A man's scream. One of fear mixed up with confusion mixed up with betrayal; the best of all worlds.

Springing back, Mikhail was back up on his feet in no time. And he now realised that there was a flaw, a massive shortcoming in his thinking. He didn't know for certain if comrade Vlad had taken the *Light* today (or any other day).

He assumed so, but you could never really tell with these radical (probably penniless) types. Maybe he was still to get around to it. And now he was pretty sure given recent developments, such was the dramatic shift in their relationship, that if he was to ask he couldn't count on a reliable answer.

For that matter, Mikhail hadn't taken the *Light*. He cursed the fact he was otherwise preoccupied, having walked past a hundred streetlights. But now he was thinking if it really mattered?

Did it really matter?

He had no solid basis to put his theory to the test. What was there to gain by hacking Vlad into tiny or any other size of pieces? What would he now be trying to prove? All that grease and blood and upset, all for nothing?

Plus, the usual reason for his daily ambulation could not be forgotten. He really needed to take a shit. He hadn't had one in over two days.

He was an idiot. He had taken on too much. Why choose to fight on many fronts rather than the sensible option of taking a task in turn one at a time? So where were the voices? Where was Trotsky? Where was Lenin? Why had they abandoned him?

Comrade Vlad scrambled around the floor for a short while before getting on his feet, stumbling and veering forward. His mangled foot, with semi-detached big toe, made a bloody mess of the shifting paper stock floor. It was a mess, truly at sixes and sevens.

One moment they were apart at opposite ends of the room. The next, Vlad, a man possessed, reared up in front of Mikhail. Vlad's face around the centre was puffy, disjointed, bruised. It was the bloodiest bruise, darkest black and blue. A hairline crack started at his top lip and finished at his brow, forming a broken trail, making it look like his face was two perfectly irregular segments crudely forced together. Just like Frankenstein's monster, Mikhail thought, near jumping out his own skin.

Mikhail brought the hacksaw down on Vlad's shoulder, predictably to minimum effect. Responding, Vlad held up an iron nail wedged between thumb and index finger which he stuck into Mikhail's eye, using his thumb to push it further in.

The pain was excruciating. A fireball where his eye used to be. How he wished for divine inspiration in the form of the voice of Trotsky, who had now fallen silent. He had fallen silent; Mikhail couldn't remember any of the quotes. That part of his brain wasn't working anymore.

It should have been Mikhail's turn to scream, and his mouth was shaped just right, but nothing came out. His head twitched as much as the nail would allow, blinding, slashing, ripping pain accompanied his every movement. His head was at an odd angle and suddenly in his line of vision was the screensaver, a smiling panda bear, the gateway to a flashing cursor. If he tried hard enough, could turn a little more, it was just within his grasp.

No one would come because of the sound of the struggle. These rooms were all about the sound of the struggle.

Mikhail wriggled his fingers. He could see they were moving but couldn't feel it. Brain working/brain not working. The bomb was waiting; the fuse a blinking cursor. A marker, a pointer, developed a heartbeat of its own. There, at his trembling fingertips, all he had to do was press execute. Then, the thought struck him, that he could have imagined the whole thing. There was in fact no glitch to be had in the *Light* network. He could have been mistaken; as boneheaded as he was over the whole sorry Vlad scenario. Equally, indeed, that the blip was real, but someone else halfway across the world, or considerably closer, had discovered it too, and they would be the first to exploit it.

Mikhail couldn't shut down the doubts; not all of them. Bile moved all the way from his stomach up to his throat up to his nose. And it was up to him. Comrade Vlad was motionless. It was enough to hold the nail firm, made slippy from the ooze.

The hacksaw fell out of Mikhail's useless grasp and to the floor. Both Mikhail and adversary were too far gone, too immersed in each other, for it to amount to any kind of distraction. Finally, after a deafening period of silence, there was the voice. Both could hear it. Both took from it what they wanted. What they needed. Vlad didn't seem to care anymore and Mikhail couldn't remember the point of anything anymore.

There was always the bomb, the dalliance of a keypad, if he stretched; if he really wanted to.

'Stick your finger in your ear. Stick your finger in your eye. Stick your finger...'

14

Opposite Of Light

It was still early morning, but gone past rush hour. Not that any in The Gadfly seemed in a hurry to be any other place else. Alfie, who lived in the flat above the pub, had assumed his customary position behind the bar, dressed perhaps less conventionally in pyjamas and dressing gown. Still, the way he poured two full pints and two half-pints—smooth—he demonstrated a professionalism that was quintessentially around the clock. Bitter all round in varying amounts, the appropriate beverage of choice for each of them.

All four sat at two round tables pushed together. Elijah had put his phone together then plugged it into a charger Alfie kept behind the bar. But it was no use, devoid of a spark, dead to the world, both Elijah and device together. The fittings were loose, warped, so Elijah respected their wishes and separated them again into three pieces, plus the battery. With due reverence, he laid them out on the table. He was morose. His face was in danger of caving in.

'The pigs,' he said, 'they killed my phone.'

Si took a moment to look around. It had occurred to him before that the pub didn't have the *Light*. There was no sign of any fitted panels anywhere. This didn't surprise him. What surprised him was that this had slipped his mind, leaving him to pick up on the fact all over again.

Using what remained of his wallet, Si had bought the round. In one gulp, Mo all but wiped out his beer. 'Cheers,' he said, motioning towards Si who was sitting at a diagonal across from him at the adjoining table.

Si nodded in response, and like a pious man acknowledging Heaven, raised a tentative finger. As soon as he'd done this, he was asking himself, *what was that all about?* The gesture wasn't him. It only served to underline he wasn't comfortable in his own skin.

He was going around in ever decreasing circles—him, his skin—but he was ready to pack it in, call it a day. If someone made an offer, slapped it on the table, the prospect that this was all a bad dream, he would leap at the chance. He would snap someone's hand off. But this wouldn't explain in the waking world why he was so cold, so tired and sore.

This didn't explain either why he was still here. Why he was still a participant.

And thirsty. He took a sip of his half-pint. Previously he had never cared for the taste of bitter, finding it acrid, biting and unpleasant. In every respect it was exceptionally well named. And while he could never say hand on heart the taste was particularly enjoyable, at least now it made perfect sense to him.

Ollie, chin rested on the back of her hands, having formed an arch on the table, stared at her drink, trying to count the number of bubbles; the number of angels standing on the head of her pint.

There was a ringing sound. Everyone looked up. It was the pub phone. Alfie, alert, reflexes of a panther, didn't let it ring long before picking up the receiver. Several grunts later and with an economical flick of the hand he motioned Si forward.

Si complied.

'Bloke phoned not long after you left yesterday,' Alfie said in that loud, booming, landlord-acquired voice of his. 'The second time,' he quickly added, 'gave a decent description of you right down to the shoes.' He nodded in Elijah's direction. 'As a rule I don't give out numbers. Not that, by the looks of it, your man and his mobile device would be any use to anyone both sides of Hadrian's Wall. I told the caller to try again and last night he rang every hour on the hour and that's him back on the blower this morning, already, yeah?'

Si wondered if using the word 'blower,' actually including it in a sentence, was written into some arcane pub landlord code of conduct. That, and crowbarring in a reference to Hadrian's Wall.

Alfie held out the receiver and Si stood transfixed at the coiled wire which connected receiver to handset. The receiver was curved and blocky at either end. It was an old friend Si had never thought out of a museum, alongside the typewriter and Sinclair C5—and small portable TVs—he'd see again.

'Just take the fucking thing,' Alfie said. His words resonated and bounced between the recipient's ears, his voice designed to clear the head of everything in-between. In The Gadfly, Alfie was king. Who was Si to even contemplate arguing?

'Simon?' enquired the voice from the receiver.

'Sofiane,' Si said.

'I take it you're not back yet?'

'No, ah…'

'You know, I was worried. You left your phone in your coat pocket. Idiot.'

Both of them couldn't help but smile at this. And know the other was doing so at the same time.

'If you were home,' Sofi said, 'you'd know I'm not there. I'm in Brighton.'

'Brighton?'

'You want to blow-off steam, then great, Simon, good for you. I waited, I phoned around the local pubs on the off-chance. I couldn't think of anything else to do, except maybe check out the hospitals. I had to do something; wanted to tell you I wanted to be with the kids. Took the car to Brighton last night. Now, before you interrupt, talk over me like you always do, I need you to listen for a minute. You know, I'm not blind. I can see it in your eyes. This wanderlust … Christ, whatever you want to call it. I don't want to be the one who forces you to change, to take that part of you from you. But you know what I'm about to say: where does that leave us? How is this going to work? What's the future?'

It was clear that Sofi had already rehearsed what he was going to say in his head. It was equally obvious he fully expected it would start an argument.

241

'No, I agree,' Si said. 'Look Sofi, I needed to get something out of my system; couldn't begin to describe to you what it is, not properly, but I think it's gone now. I know there's only one life I want, one future I care about, and it's with you and the kids. I don't deserve you; don't deserve Alex and Julia.'

This seemed like the most they'd said to each other in a very long time, at least where one was talking and the other was listening.

'Where'd you spend the night?' Sofi said.

'With a pal,' Si said, 'Ollie.'

'Ollie?'

'Relax, hot stuff. Short for Olivia. Don't worry, there's nothing to worry about. Look, I'll tell you all about it, but not on the phone. It's been a day. It'll take a day to tell you everything that's happened. You trust me?'

He could tell Sofi wanted to talk about Geoff, about the attack, living in London, everything that had come between them. And Si wanted it too. These were the would-be, could-be conversations that couldn't keep falling down between the cracks. Si was now a believer. It had to happen or else none of this, nothing of anything, would make any sense. It was a good start, but that's all it was. Anyone could be civil to anyone else while miles apart. The trick was to keep it going while occupying the same space.

There was silence, a collective pause for breath, travelling up and down the wire.

'You know I love you,' Sofi said. 'You coming home?'

'I love you,' Si said. 'Of course I do.' The last comment as much directed at himself as to his husband. 'Plan is to pop back to the house.' Desperately low on funds, he'd need to walk, not exactly well travelled, but he should be sure of the route by now. 'Then I'll make the trip through to Brighton. I'll phone once I have my phone, I promise. Heading back once I finish my beer.'

'Beer?' went the voice, incredulous, from the receiver. 'This early?' Si handed the phone back to Alfie. There would have been a skip in his step if any of this involved moving his feet.

'Glad he caught you,' Alfie said. 'Shoes,' he added with a single, efficient nod. There was a second, firmer nod, motioning over Si's shoulder towards the portable TV up on the shelf. 'King's Cross. If you're planning on going into London, there are a couple of demos planned. Something about the Falklands, and some other thing about fucking pandas. If you ask me, tossers every one of them. They'll fuck off home at the earliest opportunity, the first sign of rain, but you might want to keep an eye out.'

Si turned towards the TV, sound as always turned down. The screen took its leave of the prospect of demonstrations in the centre of London and moved on to the next news story spearheaded by a picture of the forty-fifth (or was it forty-fourth) President of the United States. The President's eyes were tight slits and Si found himself trying to remember the last time he'd seen them opened properly. It was a stillborn thought; his brain was already addled, bombarded, saturated; he couldn't possibly take anything else in. The accompanying caption read 'President denies health scare?' Si found himself focussing on the question mark up on the TV screen. Did it really need to be there? Again, this whole process of thinking, it made him nauseous.

'Seriously, what is wrong with people?' Alfie quipped. 'There is something wrong with him,' indicating the face on the screen, 'something rotten inside.'

'Go figure,' Si said, blowing some air out of his mouth, nearly but not quite forming a whistle.

From the vantage point of the bar, Si's attention turned to the two tables, finding an atmosphere very different to the one he'd left behind a telephone conversation ago.

Mo was on his feet. 'Play your favourites then,' he said with a venom that suggested he had grown fangs. He grabbed the back of his chair with both hands, throwing it down onto its side with an almighty clatter. 'Well fuck that.'

Ollie hadn't budged from her previous position, showing no sign of acknowledging an energised, easily antagonised Mo. She only had eyes for her untouched pint.

Si wasn't sure what to do, but settled for staying put. Elijah looked up from the table, meeting Si's gaze, communicating a longing to swap places.

Turning one hundred and eighty degrees, Mo jabbed a finger towards Si. He opened his mouth, prelude to articulating something appropriately vituperative, but instead he fell silent, face gone flat as if struck dumb.

Si's expression in turn was a determined one. He remained at the bar, but did not think this a weakness. His body rigid, fists clenched; laying down the challenge. The meaning was clear. It said to Mo, *you're not going to punch me again.*

There was a moment, which became a snapshot, and Mo was turned to stone. 'I thought we were past all this?' Mo said. 'I really thought…'

There was no finish to the sentence. Mo stormed out of the pub. A few seconds later, Elijah followed predictably in tow, leaving his phone in fragments behind him.

Throughout it all, Ollie still did not move. Si wanted her so much to respond in some way. He was seeking some kind of reassurance, having put his eggs in one basket. *Just move, damn it*, his unspoken thought. He willed on her displacement—would have settled for a twitch—to demonstrate she felt something for these individuals; that she was prepared to react. She was ready to suffer, and not in an abstract way, at the absence of her two companions.

But there was nothing.

He wasn't sure what to do, so he took the required number of steps back to his half-pint of bitter. He took another sip. He stared out of the pub window, several feet away, with a longing as precise as it was pure. Another sip, but at the rate he was going, the tiny volume so far imbibed, he feared he was never going to bring anything to a close, never mind his drink.

Time seemed empty. The air around them was calm, cowed, barely noticeable, not even through breathing. There was a drilling. The prevailing submissiveness was punctured by the ringing once more of Alfie's phone, the noise perhaps more poignant now there were two less people in the building. Si experienced hope followed by expectation. It was Sofi calling again; it had to be.

Now Mo had left, Alfie never far from a state of agitation himself, effortlessly picked up the baton of resident angry man. He grabbed the receiver with scarcely concealed hostility. He grunted down the phone. It was an alien sound; a second transaction this early in the morning not deserving of forming a phrase that resembled language, his patience stretched to the point of snapped elastic. But in the spitting feathers stakes even Alfie had a finite supply. There came a time to listen and it wasn't long before his face fell away, turned ashen. Droplets of sweat formed on his brow.

'You are shitting me,' he said. To underline the point, he took the receiver away from his ear and peered at it intensely as if it now transcended his understanding.

Si placed his half-pint back on the table. Slowly, reluctantly, he turned to look at Alfie. *Let it be good news*, he was thinking furiously. *Or no news. Please don't let it be anything else.*

'The *Light*,' Alfie said, his eyes wider than the circumference of the sun.

Up to a point, Si understood. Or at least he would understand once he saw it with his own eyes.

He ran out of the pub, bracing himself, and not just because of the cold air. He looked down the street. Not far from him stood one streetlight, but he could imagine a whole army of them, stretching as far as the eye can see. The lamp component, the traditional part which lit up the street, had faded now after 9 a.m., stepping aside to allow the light of a winter morning try its best to take hold. It was three weeks since the anniversary of the First Day, but this was like looking back at ancient history.

It could have been out of commission, but he would have remembered this to be the case. He may have forgotten, but only momentarily.

Occupying the central panel where the Verification Light should have been—the Light Purple, a chemical process for verification, the laying on of hands, the

Light—there was nothing, or if not nothing, something that amounted to nothing.

Was it a dark shade like raisin, not light like lavender? What purple hue was on display the last moments before the *Light* went out? He thought about it so hard, head reeling, mind hurling, could swear he could now visualise it—had in fact seen it, lights snuffed out, blink, blink, blink, blink. It had to be something that was instantaneous, gone in the blink of an eye, because he hated the idea of anything fading away. Not least the *Light*.

And it got inside his head—a crazy thought, one more to add to the collection.

If dark was the absence of light, then what was the opposite of light?

He had never felt closer to his family than he did at that moment. In reality he was so far away, and yet there it was, never stronger, never more certain.

He'd come to despise the restlessness, the relentlessness, the pleasure seeking, the *wanderlust* as Sofi described it. And yet, this also deepened the resolve to forgive.

He took a mixture of downers and uppers, hardly any alcohol was involved. He'd be dancing all night, his body caked in sweat. He caught his reflection on the mirrored wall and swore if he could have, he would have fucked himself. So it just had to fall to the next in line, the first he set eyes on.

'You okay?' The voice was Ollie's, having stirred belatedly in order to follow him outside.

'The *Light*,' he said. It was all anyone could say, he thought, would want to say at this precise time all around the world.

'The *Light*,' she answered. 'Si … Simon, I need your help.'

He noticed the colour of her eyes were green, but couldn't be sure they'd always been that way. And he felt vindicated. Something—anything—happening to the *Light* had global consequences. It had the potential to turn the world upside down, batshit crazy, and here he was taking time to observe the simplest of things. In her hand was Elijah's phone which, mirroring *all the king's horses and all the king's men*, she had put together again. But this in itself wasn't enough.

'I know where they'll be,' she said, 'but I need to give them, Mo especially, a day to cool off. I need to make a phone call. I need someone to know. Need to get this phone fixed. Will you help me? I can do this on my own, but it would be good to have someone I can rely on.'

'Mo?' he said fuzzily, aware his head was still reeling. It felt jangly inside, like his brain was a mixture of jigsaw pieces which weren't the right fit but nonetheless forced and lodged together.

'He can be overprotective, the big lug. His emotions overwhelm him sometimes,' she said.

'I have a phone, back at the flat,' he said. Same model. Maybe we can swap SIMs?'

She grew twitchy at this.

'The number I need is on the phone,' she said, 'not the SIM. There's this shop in the centre of London. If the guys there can't fix it, then no one can.'

'You can stay with me. One night's not a problem.'

'Brighton. Don't you need to be in Brighton?'

'I have money. I have some back at the …'

And then he recalled, it seemed an eternity away but it

was only yesterday, the drifting smoke. Sofi had burned the shoebox. He could've emptied the contents beforehand, but Si knew he hadn't. In all the time he'd known him, only rarely had Sofi let his temper get the better of him, but when it did so, it was a shitstorm of Old Testament proportions. Reason was the first casualty.

All that money stashed away, now up in flames. Up in smoke. Literally, there was too much smoke.

He did this, don't you remember? He fucking did this!

He had never known a life without doubt nagging away at the back of his head, a constant companion of sorts. No matter how much he tried to think ahead, he could not imagine a life free of it. The more he learned about himself, the less sure about anything else he became.

'I have no money,' he corrected himself. 'I can't even get cash out of a hole-in-the-wall. I can try but the machine will probably swallow up my card.'

'No worries,' she said. 'Alfie gave me money. More than enough. Whatever it takes for us to be safe.'

'My phone,' he said.

'You've come this far without it,' she said. 'You can use mine, I promise.'

'The *Light*,' he said. 'I can keep you safe.'

'It's not that simple,' she said. It's never that simple. I need someone I can trust.'

Her green eyes were epicentres, binary universes floating side by side. The morning light caught her back, moved down her spine, in such a way as to illuminate her. Rays of light, however faint, came out of her fingertips. He had to squint to look at her. He couldn't see past her.

And it was so very quiet. It was like they were caught in amber, awaiting the ongoing centuries. Both turned into fossils, preserved in the jelly of time. There was no *Light*. How soon before the shock abated and the quiet turned and changed into something else? Something dark and dangerous? Something demented? He was worried more for her than for him.

And he wondered there and then if the opposite of light was in fact a person. It was the one standing in front of him.

15

MD

That morning, Dek's thoughts were all jumbled up. He preferred it if he was more focussed, that he took a more *mindful* approach. Being overly preoccupied with the present meant he didn't have to look too far to the future or dwell too much on the past. This was what he needed to get him through the greater part of the day. It took a lot of mental discipline.

Presently, it was stupid o'clock in Partick, Glasgow. He had to get up early for work. For two-thirds of the year he got up in complete darkness and that sort of shit really had to mess with your head. Maybe that's why there were so many crazy Scottish people around—although it was difficult to be objective when making such comparisons as it was mostly crazy Scottish people he was around.

'Abandon all hope,' the clock radio chirped.

It was the same clock radio that woke him. As way

251

of prelude to the local radio station merrily assaulting his senses, projecting the vacuous, semi-excitable voice of a DJ (who he imagined had a half-arsed hipster beard) droning on about the dreich Scottish weather; wondering if this was the day when the sun finally didn't come up; then segueing into the First Minister's choice of clothing, cat videos on YouTube, and speculating at length on Katy Perry's inside leg measurements. The inane chatter was interspersed mercifully with some old hit single, usually but not exclusively from Bananarama. If Dek could have, right at that moment in time, if the DJ was to somehow materialise into the same room as him, he would have happily smashed his head in. But it was easy to have psychotic impulses when there was no one else around to put such convictions to the test. So instead, he fed on such feelings of violence. He rolled with them. He converted negative psyche into rocket fuel. He needed the motivation from somewhere to get out of bed. You see, he wasn't the only person who hated his job, but he'd argue he had more reason than most. He was the MD and he worked in the National Health Service.

He showered and breakfasted. Heavy breakfast was a no-no, so he ate light. Fresh fruit and natural yoghurt. He lived alone. Too young to settle down, and if not wildly ecstatic about his lot, resigned to making the transition to too old to settle down. He couldn't imagine providing for anyone else, only himself here in his flat in the West End of Glasgow. He was the MD, but not *that* kind of MD. There wasn't enough room in his flat to swing an imaginary cat, never mind a real one. It didn't matter anyway, he had his bike. If you believed some of the rumours around work you'd think he loved his bike, wanted to marry it the same tri-sexual way some Americans marry their horses, or the case of the woman who married the Eiffel Tower. He laughed these kinds of things off, for the most part.

He got ready for the cycle commute to work. Waterproof trainers, jacket, shorts, rucksack, and bottle. He had no time for Lycra; despised anyone forever, no exceptions, who'd even think about wearing it. That kind of crap was for posers only. Wankers and tourists. Who did they think they were, the fucking X-Men?

If it was raining (and let's face it, it was constantly raining in Glasgow) there was always his trusty waterproof trousers to fall back on. If it was bucketing down—and the heavens would have to open, no mistake—he would probably just chuck it in and take the bus or underground into the city centre instead. The bike was more a means to an end. He wasn't a cycling nut. Nothing was worth getting soaked to the skin for, contracting pneumonia or something equally nasty. He didn't want anything like that—who did?—not on top of everything else.

Oh, and he wore a cycle helmet, ventilated, with helmet camera attached. Not compulsory, but sometimes it was war out there. He remembered one time when a car came out of nowhere, crashing into him, sending him hurtling head first off the bike. Off the edge of the world, or so it seemed. Ever so groggily, he picked himself up off the ground and inspected the bike, miraculously unscathed except for a few scrapes (as he was himself). As for the driver, he got out of the car. He was screaming; a face of pure murder. He jabbed at Dek with his index finger, wanting his address so he could come pay him a visit and teach him a lesson.

'You don't need my address to teach me a lesson, I'm standing right here, ya eejit,' Dek responded.

'Don't call me an eejit,' the driver said, 'you cyclists are a menace. If it was up to me, I'd ban the lot of you.'

'It was you who hit me!'

'You didn't signal.'

'How could I signal? I was too busy being thrown off my bike!'

And so it went on for a few minutes more before Dek, composure returned, got back on the saddle and nimbly cycled off.

'I want to know where you live!' the driver hollered after him.

Dek had filmed everything on his helmet camera and put it up on YouTube. He was half in expectation, half in hope that it might go viral. Forty-seven views so far.

That morning there was a little rain, nothing drastic, so he took to the streets in his trusty road bike, grade alloy. Even though it was early, there were always cars about. His every sense was strained, dedicated to the detection of these metal beasts which were unpredictable, quick to anger. Car drivers seemed oblivious to his existence at all. He would weave in and out, take the cycle lanes where available, the pavement if he had to, jump red lights where necessary. But consider this, the transformation underwent by motorists, the strange twisted metamorphosis. At the point they set off, even the mild-mannered ones—kissing the wife or hubby and two kids goodbye, embracing a new day and all the stunning possibilities this might entail—become something else behind the wheel; something sinister and twisted, a hot-headed monster, a road-owning psychopath. When Dek was on his bike he felt like he was a different species. The petrol and electric guzzlers were the predators. He was the hunted.

This particular morning, it wasn't raining bar the odd shower, so he cycled without incident to the Royal Infirmary, his place of employment. Even so, under the shadow of the Infirmary's great Victorian cathedral façade, he had no cause to shrug off the feeling that he was different, alien. Nor was it any time to start becoming human. Or maybe he was the human one and the rest of them were something else. There was a mantra which went off periodically inside his head.

'You're not like them. You're not like them. You're not like them.'

He locked up his bike. He didn't easily sweat. All he needed in the changing room were some baby wipes to wipe him down. He changed into his uniform. It was all terribly perfunctory. Officially he was at the level of medical tech, but his present role was far more specialised, instantly setting him apart from the rest. A couple of other techs, working in critical care, were changing for work at the same time as him. They avoided his gaze as if ingrained into them not to notice or acknowledge that he was in the room. Dek was like the Greek mythical creature Medusa. If you looked at him, set your gaze, you'd surely be turned to stone.

He made the morning meeting in good time, where one or more managers would brief the techs and senior nurses. As usual it was packed, standing room only. Dek didn't need to be self-conscious, just not blind. He couldn't ignore the space around him. He could step forward or back and still not come into direct contact with a fellow member of staff. The others in the room by contrast were giving an impossibly close-knit shoal of small fish a run for its money. They barely gave themselves room to breathe. It was instinctive, doing what came naturally. He didn't blame them for responding the way they did. If he was honest, he would probably react in similar fashion if he wasn't him. If someone else was him instead.

Dek's heart sunk when he saw it was Malcolm taking the briefing. Malcolm had a nasty habit, right at the end, of wanting a quiet word. Briefings were rarely more than ten minutes long. On the agenda this morning, a reminder of staff obligation to challenge smokers on hospital grounds; some minor changes to the annual leave process; the latest changes to staff car park policy. And then it was over and done with, with everyone shuffling back to their wards.

'Derek, a word,' Malcolm the manager gave a shout-out. 'You've got a minute or two or three…'

He knew he wouldn't stop counting until he got over there. Dek, so resigned, dipped his head dutifully and answered the summons. On such occasions, he hated the fake smile and the small talk most of all, but on they came.

'Good ride in?' Malcolm said. 'Encounter any crazed muppet car users? Next stop: they'll probably end up admitted here?'

'Nah,' Dek said, 'pretty quiet. Maybe all the lunatics are on the school run this morning.'

Malcolm laughed. The more extended the laugh, the

less genuine it came across. And this one went on for a long time.

'Listen, don't want to keep you,' Malcolm said. 'You've got a full day ahead of you. Geriatric and maternity wards I understand are full to the gunnels. Hope to God you don't get any crosses, of course I do, but if by some disaster you do record any, we could do with a couple of beds freed up. God forbid, you understand, but we'll take anything we can get.' Malcolm smiled, firm in the belief that 'pep' and 'talk' were his middle names. 'It's important work you do, Derek, incredibly testing conditions. Don't let anyone tell you otherwise.'

Dek grunted in reply. He hoped the texture and throatiness of the grunt conveyed adequately the total disdain he felt towards both the man and his words. He knew that management was no different to anyone else. They too behind his back referred to him as the MD.

MD, which for the uninitiated didn't stand for Managing Director.

Nor even closer to home, Doctor of Medicine. In the case of Dek, he was *Master of Death*. That was the trick. Fucking ha-ha-ha.

Malcolm arched his arm to the point his hand rested on the small of Dek's back. Dek experienced a measure of force, not much, but enough to push him forward. 'Don't let me keep you,' Malcolm said. 'Chop-chop.'

'Well, Malcolm the Manager, sir,' Dek might have said, if not so intent on his grunt doing the talking for him. 'Out of the both of us, it's you I feel sorry for. What kind of pressure from up on high must you be under to be able to live with yourself? It's all crap. The NHS. We're no longing in the caring business. Just say so and we can all shake hands, shut up shop, and be home in time for tea. Chop-chop.'

Dek was sure he'd ask Malcolm or one of his management cronies this one day. He'd use those exact words. He'd muster up the courage, grow a spine. He'd do so when the desire to live in the upmarket part of the West End wasn't so strong. He'd do so on his last day of work before retirement, or on his actual Last Day. But, alas, this particular morning there was nothing of the kind to spring from his lips. Not a peep or a squeak, just a grunt and a willingness to use the nudge on his back courtesy of Malcolm the Manager to launch him forward...

...and into the future.

He stood at the swing doors leading into Ward 18. In his grasp was the hand-held certification device, aka a *Lighter*. He inspected the *Lighter's* screen to check if it was working properly. Usually, the emitting of a functioning purple light was all that was required. The overriding preference as always would be to work though the wards, the priority ones certainly, before the start of visiting hours. It wasn't always possible. He didn't always have a clear run at it. In fact, it could get quite haphazard having to zigzag from one ward to another. It wouldn't be the first time he was physically removed by hospital staff while an emergency procedure was taking place. He didn't care to be manhandled, but he endured this, he thought, with a quiet dignity. In his mind, he went to another place. Not necessarily a quiet place. Quite an excitable one, in fact.

'*You're not like them. You're not like them. You're not like them.*'

That morning, Ward 18 (Medicine for the Elderly) was quiet. It was deathly still for want of a better way of describing it. In the first room, all four beds were taken. All female. None of the patients seemed to register his presence. There was no turning of heads. Normally he wouldn't have time to use the privacy curtains but considered it a tiny victory when he did. For the fourth patient, like the preceding three—Doris, Eleanor, and Angie—he checked her chart, then he drew the screen around her. Her name was Elizabeth; aged eighty-seven, a smoker all her life, experiencing respiratory problems and other complications. He stood over her and could hear her ragged, broken breathing. Her hair was thinning and white, and recently brushed. The lines on her face told a story of a life well lived, and the thought of this pleased Dek greatly.

Elizabeth's right arm, bent at the elbow, straddled her chest. Gently, he moved it so it rested on her side. In the same motion, he carefully turned her arm so he could see the palm of her hand. Using the *Lighter*, he screened the area from her wrist to the tips of her fingers. Once done, he turned the business end of the device towards him.

At this, Elizabeth opened her eyes. 'Doctor,' she said. Her voice was near-transparent, next to nothing, same volume as her beleaguered breathing.

'Good morning, Elizabeth,' he said. 'Just some routine checks. Try to get some rest.'

'Thank you.' Her eyes fluttered shut once more.

'You're welcome.'

His eyes fluttered also, but did not shut. He didn't think he had tear ducts because otherwise sometime surely during his six months in his current role he would have had cause to tear up. His face throughout remained implacable; as dry as the desert. Still, he wasn't a machine. Nor was this a requirement in the job description. (He'd checked.)

Where before there were three patients, three ticks on the *Lighter*, in the fourth case with Elizabeth there was now an 'X.' He wondered how much of her remaining life force she had expelled in the course of their conversation. The more he pondered such things, the more he marvelled at the human spirit. How people stayed true to themselves right up to the end. He had the briefest of chats with this woman named Elizabeth, but inside, as way of contrast to his craggy, dour exterior, he felt nothing but love for her all the same. As emotions go, it was short-lived, but he'd insist no less powerful for that. No less important. He had to cling onto something before taking a deep breath and moving onto the next room. He was already woefully behind schedule.

He was called to the Jubilee Building, which housed the Burns Unit. They wanted him to test a patient who they suspected had less life than skin. And who, as it happened, had very little skin.

Born in 2000, Dek had never known anything different. He heard older colleagues chat about the time when death was random, right up to the end—when death could take the form of a genuine surprise. The tone of their voices seemed to attach real nostalgia to a bygone age. As much as Dek tried to, he couldn't fathom it, couldn't get his head around it. What was so great about not being certain? *Fair enough in terms of a game of football or snooker*, he'd think. *But something like death, I mean come on.*

A shape was laid in front of him—he thought about it, but decided against checking the patient's name—heavily sedated, with third-degree burns covering most of the body, lungs full of carbon monoxide, infection having set in. A figure of sterile Vaseline gauze, ready to transcend from this world to the next. And now it was up to the MD, *Lighter* in hand, to divine whether he was ready to be sent on his way. It was true, occasionally, even he referred to himself as the MD. Sometimes he even toyed with the idea of acting out the part, like some grotesque, bounding hunchback. A Quasimodo for the modern age. Would the other techs relate to him more if he did?

The doctor had cut away at the gauze to expose some palm. There was enough undamaged skin to take a reading. 'X,' the *Lighter* read. *X marks the spot* was the common refrain. Something Dek might have been tempted to say if all sense of decency had deserted him, which wasn't the case; at least not yet.

That morning as ever, he braced himself, his whole frame shuddering if only momentarily, before entering the Intensive Care Unit's Neonatal ward, where arranged before him were all those tiny shapes. Rather much like the geriatric wards, there was no movement. The little ones couldn't turn their heads even if they tried.

He was not immune. If he saw his reflection, his expression would be one of horror. He'd barely recognise himself. Trying especially hard not to stumble, he walked towards the first incubation unit. Morality apart, how practical was it to test babies in such conditions, immersed in a plastic box, regulating temperature and oxygen levels, alleviating the risks of life-threatening infection? Wasn't it the point of the box to keep them alive? Wasn't the whole point of a hospital to keep everyone alive?

He did not require an answer. He was well-versed in the argument, in an environment of interminable waiting lists based on terms of need. How could it be fair to withhold a bed occupied by a patient, having now established they were beyond help? Instead, those who failed the *Light* were moved to the hospice on Glasgow Royal Campus, family notified, everything done to make their remaining hours as comfortable as possible. All that—and the bonus of having freed up a hospital bed. It sounded so simple and straightforward when spoken from the mouth of a smooth operator from NHS management.

But the reality was nothing of the kind. He was the MD and he had a purpose; always to take, never to give life.

'With so many staff shortages, how can this go on? He could be doing a real job. What do you expect? It's the fucking MD.' He wasn't sure if these were his thoughts—or if it was his mind echoing what everyone said about him behind his back, but close enough to earshot—about the position he was in.

He stood over a little one. There were so many cannulas and tubes sticking out of the baby, an overwhelming number considering how unbearably slight the patient was. He wasn't in the mood to check the chart for a name here either, which had nothing to do with his being horribly behind schedule, which incidentally he was. The only evidence that the baby was alive was that the monitoring equipment said so. But to read and record current readings was not the purpose of his visit. He was here because of the *Light*. There were ports on the side of the incubator and he was adept, *Lighter* clasped, at quickly popping his hands in, a little twist to follow and out again, allowing him to do what he had to.

And job done, he made a cursory check of the *Lighter*. There was no purple light. In its place, there was a thin, emaciated reddish light, little more than the coating on the bulb.

Faulty connection? He gave it a shake. There was no change to it.

Gripped by the most bizarre, most wonderful of notions, he ran out of the Neonatal ward. He took a quick right and then a longer left, before using his key to enter a storeroom. There on the shelf were several boxes of *Lighters*. He grabbed the first box, examining the device inside, before tossing it to the side and repeating the process with the next one. As the realisation sunk in, tears were in his eyes. He was actually crying. He was human after all.

There was no *Light*.

That morning he found four hospital staff in the tea room, including Malcolm who was mulling around the kitchen area, rooting around the cupboard searching for his favourite mug. The TV was off. It didn't get much better than this.

Dek barged in and threw a *Lighter* at Malcolm, who instinctively ducked, but not before closing the cupboard first. The *Lighter* made telling impact against the wall close to Malcolm's head, shattering into several pieces, which tumbled into the sink below.

'What?' Malcolm said, turning, staring daggers at Dek.

Dek for his part was panting, momentarily out of breath.

'What the hell?' Malcolm continued, 'Do you realise how much that kit costs? Are we now in the business of cutting our own throats?'

A nurse ran into the staff room. 'Turn the TV on. Switch on your phones,' he said. 'Turn the TV on.'

Dek laughed in such a way he mimicked Malcolm's laugh. It surprised him, as much as it did surely Malcolm, how pitch-perfect it was. Dek realised then that he had been wrong all this time. He was just like his manager, just like them, just like everybody. There was no such thing as master of your own fate, not in this scenario.

'I'm fucked,' Dek said, sneering. 'But if I'm fucked, you're all fucked, too.'

16

World Shut Your Mouth

He was dreaming. He was at that stage in sleep where he was aware that he was dreaming, but prepared all the same to go with the flow.

This was what the dream was telling him.

He was in a state of suspension of disbelief—typical of dreams— replacing the cold snap of London for the sapping heat of Egypt. The heat spirited away his every breath, made the air around him hazy and unreliable. He was with a boy of around twelve, perhaps younger; it was difficult to tell with children of that age. The boy had flat dark hair, which made his head appear squarer than it was. The boy slapped his arm; there was a look on his face. A bright red spot erupted there; result of a mosquito bite. The boy's left eye was opened wide with fright. They both stood still, him and the boy, rooted to the spot like they were captured in a photograph. He was basically an onlooker, but it was the shock of it—of seeing it. A mosquito, the biggest one he had ever seen, had planted itself on the side of the boy's face, biting his eye. The insect seemed to pulsate, luminescent against a backdrop of the fullness of day, as it fed on the yolk of the boy's eye.

He woke with a start. He was on the London Underground. A quick look outside confirmed that the train hadn't moved yet. They remained for the time being in Leytonstone tube station.

It was Ollie who had nudged him awake, gently rocking him by the shoulder. 'You were making this funny noise,' she said. 'You were moaning.'

Si mumbled something too low and incoherent to be understood, although it served to confirm that he was awake. He tried again, to properly move his lips this time. 'How long has the tube been stuck here?'

Ollie stuck out her bottom lip. 'Ten minutes. There hasn't been an announcement.'

Si looked around the carriage which was empty apart from them.

He struggled to think he'd ever encountered such a thing before; an empty train. 'Anyone else get on?'

'Nope,' she said. 'It looks like it's just us—and the driver, hopefully. Do you think we should get out and ask?'

Si was about to suggest for the fifth time that they should go back to his house—on this occasion, to better distinguish from those other times, he was building up in his own mind to sounding more forceful—when the train at last juddered to a start. Si winced internally then resigned himself to the fact that his immediate future, at least, was in the hands of the Central Line to North Acton.

'Mo? Elijah?' he said. 'I still don't understand.'

'Unnh?' she said, her face gone blank as if the two names had lost any significance they surely possessed up until only recently.

Recognition soon followed—thankfully, as far as Si was concerned—but the fact there had been any kind of delay was unerring enough.

'What about them?' she said.

'Do you know where they've gone?' he said.

'Yep, and you know where, too. That flat vacated by the Last Dayer, the dude who got the air gun pellet in the neck. Ideal place to squat, I'd say.'

Charlton Heston, Si remembered.

But even this snippet of memory wasn't enough to prevent him plunging into a world of confusion. 'Won't the police just evict like they did at Charlie's?'

She smiled.

It was a difficult smile to pin down. He couldn't tell if she found his last comment endearing or contemptuous or anything at all, really.

'It's a much smaller place,' she said. 'Not a big house like Charlie's. Trust me on this; it'll be weeks, maybe even months before the boys in blue and all those official fucks get round to it. Mo and Elijah will be fine. Together they're an unstoppable force. They're survivors.'

There it was, the word *trust* again. She had opened the floodgates on that one. Having said it first outside The Gadfly, she had repeated it several times since as if trying to force a point home. If she was a superhero with only one power to call her own, he thought it would be the power of suggestion.

The tube had reached Mile End Station. Still no sign of another soul.

'The boy from Egypt,' he said, 'the Valley of Kings I think you said, what was his name again?'

'Why do you ask?' she said.

'Does there have to be a reason?

The tube shuddered and shook. His body felt the drag that came with each stuttering start. From his exterior, there was the urge to implode and hide under his skin. But then he wondered if this sensation was purely down to the effect of the train, or if everyone—wherever they were, all around them—was experiencing something similar; heavy gravity, ominous punitive forces, dragging them back, stopping them, compelling them to stay in their home, place of work, coffee place, shop door; to stay in one place.

After a few moments of frenzied self-examination, the train started moving again. He looked out of the window and saw only blackness, the dark shuttling of walls. The sight of it scared him, but then he considered, if not this, then what was he expecting to see?

There was no sun. No hint of natural light. He was travelling underground.

And he could have sworn that something was missing, was certain somewhere out there was a gaping wound. He could sense it—don't ask him how—weeping, growing; nothing outside of nature capable of stopping it; a hole, if unimpeded, it would threaten to swallow the world.

'What do you think has happened to the *Light*?' he said.

She was beaming. Her eyes flashed fiery jade. Her face lit up the carriage.

'Revolution,' she said.

He glared at her. 'Don't you take anything bloody seriously?' He was annoyed at her. He was furious at the situation he found himself in. He thumped with his fist the top of his leg in frustration. 'If you're so clever, why can't I say right now that I don't like any of this? What's stopping me from saying I'm worried? I'm scared?'

The outburst took her by surprise, but she was prepared for it all the same. 'You knew what you were getting into with me,' she said. 'You're not daft. You walked into this with your eyes open. You ask so many questions and I've tried my best to answer every one of them. I like being around people. I don't take the *Light*, not that it's an option, not right now. I live in a squat or I'm between squats. I have doubts. It's not enough to want to be better, I realise this, but it's got to help. I still wear the same clothes. I've not changed from yesterday.'

Which was the first time we met, so went the unspoken words rippling out from both of them.

His cheeks were flushed. He felt the awkwardness of the situation spread over him, but he fought against the compulsion to take the easy way out and say he was sorry.

She reached out smiling, if you could call it that, a tiny upturn of the mouth, and took hold of his sleeve between thumb and forefinger.

'Ako,' she said. 'That was his name.'

Eventually, she had answered his question from earlier, but this couldn't mitigate the prevailing sentiment of too little too late, nor was it designed to. Wanting to appear that he was no longer listening, he looked out of the window and was rewarded with a welcome distraction. They had arrived at the next station.

'Bethnal Green,' he said.

He was still sleepy. His body ached with tiredness and he couldn't steer his mind away any longer from the discomfort he was feeling. There again, pulsing, beating, flashing, a pain originating from the back of his head. It was as if a miniature person delivering a karate chop at regular intervals was nestled in there.

'I'm not even sure we're meant to stop here,' that familiar voice said, cutting through the background noise, all those thoughts.

They sat peering out of the window, an uneasy silence descending on them. It was so quiet, Si was sure he could hear his heartbeat, which seemed to race too fast for someone in a stationary position. The platform before them was empty, nothing to see, not from these seats.

'We should get off,' she said.

The train doors were open. The train itself was stationary, in a state of permanence, opted out, not going anywhere; like it had no need for time. Si didn't want this for himself. He wanted to keep moving. Maybe, now he was thinking, there was an opportunity. He could initiate a parting of the ways.

Some customary hand movements prefixed them getting off the train in silence. They stood on the platform, both sets of feet planted on an echoey stone surface. Facing them were long white curved tunnel walls, interspersed with red circles and blue lines, which not only carried the station name but provided an imprint fed straight into the brain; a sense of the familiar; the links of a chain. Hanging down from the ceiling was a large electric clock face, like something from the mind of Lewis Carroll. Si had to glance at it a second time to convince himself he wasn't hallucinating. That there would be no white rabbits to follow.

He was trying to think logically, not allow the tiredness to creep in, but such a thing seemed beyond his capability. He was hunched over, struggling to even straighten his back.

They were a hundred feet underground; insulated; wrapped up in cotton rock. If there was mass panic at ground level high above—the screaming, the stampeding of feet—would they hear? From all the way down, would they be remotely aware?

Ollie, hands tucked behind her back, turned on her heels three hundred and sixty degrees, revelling in her surroundings.

'Bethnal Green,' she repeated, 'site of the worst civilian disaster of World War II. It doubled up as an air raid shelter. Imagine it, pitch dark. One hundred and seventy-three lost souls killed in the crush as they tumbled down the wet steps. Sheer panic; sirens bouncing off the walls, sounding in their ears. Some of the bodies were unrecognisable, they had so many bruises. There's a commemorative plaque somewhere. And the worst thing about the tragedy, it was human error; an honest mistake. That's what caused it. All down to a false alarm.'

Si was barely listening but he got the gist of what was being said. Initially, for a second, a hard stare took over his face, threatening to give away his true feelings. *What is wrong with you? Why feel the need to bring up such a thing now of all times?* He wanted to shout this out; scream into her face, but as soon as he felt the need bubbling and boiling inside, he forced it back down. It didn't fit in with the new plan. Time to play it cool, confident she hadn't noticed his mask having slipped, if only for a moment.

'During the war they crammed thousands of people in here, seeking refuge from Nazi bombs,' she said, her tone less giddy than before. 'So where are they now?'

Such was the ever-changing, stop start nature of their relationship, he had to admit he knew what she was getting at. He could follow her line of thought. There was absolutely no one around. Where was everyone else? Where truly were they now?

'We should get back on the train.'

He could have sworn at the start of her sentence there wasn't, but by the end there was movement. The train was shuddering, creating vibrations of a mechanical kind. The electronic notice board hanging overhead made its apologies to the world, or more specifically Si and Ollie, for the train running late.

He had got her this far. Job done. Mission accomplished. They were standing side by side about to enter the train. Ollie pointed out a rat scurrying about the tracks below them and gave out a childish giggle.

'If we were the last man and woman on the planet,' she said, still pointing, 'we could take it as a pet. Be a family. A dysfunctional family.'

She never looked at him for the duration of those last few sentences, kept her gaze fixed on the tracks, but she hoped he was smiling at this. From the corner of her eye she could detect a slight shake of the head only.

He adjusted his frame, now a step behind so logic demanded she'd enter the carriage first. He was aware of the tightness of his smile, could feel the tension around his face. He hoped she would accept it. There would be no need for words. When it came to it he'd hesitate and wait for the doors to slide shut.

They would be on either side of the door. He'd wave to her as the train moved off like an unsteady metal slug before picking up a head of steam, a shutter-frame effect, chopping up the ether as it shot up the tunnel with a flurry of sound, leaving in its wake an engulfing, artificial, entirely circular gust of disgruntled air. She'd understand, he was sure of it. She'd respect his decision. It was time. She'd be gone, carried away, and he'd be obliged to wait for the next train. Perhaps he'd make his way home. He hadn't given much thought what he was going to do. What mattered was there would be distance between them. And then there would be time.

What time of the day was it? What day was it? Nothing on a basic level seemed to matter. Events would now be defined by the period before he met her and the one having made his farewell. Everything that fell between was timeless.

***

It was dark. He was in a tunnel of some kind. He could feel it in his legs and spine, the vibrations, the sensation of travelling; a feeling of displacement. He knew it was waiting for him at the end of an edifice. Maybe it had grown impatient. Perhaps it lurked not quite at the end, but closer along the tunnel eager to make his acquaintance. It was all to do with movement.

273

His mind was floating. He was elsewhere, back home, trying to put his son Alex to bed.

Alex was typically asking one hundred questions: 'Are butterflies made out of butter? Why can't Captain America fly? Will your nose really fall off if you pick it?'

Suddenly, exasperated, Si grabbed and started tickling him. 'Where's your off button? Let me find it.' Alex was laughing. It was a real belly laugh and Si was laughing too. It was infectious…

Shifting sands, his mind changed to Sofi. It was days later, or maybe days before, placing his hand, weaving his fingers into the hairs on Sofi's chest. He exhaled slowly, but at a sufficient volume to be heard by the man lying next to him.

'Are you happy?' Sofi asked.

***

His eyes opened once more. From the seat opposite, Ollie leaned over to him. He was still underground on a moving train. The realisation came rushing then crashing into him.

'Are you okay?' she said. 'You keep nodding off.'

He looked out. They were heading into Moorgate station, which meant he must have slept through—

'Did we change lines?' he said.

'Sure did, at Liverpool Street,' she said. 'You were pretty quiet. You remember me taking your arm?'

She wasn't sure if she should expect an answer. Instead she looked around the cabin, not wanting to say any more, giving him as best she could what space he needed.

He couldn't understand why he was still on the tube in

the first place. His head felt loose; taking a downwards, sideways trajectory until it rested on the train window. He was beaten, bowed, and had a desperate need to swallow. He wanted to drink an ocean, his mouth was impossibly dry.

He looked around. He looked past Ollie, even though he knew ultimately it was pointless to do so.

'Where are all the people?' he couldn't help but say.

'It's all part of a government conspiracy,' she said.

'I don't want to hear it,' he said.

She cast a little look to the side. 'Obviously,' she continued, 'without the *Light* people will be confused, scared, disorientated; they won't go out. There's something comfortable, safe, to be surrounded by familiar walls, but it won't last.'

Si brushed his head against the window. His brow squeaked against the glass. 'I'm sorry, you're sort of freaking me out. I mean it was different at first, but it's all too much now. It's getting really tiresome.'

In response, she took his hand in both her hands. 'Look around you,' she said. 'We can't be the only ones who are out, but here we are. It seems to me that we have more in common than maybe you're prepared to admit. What do you think?' She rolled out the last four words together, without any pauses, like it was one word.

'I can't feel your hand,' she said.

'Are you feeling okay?' he said. His previous resolve had peeled away. Broken. There was even a note of worry to be had.

'Like I said, it's this condition I have,' she said. 'No sense of touch, but in an *"I'm not going to die"* kind of way. It's really screwy.'

She looked down at her hands on his and was hopeful of something passing between them. They sat in silence as the train moved from Farringdon station to their final stop of King's Cross St Pancras. Si wearily removed his hand. He had done his best to ignore it, but the taste of cigarette was still in his mouth.

The train came to a ragged stop with a shunting motion, metal screeching against the tides.

The doors slid open and out they got. Si looked towards where he thought the driver might be, but there was no sign of life. His head seemed clearer, the fog had lifted, but searching for any trace of people—staff, commuters, bystanders—was too much like mental torture, so he kept his head down. They stepped onto escalators that rumbled as they ascended.

There was no peripheral vision. He'd shut down the rest of the world for fear of what it might tell him. Any suggestion of movement was put down to the many drafts, the gusts of wind, which originated from below and beyond, that whipped through the tunnels and apertures. It took a double take before, looking down, he realised they were holding hands. They passed open barriers and went up the last set of stairs before reaching the exit.

They had returned to the outside world. They walked from St Pancras towards King's Cross. The expanse of King's Cross concourse stretched out in front of them, but the implications of this could not be ignored. There was no one else. It was a ghost concourse.

This was one of the busiest train connections in Europe. It should be sprawling with bug-eyed commuters. There should be so many people; a biblical horde of lurching, swerving, sliding, buzzing humanity. There weren't enough buildings in the whole of London to hide all of these people in.

Si's head was reeling. Everything was blurred before his sight latterly, cloaked in terms of surrender rather than triumph, drifted back into focus. He searched frantically for his companion, if only for a moment, then realised she was standing next to him. She pointed, arm at a diagonal, towards the other side of a street across the far end of the concourse.

'There, that's the one,' she said, 'there's this shop, convenience store. They do a little side business in fixing phones if you speak to the right chappie. A real miracle worker. Thanks for taking me this far. Best to your family.'

She reached out with her hand and passed him something before walking on, never to look back. Si watched her go. She left a trail of light particles in her wake, like space rock entering a planet's atmosphere heated to incandescence, a weaving crystal shine. On watching her finally take her leave of him, he wasn't sure how to react. Relieved? Anxious? Unprepared? Still, he couldn't see past her.

He straightened out the folded banknotes she had passed his way. Three twenties; sufficient funds to take him one-way to Brighton. Maybe even get a taxi from the station. He stuffed the notes into his back pocket and started walking to King's Cross railway station.

He took an exaggerated, curved path across the concourse. This, at least initially, took him further away as the crow flies from his intended destination. He wanted a clearer view on his approach of the famous old front building; the terminus, the granite heart; the centrepiece clock tower with two great arch-shaped portals either side. He wanted to see what he was getting himself into. He was looking for signs of life.

Something wasn't right, clearly. He wasn't right. He sensed his head was filtering out important information. He was aware of the book inside his coat pressing against his chest and was assured of at least one reality he could trust. He had always wanted a London with no people; to walk the streets without fear of interaction, nothing to see, nothing to dodge or avoid; nothing to invade or butcher his personal space. Even Ollie was gone now, eviscerated from sight. Be careful what you wish for. For was this not *The Land of Do-As-You-Please.*

That was it, but that wasn't it. Thoughts coming fast, propelled outside his comfort zone, not what he was used to, a dishevelled reality.

He was presented with two worlds. The first was right in front of him, the grand terminus that would take him to his family, the normalcy of domestic life. A life he could be certain of; security, safety, all that jazz. The second was behind him, with the promise of delivering everything the first world could not. He had no idea what shape his next step, backwards, forwards, would take. There was something terribly alluring about not knowing. It excited and terrified him. It made him feel alive.

And wasn't that the point?

A pigeon flew suddenly into his peripheral vision, which seemed now to be working again. He dragged and turned himself around, searching, grateful for the distraction, conspiring to follow its flight path. But that's not what caught his eye. In a pixelated, unreliable sky, he observed a sizable chunk of concrete dropping, falling towards him.

At its highest point, the concrete blocked out the sky. Rays of light began to break through as it fell, tumbling towards him until he could look at it no more.

Too close, too quick to fully react; he did his best to step to the side. The world shifted as concrete cracked into his shoulder. Stabbing, coiling, his whole body hunched with localised pain. A puff of jagged dust intruded on his eyes.

Next thing he knew, another object, a much bigger one with gangly limbs, hit into him. It winded him, knocking him down. He was back on his back.

There were people all around. So many feet, misshapen and turned at the ankles, neither coming nor going, stamping the ground indiscriminately. There was the clatter, thumping, thunder like human rain.

Instinctively, protectively, he wrapped both arms around his head. A trainer with rubber soles came down on his chest. Reacting, he turned on his side. A hand came down and grabbed a bunch of coat and started dragging him up. To aid him on his way, he grabbed someone's leg. Blind hands, he climbed it like a pole.

He was back on his feet, as vertical as his shifting surroundings allowed. Circling him, squeezed up close, occupying the busy dizzying space, ever more evidence of the ensuing melee. Spinning wheels, bodies colliding, bouncing off each other, everything compacted and compressed, whether possible or not. It was too much for the senses, which were falling away from him one by one.

Amid the human revolving doors, Si was face to face with the guy who helped pull him up. Or, as face to face as possible when encountering someone half a foot taller. He was young, remarkably fresh-faced, hair slicked with sweat.

'Who are you with?' Fresh-Face asked urgently.

Si was plunged into confusion, his face was fragments of wildly differing expressions all tangled up with each other.

'Are you with the pandas or the Falklands?' Fresh-Face said, as way of addition, very fast.

'Can't … can't I be both?' Si stammered back.

He tripped over the chunk of concrete which wasn't completely done with him, not strayed far from his feet. His legs were like jelly.

He would have gone straight down if there weren't so many others around to break his fall. His damaged shoulder collided with a spinning top. He gritted his teeth, inadvertently biting down on his tongue, converting his mouth into an eruption of hurt.

Who threw the concrete? A voice was yammering inside his head. *Who threw the concrete?*

And with this, Si was swept away—further away from King's Cross station and from fresh-faced youths—further into the bowels of the concourse.

A mass gathering, in fact two mass gatherings, had been trammelled into a confined space. A cordon of police employed the tactic of kettling, pushing a crowd of demonstrators (it didn't seem to matter who was demonstrating for or against what or whom) into a limited area so better to control them.

At the centre of the maelstrom, his body not his own,

both pushed and pulled at the same time, like a rag doll in a hurricane.

If he ever had cause to imagine what purgatory was like, the halfway house from Heaven to Hell, then this was as good an approximation as any.

The crowd was thrust together to the point you couldn't see the join; an organic, thrashing, convulsing creature. But Si did not belong, set adrift, trapped inside the belly of the beast. He was the lone wolf; the bacteria in the tissue of a living giant surrounded by white blood cells whose only role was to ingest him. The neutrophils, eosinophils, basophils, and lymphocytes all had him in their sights.

His head was fit to burst, constant, on the move, falling headway into randoms. His frame bounced off one clump of demonstrators, then another; a blur of human limbs. He couldn't distinguish the children from the adults, so he gave up trying.

Pushing and shoving, pushed and shoved, returning to an earlier cluster, condemned to repeat the same variables, the equivalent to a flight of madness. But through it all, he could feel the pull of the undercurrent. For too long he had wished to be rid of her, and now he couldn't stand to be too far away from her. She was like a potion that was beginning to wear off, the only thing that made his existence bearable.

The more he wanted to push them away, the more he realised he needed to be with them.

And he was terrified, but still unsure exactly how to vocalise this.

'What's stopping me from saying I'm worried? I'm scared?'
So like the best of them, he tussled and jostled. He

submitted to the currents, buffeting him, certain that they would take him…

Would take him to her.

'You promise no one's going to hurt me again?'

The thrum of the crowd was now reduced to that of a murmur. There was fear. There was a strange kind of expectation.

Three sides of the concourse were blocked off, curbing a motley crew of unlikely men, women, and children. There were demonstrators dressed in union jacks holding up banners of the Falklands Islands. There were families clutching toy panda bears. There was no more concrete. It seemed the furthest thing from their minds. No one wanted to cause trouble.

Police on horseback from the western side of the concourse charged into the crowd, causing the beast, the whole monolithic creature, to suck in its belly. The crowd accumulated scrapes and injuries. There was blood. The whiplash threw people down on as much ground as could be covered. Si found himself on his knees. His hands were clenched and he sensed that his time was up. Still, from A to B to C, sometimes back to B, he had circumnavigated a fair distance.

He was losing air. Whirly burly bish bash bosh. Bobbing and weaving through the shifting, exfoliating outer skin of this creature of ten thousand limbs. Maybe it was down to his faltering senses, his fading touch, head space unnaturally restricted. Maybe it was withdrawal pangs. Maybe he had no time for maybes. He grabbed whatever human flotsam presented itself before him. Arms, legs, torso; he had to use what came to hand to drag and clamber and lever himself up. As the hullabaloo played out, he took a glancing knee to the temple. He just had to shake it off, along with prior injustices to shoulder, head and mouth, just had to get on with it. On he scrambled, and a miracle bestowed itself in the form of forward momentum. He was climbing, stepping on unsteady ground, shifting sands. And then everything around him grew still, frozen in unreliable time. He looked up and saw *all the king's horses and all the king's men.*

He was at the frontline.

The police officer directly in front of him wore an orange high visibility vest and helmet with a visor. He looked like how we imagined an alien visitor would be back in the fifties, obviously humanoid, but all the same eager to hide as much of its true form as possible. Friendly overtures at first, mysterious and duplicitous; otherworldly; probably had a killer robot tucked away somewhere. The helmeted officer was one of many, forming a line indefatigably linked; the featureless definition of impenetrability.

Si didn't realise how terrified he was until he heard his own voice. 'Please,' he said, 'you have to let me pass.'

The officer was saying something. He could see his lips move, but nothing escaped the visor. Nothing reached his throbbing eardrums. Clearly an advocate for actions versus words, the officer pushed Si back, but there was no space to be pushed back into. Si didn't know how to respond. He was fearful of pushing back; of lifting his hands.

It had taken him so long to get this far, a torturous journey not without its perilous twists and turns. Not without its heartbreak. He was crying like a baby, all for himself and what might have been. He was up so close, up on his tiptoes, neck muscles stretched. It was all he could do to stop him being pushed up against the hard plastic that shielded the officer's face.

'Just give me this one thing,' he pleaded.

'Step back,' the officer said—and finally Si could hear. 'Step back,' so repeated, stuck in a loop.

Si's lack of movement threatened to escalate quickly as the officer grabbed him by the shoulders—one good shoulder, one bad. Si did not resist as he was shaken and shoved, a puppet attached to a marionette's death rattle.

Behind him, the great beast heaved and bellowed. Its individual parts starved of room, of oxygen, writhing and thrashing, squirming in the inadequate area afforded it. *'Step back. Step back. Step back.'* And in this way, sure and steady, the beast's life was squeezed out of it.

An arm came out of nowhere and Si was punched in the chest. Bent over as best he could, a mix of shock and instinct, the need for self-protection leading to a single arched convulsion, led to the book slipping out of his coat, tumbling harmlessly and spinning to the ground.

Si feared the whole of him would follow suit. Would a truncheon, he wondered, come down and crack open his head? Would a kick be dispensed that broke a rib which then punctured his heart? Would component parts of the beast fall on top of him and steal all the air from his lungs? He just hoped; *please, please anything, but don't set me on fire.*

An officer close by broke from the ranks. He crouched and scooped up the book, clasping it in heavily padded hands. He scrutinised the cover, staring at the three children sitting on a branch of *The Magic Faraway Tree,* and felt something gnaw away inside of him. It signified a different time, a different place; a world of innocence and happiness he hoped against hope was not long forgotten. But if nothing else, the book was testament to a frame of mind, a point of view having at least existed at one time. If what it represented was an imperfect reality, it was a child's reality. He'd make a single gesture, he decided, and maybe, God willing, he'd find a way to sleep that night.

A product of his time.

The officer handed him back the book and Si took it.

From behind the riot gear, beyond the visor, beyond the hard plastic, Si identified a cleft chin. PC Spartacus motioned to his fellow officer to step aside.

'Let him through,' he said.

It was a tight squeeze through the cordon, but Si didn't hesitate to take the opportunity to wriggle free. He was aware of a tidal wave at his back, halted unceremoniously in its tracks as behind him the cordon joined ranks once more.

He stumbled as he reached the other side. Perhaps, he pondered ruefully, this marked his wanderlust days as come to an end. Finally out of his system.

He didn't adjust right away to the opening up of space around him. His brain was still attuned to taking baby steps. There were stragglers just like him having escaped the belly of the beast.

They were dazed, shattered, bloodshot eyes; the blood having drained from the rest of their faces. He glanced back and his focus settled on a woman begging one of the drones on the police lines to let her fourteen-year-old son through.

Si turned away, swinging his leg theatrically, banishing cramp and driving himself forward.

She was there, standing, waiting. She seemed different to him somehow. He wanted to hug her, but the stiffness of her body language put up an instant barrier. And he'd had his fill of barriers.

'We can't stay here,' she said. 'We need to find some cover.'

She strode off and he did his best to keep up.

'What the hell is happening?' he said.

'The authorities are better prepared this time,' she said. 'They've had years to plan for this.'

'Years, I don't…?' he said. 'You talking about the *Light*?' They weren't even protesting, not about that.' He patted his forehead furiously. 'My head is full. It hurts. I can't think straight.'

She turned to face him. They hadn't walked far, but far enough, unearthing a backstreet, a narrow one, deserted, quiet; a blessing by contrast to all that had gone before.

'Find some sand,' she said. 'You draw a line in it. You step over that line, there's no going back and nothing else matters. It's all about the *Light*, this supersedes everything. Even the lack of it.'

He tried so hard to follow her words, every one of them, absorb the thread and find meaning. And maybe there was some truth to discern from them, or maybe it was the usual bats in the belfry conspiracy nonsense. Everything was swimming in front of him. He wanted so much to sit or lie down and rest his beleaguered, embattled physique.

'Olivia,' he said. He couldn't call her Ollie, nothing so informal at a time like this. 'There's no feeling in my hands or feet. There was when I was with you on the train, and before, but not any longer. What this means … I'm too tired to think.'

She smiled at him. It was a perfunctory smile, on the lines of a local official fulfilling a public service. Perhaps aware, seeking to compensate for her recent standoffishness, she reached out to take his hand. Sensing bad vibes, Si snatched his hand away.

She took a breath. She couldn't take her eyes off him.

'You're dying,' she said. 'You've been dying from the moment Mo punched you.'

17

Turnberry

'World's gone to shit and I'm going to die and I don't care.'

Logistics was a funny word. Every time someone mentioned it—no matter how rammed the meetings were, no matter how exalted the company, or the amount of stars on the generals' lapels—he laughed inside. He enjoyed the act of laughing inside. It was one of the few things that had kept him sane all this time. Although with him it wasn't so much a laugh but a guffaw.

He usually checked the *Light* without fail as the new day dawned. At one minute past midnight if he could, usually between Tweets. He'd requested a cell, one of those new-fangled *Light*-enabled prototypes, but it wasn't always reliable, causing him to double check with the ones in place on the White House walls. And should it ever come up with a negative result, he would be ready.

His family motto, one of them at least, was *natus est paratum.*

Born ready.

Irony, on the other hand, was a word he took very seriously. Was it even twenty-four hours since news reached him of the fate of the Baumann fella? So much for the dream ticket for that brave, great new world that was his re-election. So much twice over...

And so it fell to him. It had to happen at some point he supposed, and the older he got the more likely the eventuality. Just like the time he became President, it was a question of probabilities. So when in the early hours, on registering then digesting a negative result, perhaps surprisingly given his public persona and reputation for being quick on the draw, he felt very little. He had considered how he would react for so long and to such an extent, racing through all the permutations like a Grand Canyon assault course, frankly he had squeezed all the emotion out of it.

Everything was in place. A phone would ring, answered by his successor (he had forgotten her name) to enable a smooth transition at least up to the next election. They had plenty of time to get their shit together; that wasn't until November. As for now, it would be a case of deciding on the right time to make the announcement, probably to coincide with the news of his actual death. He was strangely reassured by the fact that, for this one, it wouldn't be his call to make. At least he wouldn't be around to claim it was fake news.

So, the naysayers were right, he wouldn't be sticking around for a full term, but wasn't that the case with JFK and didn't he turn out okay?

He had considered taking Air Force One to Anchorage, Alaska, which was four hours behind Washington DC. He reckoned he could make the journey in less than four hours with some loose change to spare, effectively taking him back to yesterday, where at the very least he could have a second opinion. He thought he might be able to get into the sky and fly in a direction away from the sunrise and take advantage of all the fucked up vagaries presented by the world's time zones. In this way he could gain, in theory, the king's share of an extra day. When it came down to it, bottom line, the President of the United States was not one to run away from anything—where death was concerned, that scary little godless motherfucker, well, one could make a different case entirely. Christ, he was tempted, but this was his Last Day, and he'd already set his heart on something else. He'd planned it for a long time. All told it cost him one tenth, give or take, of his personal fortune, paid directly to the Chinese government.

No time obviously to lose, so still dressed in his presidential bathrobe he slipped his feet into a pair of sneakers. In terms of clothing, it was sufficient to brave the unseasonably cool Washington DC climate and negotiate the short route to the helicopter pad. He left his wife sleeping undisturbed in her bedroom. God willing, he would see her again before the day—*his* day—was out.

There was no precedence for this, except that it was his day to do as he pleased. Even the President could have a day like this. No one was going to stop him.

It was a question of logistics and no snickering behind his back there. Helicopter would take him to Air Force One, which would be up in the air in half an hour. And you could say what you like, in Mandarin or French for all he cared, it was always a relief, no matter the circumstances, to get out of the Swamp. Away from the clowns. The surrender monkeys. The impeachment-crazed flakes and phonies.

Upon navigating US airspace, he changed into his golf apparel; white shirt, charcoal top, cream pants, belt. He rounded things off with one of his many red golf caps; the one with a single word imprinted above a lion's crest which read simply *Turnberry*.

Before Air Force One had even set off, it was already 6 a.m. in the UK. They were airborne for less than four hours when confirmation reached them that the *Light* network had experienced worldwide catastrophic failure. He couldn't help but smile at this; it was a tiny crooked smile for his own gratification only. He always suspected that one day this headfuck would come home to roost, tumbling down like a house of self-righteous cards. Actually, this could make the transition period for his successor that much smoother. A case of shutting down the country until they could find out what the hell just happened. At least they'd still be around to see what the next day brings. Everyone had their problems. One man's crisis was another man's possibility.

It was inevitable after a period of shock, playing statues, humanity would take to the streets en masse. The vast majority of people had never properly come to terms with all this death business. The trappings of the new age, the Church, the *Light*, they were all just a stopgap; an elaborate placebo. It occupied people's minds; distracted them from the true facts. It didn't replace the need to fuck up and tear everything apart, not completely. And now something like this, you take away the bullshit—you take away the *Light*—it was gonna get messy and very soon. It was gonna get fearful.

If you thought about it, it was truly egalitarian. On one hand it brought ordinary Americans and Europeans and Brazilians and even Mexicans together. And on the other it brought all the governments together as well, even Iraq and Iran—even the fucking Venezuelans!

Michael, one of his White house staff, perambulated forward into his line of sight. Air Force One could comfortably accommodate a hundred passengers, but for this trip, President's orders, numbers were limited to strictly a skeleton travel pool. So from the anonymity of forty-thousand feet up, Michael literally stepped out from nowhere.

'Mr President, sir,' he said.

Three words, six syllables, but at syllable one, the inflection of Michael's voice told the President everything. He didn't need to be a mind reader to know what was on everyone's mind.

'The country is in ferment,' Michael continued. His face was straighter than a Jack Nicklaus drive off the tee. 'No one can access their savings. People won't be able to tell for sure if they'll live or die until they do, ahem, live or die.'

It occurred to the President that maybe he was the last person in the whole wide world to have used the *Light* before it broke. He liked the sound of that. Maybe it was the fact he failed the *Light* that caused it to blow up in the first place. He was a big man, most powerful person on the planet. He liked the bombast, and he'd earned it. On this occasion, though, about to unleash his latest epistle, he was of the firm decision to err on the side of presidential.

'It's a clusterfuck,' the President said. 'The *Light*, I know, I heard. All that anxiety of not knowing. Why would anyone go to bed before midnight? Why would any sane person not choose to find out as soon as they possibly could? People, ordinary people, can make strange decisions. They can make up so many excuses, wait until the last minute to do anything. Where does all that pressure go, that unease? It's swept under the rug where you're kidding no one. Then rearing up all of a sudden there's a massive bump size of Mount of Beatitudes and that's when you know it's ready to blow. In my experience, folks don't need much to take to the streets. If this is the last thing I say as President, so be it.' He waited a few seconds, suddenly in the grip of impending doom, anticipating a bolt from out of the blue to come strike him down. But no, there was nothing. 'Go find the fucker who can switch it on again.'

So briefed, Michael about-turned and was swallowed up by the bowels of the plane once more.

For the remaining duration of the flight, the President sat steadfastly at his desk. He wanted some time on his own.

It was 11 a.m., or as near as, when Air Force One landed in Prestwick Airport situated in South Ayrshire, Scotland. The landing was bumpier than usual. He rolled in his seat, felt the vibrations climb up his chest, and looked down and noticed he hadn't touched his scotch. Laphroaig twenty-five-year-old, if he was not mistaken. He picked it up, couldn't feel the glass in his hand. He was the forty-fifth President of the United States, some would argue the forty-fourth as if it really mattered, but those third-rate jokers on Capitol Hill would contest just about anything. And with this sobering thought rattling around his brain, he promptly drained his glass dry.

It was late morning and everything around the place was pretty calm, pretty sleepy in fact. He'd never known Prestwick to be anything but. The trip was on the QT, but as he disembarked down the steps, as way of welcoming committee, the airport had rustled up a ragtag collection of staff. Christ, it was freezing. Any of those dummies in Washington wanted to argue about global warming, they should take a trip to Prestwick come a January morning. But at least it was dry. He was thankful for that.

Looking across this makeshift guard of honour he set his sights on a member of catering, going by the square cap and off-white colour of his overalls, shirt only half tucked in. The President made a beeline for the man, shaking his hand vigorously and whispering into his ear.

'What are they going to do, it's my Last Day, impeach me?' the President hissed, the tip of his tongue sticking out from between his teeth.

The catering guy's eyes widened, but he resisted the urge to say anything. Then the moment was gone, ephemeral, and the President proceeded to walk on by.

On a parallel runway, a helicopter waited for him. He was accompanied from the plane by a couple of secret service dudes—Frank and Ted, two of his favourites. As was the custom, Frank was entrusted with the golf bag which he diligently carried strapped over his shoulder.

On the approach, the President's heart was beating in line with the slapping of the helicopter's rotor blades. It got faster, more irregular. Sandwiched between Frank and Ted, he climbed on board.

He was back in the air, but it seemed different somehow, and not just because he was in a helicopter. Scotland was the land of his mother's birth. He once toyed with the idea of coming to live here, if only it wasn't such a crappy little country. It was a clear day and there was nothing in the sky except a vista as fiercely blue as the colour of his eyes. There was that and a defiant yellow ball, too far away in the distance to do much in the way of anything, but at least, credit where credit's due, it had decided to show its face. The approach to his golf course, the hills, the green, the craggy rocks, the sea, the volcanic island of Ailsa Craig was a picture, all quite stunning. And there it was: the Turnberry Point Lighthouse, sporting a new lick of paint, an erection of perfect white. Repackaged as luxury accommodation and available at a snip for seven thousand dollars a night. No longer operational, but should you decide to peer into it, the lighthouse lamp could still make a connection. It could still burn a light, symbolic to be sure, deep into the depths of your soul. The scene was perfect. Some would claim he didn't have a heart, but they were wrong, so wrong. It was a picture and it took his breath away—but not, he determined thankfully a moment later, permanently.

Correction, it wasn't his golf course, not anymore. On becoming President, he'd passed everything, along with his other business interests, onto his sons, Junior and Junior-Junior. But undercutting all of this was a clear understanding that he was still the Daddy who'd paid a million bucks for the new chandelier hanging down from the clubhouse ceiling. Turning up announced or unannounced, the toss of the coin, the folks at Turnberry weren't exactly going to turn him away, now were they?

He arrived as discreetly as his front door manner allowed. He marched onto the first hole stridently, belying the heart condition which surely would be the end of him. He wouldn't need a driver, not for this hole. He nodded in the direction of secret service caddie Frank, barking out the order, 'Five iron.'

Frank had come to regret, during the long hours of service, letting slip the fact he'd been a caddie in his youth. He knew the score and searched the golf bag before handing over the correct club. The President pressed his tee perfunctorily into the ground. A golf ball emblazoned with his initials soon followed suit.

A golf buggy appeared from the direction of the clubhouse; its engine crackling with electric, purring apologetically. Out of the buggy jumped one of the Turnberry managers, appropriately flustered as he approached, at least officially, his ex-boss. He was unsure what to do, so caught himself in mid-salute, giving the appearance of someone not in complete control of his limbs.

'Sir, Mr President, sir,' he said. 'You've arrived.'

Sir, Mr President considered responding with a customary caustic response, but instead experienced a strange and unfamiliar level of compassion for the quivering, uncoordinated wreck of a man standing in front of him. So instead he let it fly. He released such thoughts, such bad karma, to the biting sea breeze. Let *it* decide, he decided; let *it* cast judgement.

'My guest has arrived?' the President said, making a

statement sound like a question. 'The guys from the zoo put it where I wanted?'

'Yes, sir. Mildly sedated on arrival, but it'll be up on its feet in no time,' the manager said, eyes bouncing around the sockets. 'But the clubhouse, I tried to empty it, even went as far as…' he gulped, '…claiming we'd failed a health inspection, but it was such short notice, sir, there might be some stray golfers still on the greens.'

The manager stopped talking and instead stared into empty space before realising, stretching out as far as the eye could see, was an empty golf course.

'Of course,' the manager spoke as quietly as one of the mythical mice he was prepared to blame for failing a bogus health inspection. 'Of course that was before the *Light* and now there's nobody, not a soul to be seen.'

'You want a soul?' the President said, 'Go check a room, hiding below the bed, that's where you'll find it.' He chuckled under his breath.

He'd already spent too long prolonging the meaningless chatter. This was clear indulgence on his part.

What did he, even now, have to constantly remind himself of? You seal the deal then get the hell out.

He couldn't rely on the sensation of touch. He had to go with instinct, but if he was anything, he was a creature of instinct. Revealing graceful balletic movement, belying a man of his shape, he hit the golf ball. He hit the sweet spot. It made a clean zipping sound, which immediately informed him he'd hit the perfect shot. He looked up so his eyes could confirm what his ears had already told him. He had nudged the shot towards the left, travelling two hundred yards, past a wall of gorse.

The ball landed in one of the bunkers, which was where he wanted it to.

Rising from the sand trap that was the bunker there was a whirling, sombre sound; a waking of sorts, which soon developed into a roar. Something bulky scrambled to climb out.

'Iron,' the President said with a piercing glint in his eyes (one of many family traits he prided himself on). 'The other type of iron,' he added.

He was handed a hunting rifle, a *Remington 700*. Steady on the shoulder, bolt slid back, he looked through the sights and concentrated like he had never concentrated before. Although, even then, he couldn't prevent the intrusion of a random thought or two. Was it *Mother Nature* or *Father Nature*, he could never remember? Wondering why he'd never put that bitch Hillary in jail.

He had shot wolves in Alaska and a Grizzly in Wyoming, but never something from as far away as two hundred yards.

The creature was still making heavy weather of climbing out of the bunker, so he allowed his concentration to wander some more.

'People have got the panda bear all wrong,' he said. 'Folks think they're kind of cute, cuddly; the animal equivalent of Mother Theresa or that Julie Andrews woman out of *The Sound of Music*. They just don't understand that these are wild animals. They have one of the biggest goddamned bites among any of the carnivores. I'm talking the whole goddamn animal universe. Thank God for the English prof for opening our eyes. Thank God for Professor Arnie.'

The panda, having been appropriated from Edinburgh Zoo, was now out of the bunker. It was male and went by the name of Yang Guang, aka *Sunshine*. A shot rang out in the Turnberry sky. Sunshine's rear end snapped to the side like an elastic band, whiplash of sinew and fur, to revert back a second later to its normal position. But the President had left his mark. The panda bounded from the first hole towards the eighteenth which ran parallel.

It was the perfect scenario. It was the home of golf. Turnberry had hosted several Open Championships, but none as famous as the *Duel in the Sun* where US golfers Tom Watson and Jack Nicklaus took the Claret Jug down to the wire. It was the stuff of thirty-foot birdie putts; the taming and breaking of the old famous links course. They dinked and drove, two giants mastering the hallowed greens and roughs, linking the sea to the land, carved by the hands of God Himself.

The President, or so he claimed, was a spectator (fact) part of the crowd that watched The Duel that day in 1977. He spoke of the crescendo, the oohs and aahs of the crowd entranced by every dip of the shoulder, every adjustment of the hips, every droplet of sweat, every majestic swing. You could cut the tension with a knife and serve it up to your favourite aunt with a dollop of cream for dessert.

Gentleman warriors, civilisation personified, men of grit and determination. American men. Men just like him, so he fancied. Men who sweated on the inside.

He turned to his own personal dynamic duo and thumbed back towards the buggy. 'Frank, Ted, move your asses and get in,' he barked.

The beast was deceptively lithe as it headed in the

direction of the main stand on the eighteenth. Beyond this was the clubhouse and beyond that, overlooking the greens, were the villas. Accommodation for the ordinary people. The President was conscious of ensuring the situation didn't get too out of hand. When he was gone, he didn't want to saddle his family with yet another suite of punitive lawsuits.

The buggy moved at fifteen miles an hour. A panda in full flight could top twenty. But this bear was clipped. By small but telling increments, the buggy closed the gap. He considered taking a potshot from the moving cart, but frowns two-fold from Ted in the back seat and Frank who was driving caused the President to reassess his next course of action.

'Can't this thing go any faster?' he said. His tone was drier than ancient parchment. 'Ted, can't you get out and push?'

The panda seemed to disappear, swallowed up by the looming main stand. At this, the President was clearly agitated. He wanted his rifle finger to apply pressure, but in his present condition had no way of gauging the right amount of pressure. Now the adrenaline of the first shot had worn off, he understood his trigger finger was next to useless. But this wasn't the time to feel sorry for himself. This wasn't part of the schedule. He scowled half-formed words, reminding himself that this very different take on panda diplomacy was what he wanted. It had cost him a fortune by anyone's standing—even his own. He should enjoy the moment more.

The buggy came to a stop and the President, rifle in hands, shoulders rotating, was rejuvenated. Like a man possessed, he sprang out the buggy, almost clicking his heels together as he did so. He didn't wait for the dynamic duo. They were professionals, they were half his size; they could catch up.

He was good at retaining facts. The ones that most appealed to him, that is.

His mind wandered.

White Mound Black-on-white. He'd went through a phase a few years back of collecting Ancestral Puebloan artefacts. In fact he owned a bowl, a genuine one, black-on-white. It sat pride of place on a shelf in one of his New York apartments. He was sure of it. Or maybe in one of his properties in Florida. *Course quartz sand, crushed sandstone.*

Returning to the matter at hand, there were swatches of blood around his feet among the polished grass. He had hit his quarry in the rump, but that was okay. He wasn't interested in that part of its anatomy. Up front, slumped, as clear as day, under the shadow of the main stand, there was a black and white mound that made him think of the bowl. It made him think of—made him pine for—NYC.

Right now, as many family members as humanly possible (at least, the ones he was on talking terms with) were being rounded up, informed of the news and taken to the city of his birth—Midtown Manhattan to be precise—for a final shindig back at the Tower. Jean-Georges would be on hand for the cooking.

Upon concluding his business here in Scotland, he would be hell-bent on joining them. Travelling back to the US from the UK, surely he would claw back all those hours? He would get them back again?

The black and white mound moved slightly, accompanied by panting, softly undulating. It was *Mother Nature*, he decided, that was the one, it had to be. He took more steps forward. *Just finish it*, he told himself, *you've made your point, just get back on that plane and back to your loved ones.* He raised the rifle and aimed, then hesitated. He lowered the weapon, adjusting his grip, holding it out with both hands. He studied it top to bottom with an inquisitorial eye.

Course quartz sand, crushed sandstone.

In one movement, like a cheerleader's baton, instinct, all instinct, he twirled the weapon the other way around. Holding the rifle by the barrel, he transformed it into an over-engineered club. He advanced some more.

They were all part of the global village. Here he was hunting a Chinese panda bear on a US-owned (and refurbished) golf course located in the West Coast of Scotland. It was logistics again, that was the thing that took him all the way here. Not ideal, and thinking about it not that funny, but he had a window and an Edinburgh panda was the best option available. There was a release clause triggered by the Chinese government, one those fuckers in the Scottish government could do nothing about, except maybe delay the animal's travel documentation. It was his money that made it possible, but even then, just like Muhammad and the mountain, he would have to go to Sunshine rather than have Sunshine come to him.

It was his Last Day, and he'd never tire of saying this to anyone in earshot, so what was anyone going to do about it? There would be outrage of course, although not as much as there might have been a couple of years ago. People had a lot more stuff to blow their tops over. A lot more stuff.

At the end of the day, there would be one less panda in the world. There would be one less President, too.

The green was so smooth underfoot, he was practically moonwalking Michael Jackson-style as he raised the rifle butt high above his head. The mound moved suddenly, quickly, deceptively fast, a black-and-white blur. Sunshine lifted its bulky skull. The animal opened wide, lethal maws designed to tear strips off and chew the toughest of bamboo. And bamboo was sturdy; tougher than you'd think. The panda bellowed, the sound turning the area around it into a defensive barrier. The President no longer had the rifle in his hands. There came the realisation it must have slid from his inert, unfeeling fingers.

In golfing terms, a bad case of the yips.

Jaws remaining open, the panda lunged. Round, ringed, hypnotic, crazed panda eyes ascended. Ready with carpal bone—the panda's 'false thumbs', a product of evolution—to grip and shake, and bite right down.

The President was rooted to the spot. Not that he could do much about the situation. This was his time after all.

Two shots slammed at an angle into either side of the lunging creature's head. It brought forth an explosion, releasing a fountain of panda skull and brain. Sunshine, killed instantly, in the grip of a slow-motion fall, collapsed at the President's feet. There was a lumpy puddle where its head should have been. Which was fine by him; he wasn't interested in that part of the animal, either. He looked down and saw there was panda splatter all over his shoes and cream pants. Initial thoughts of disdain soon dissipated with the realisation that things were about to get a whole lot messier.

He glanced down at his hunting rifle, sprawled out on the ground. A funny thing popped into his head; a smiling man named Bernie. He shook his head violently like a cartoon character until the image was replaced by a man with a scowl named Steve.

The President turned towards Frank and Ted, both statuesque, both still aiming their officially sanctioned firearms at the virtually decapitated Sunshine. His golf bag was leaning against Frank's leg. Standing close enough to train one eye on each of them, he was expectant. He held out the lifeless palm of one of his hands.

'Knife,' he said. 'A big hunting one. You'll find it in the bag.'

He got as far as back up in the sky with Air Force One. That was the point the stabbing pain in his chest would not go away or be alleviated. He died with a half-eaten panda's heart lying dormant and largely undigested in his belly.

18

Last Day On Earth

The *Light*. It was always the *Light*. Every day between the flossing of teeth and taking a shower, you would check yourself against the *Light*. You'd pass, beneficiary of a big tick and magenta glow. And as you put a comb through your hair, not giving it another thought, you got on with the rest of the day. You got on with the rest of your life.

But the *Light* was so much more. Once it was satisfied by dint of simply being there, a miasma of brightness; as a culmination of events at the business end of a long, dark passageway. Something you swam to, or ran to, or floated towards as the last remnants of conscious thought drifted before departing this thin, fleeting, gossamer thread we called life.

Compared to the natural life of the universe we were virtually and statistically nothing at all, but no less powerful for this; no less meaningful. It moved Chinese philosopher Lao Tzu to utter the immortal words: *'The flame that burns twice as bright burns half as long.'*

Front door to heaven; a translucence; a shimmer; formed in the distance; designed to snuff out the last embers of existence. You reached for it; a part of you had to want it. But that was in the past, when it was happy just to be the light. Was this enough? Perhaps it should have been.

Sometimes you would head to the light but win a reprieve; your consciousness bundled and swept up, and propelled kicking, coughing, and screaming back to the world of the living. Where then was the light to go? Should it merely content itself with staying put? Or could it assume a more active role, not too distant. It could take its place in the realm of the living. Every reprieved consciousness had shown a way back. Could it not follow?

Could it become something else; something more? Could it become the *Light*?

Surreptitiously, it moved into your streets and into your homes. And it stayed there, a dazzling afterthought, nuzzling behind your eyelids. Plum, violet, orchid, amethyst, and lavender; assumed all the colours of purple. Always on the periphery, taken for granted, reconnecting on a daily basis; and before you knew it, you were in its thrall.

And now it was gone.

Inside Si's head was a reflection, something mirrored. It was the end of worlds. He knew that time could not be stopped, so did not wish for this, but sensed from somewhere all the same it was possible to slow time down. Time could be stretched. It could be made to seem endless. To hear her voice, to hear anyone, he was thankful.

It was his Last Day. Was it only a day ago he had been punched? Everything since was a delayed reaction.

He remembered falling in instalments; his head connecting with concrete. Somewhere along the way there was an involuntary twist of the neck. These types of things were to be expected. He was a big boy. You just shrugged them off.

If there was lost time, blurred vision, it would have only been seconds. The simple things you do in life, then instantly forget about them. But the one thing he couldn't get away from was the reinforcement of certain behavioural traits, the nagging sensation that recently he wasn't acting completely himself.

What he wasn't to know, not until now, was that it was a trigger. It set off the formation of a haematoma of the right vertebral artery in the atlantoaxial region. It was a single punch. It formed a clot. All so innocuous—and insidious. A shadow emerged inside his skull. A black hole within, ready to expand and devour him. Ready to take everything he was; everything he could have been. It would take from him his entirety, leaving nothing in its wake but lifeless decay.

It was a lifetime. It was one day. And now it was gone.

His head was hurting. He realised the pain had been there since the incident, a constant companion, building up to something. He had either ignored it or just got used to it, or a mash-up of the two—jumbled, jumping in, jumping out. He was so close to making sense of it.

Ollie … Olivia … She had been his ballast, his shield. Just by being there, she kept everything at bay. But she couldn't ultimately stop time. Eventually it would have to reassert itself.

His face was wet and he used the back of his hand to wipe away the drool from his mouth. He could still feel with the dorsal part of his hand, which made the contrast with the other side of his hand even harder to take.

They hadn't moved from the backstreet. The temperature was a couple of degrees up on the seasonal norm. Not exactly comfortable, but certainly less uncomfortable.

Si was sat on the ground, back leaning against brickwork, legs stretched out so far in front of him he couldn't see his feet.

He leaned back and could feel his shoulder kick back, but that was the least of it. He was tired, drained, sapped of all vitality. It was as if Delilah had come to him while he dosed and left him a haircut.

Ollie, legs bent, knees tucked in, was next to him. Diligently she opened a fresh packet of cigarettes. She thought twice about offering him another one. 'Did I say it was a yellow taxi,' she said?

He was feeling sleepy. His eyes were watering. He tipped his head back and looked to the heavens. Disappointedly all there was to see were thick, poppy-shaped clouds. 'Yes, New York,' he said. 'I remember you saying.' It was still in his gift to remember.

'Not a taxi. It was a bus, a yellow school bus,' she said. 'I say it was a taxi that hit me, threw me up in the air, put me in hospital, because it lends more credibility to the idea that I might have survived. But it was a bus, empty except for the driver that smacked full pelt into me. The impact crushed my body, shattered my organs. It killed me. I was aware I was flying through the air, even though at that point I was out of my body. I was already dead.'

She now looked at Si. His head was at an incline, breathing erratic, nostrils red and inflamed. Even if Si wanted to, he wasn't in a fit state to reciprocate and look back.

He thought perhaps he owed her an explanation.

'It started as a pinprick,' he said, his words given the circumstances remarkably lucid. Emboldened, he attempted to lift his hand, hopelessly shaky, before giving up on the idea. But the words they kept on coming, elegant, poetic even. 'A dot inside my head, like a beacon, a light marking out the coastline. A tiny fragment of pain, hardly there unless you had a mind to notice, I suppose. A warning of all the big pain to come.'

'Pinprick,' she said, 'such an odd sounding word.'

'It's not to me.' He tried to smile; so fleeting it barely registered, strangled at birth.

'I know all about pain,' she said, nodding. 'I was dead. Do you know what that feels like?' She stopped abruptly, realising that he would know soon enough. But he didn't seem to pick up on this, or didn't care enough, or possess enough energy to see any kind of reaction through. She took this as a sign to continue. 'I died mid-air, but when I hit the ground I was suddenly gripped by life again, sharp intake of breath, eyes open as wide as I could make them, limbs aching, the most terrible feeling of cramp taking hold of every part of my body. Something was shrieking inside me; pain breaking out everywhere.'

'I looked over and I saw the guy from the shop,' she said, 'the one who had given me such a hard time shouting and screaming at me. He was on the ground on his side, his whole body contorted, but also ... he was sort of flat and compressed. His hands shaped like claws. Not breathing. There was nothing in his eyes. Some sort of seizure. Shock, probably. Served the old bastard right. You could say that, but that wouldn't be right; that wouldn't be decent.'

Si coughed. He tried to hide it, but around the eyes it was obvious how much pain he was in. It was as if Geoff's hands had never left his throat. Thought processes remained robust, but he wasn't sure if this was a good thing.

If this was all he had, though, he reasoned, it had to be worth holding onto. 'But you were in a coma,' he said, croakily, wearily. 'Four weeks you said.'

'Yes,' she said. 'Everything I said was true. I came back, but I still had to heal. No such thing as a free lunch.'

'No such thing as a free lunch,' he repeated. He wanted to keep repeating it for as long as he could. If there was an afterlife lying in wait, he wanted this to be the first thing they heard him say. 'No such thing as a free lunch.'

Instead there was silence. A calm had now enveloped Si and Ollie—Simon and Olivia—the invariable, quintessential calm before the storm.

Coming from nearby, an adjacent street, there was shouting. The quickness to anger, from men mostly by the sounds of it; followed by running.

She smiled. Her nose twitched as if she was going to sneeze. 'What do you want?' she asked him.

'What?' he said.

'Exactly,' she said. 'Not a free lunch. But seriously, what do you want?'

He knew exactly what she was getting at—and she

knew him. Part of a running joke started the first moment he met her. He couldn't shrug her off if he tried.

'I had a shoebox, a mattress fund,' he said. 'Christ, I stuffed it with cash and hid it from Sofi. I mean, I knew what it was for. It was to spend at the Church, doing something, I don't know, illegal or immoral, however you want to describe it.' He raised his arms to cover his chest following an imperative, the instinct to keep warm. 'Do you think that's why you can never get a taxi? 'Cause they're always running some poor sod to the nearest Church of the Last Day?'

'What do you want?'

'I don't know what I want. Take drugs, shag a stranger, drink my bodyweight in tequila? I always thought, *don't need to decide now*. Pushed it to one side. One for the future—way off in the future—still plenty in the tank, I can decide later. My husband and kids didn't come into it. Never entered my thinking, not really, not where that was concerned, that whole thing about …'

He didn't want to say the word, so decided that he wouldn't. His head was swimming. 'I pushed them aside, too,' he said, regaining his composure.

His face became less slack; was suddenly gripped with an idea, a thought. 'You said when we first met that we didn't have to die. It wasn't that long ago. You said there was no such thing as a Last Day.'

She closed her eyes. 'None of us should die. None of us should have to face a Last Day.' She opened them again. 'Not alone.'

Another period of silence fell between them, one that felt like they had all the time in the world.

'What do you want?'

'I want to wriggle my big toe like I'm John Wayne, boil an egg, and see my family,' he said, his teeth biting into an already swollen tongue. 'Not necessarily in that order.' He winced through the pain and turned it into a smile. It was a glorious feeling.

She handed him Elijah's phone, fixed and fully functional courtesy of a Kings Cross convenience store—it seemed not all the world had come to a standstill. 'It's *The Land of Do-As-You-Please*,' she said.

In order to do so, his arm had to move in stages, but he took it nonetheless. He knew Sofi's number off by heart, which was more than he could say for his own. Before he knew it, muscle memory taking over, he thumbed it out on the touchscreen.

He let it ring once before hanging up. 'No,' he said, handing back the phone. 'No, I've already said all I had to say on the phone at the pub. That was the moment. I was the best I could have been. Would just be repeating myself now.'

'The kids?' she said, taking back the phone all the same.

He said nothing. He bit his lower lip.

There was a black mark, a shadow, overrunning him, ready to tear strips off him.

'You know what?' he said eventually, 'I spent my whole life dissatisfied with what I had. I was convinced if there was a point to it then I'd need to go look for it. And now I've looked and I know there's nothing else—absolutely nothing else—and now I can tell myself to stop.'

But it wouldn't stop and now there was only torment, excruciating and agonising. Now, suddenly, he was screaming with pain. His head was swollen; expanding, rupturing, splitting in two. His face leaked blood, but he couldn't say from where. He clawed at his face, such were the levels of pain and frustration now endured. There was nothing to be done about it.

Ollie slid her hand in between his. 'It's okay,' she said. 'I won't leave you, not like this.'

It wasn't that he wasn't listening, but his mind was on other things. Couldn't see in front of him; couldn't feel his feet. Could have been wriggling his big toe for all he knew. A single random memory ran roughshod over his mind; the tiniest of dogs struggling on the leash; a miniscule head twisting one way then the other to utterly no avail. He remembered at the time thinking it was the most pointless thing he had ever seen.

But he could feel her; could feel her touch. She was his shield, coming between him and cold, hard reality.

And he wanted to tell her, but there was something missing and he was robbed of the power of speech. He could not control one side of his face, which fell from him and melted away.

It was too aggressive. It was happening too soon. His thoughts, the joined-up thinking, everything worthwhile, hopelessly turned on its head. He tried to remember his name. It couldn't take that away from him.

Si …

Fi …

Oh, fuck off and leave me alone, he was screaming in his own head—at his own head.

He thought he was on fire. He could see the smoke, but could not scramble away. Where was there to go? It was everywhere, the burning London air. The stifling, filthy sky. And then, quite unexpectedly, piercing the smog, cutting a jagged line across the sky, there was something else.

'Can you see anything?' she said, but it was much too late to expect any kind of response.

She looked past his shoulder and saw a crowd of people rapidly appear at the narrow end of the street, bouncing off each other such was the lack of room. Shuttling, bending, scrambling forward, creating an irresistible momentum. There was no way for the mob to go other than straight on.

At times like this, some feeling seemed to return to her hands. Enough for her to confirm, at least, his grip on her hand was gone.

'It's here,' she said, her voice hardly registering; barely a whisper. No matter how loud she spoke, he wouldn't hear her, but that wasn't a reason not to go on.

'The world is a shoebox and it's time to help yourself. Last Day on earth.'

19

Look To the Light

She lit the match. She would wake in the middle of the night with a fever and find Charlie standing crooked, peering over her. His face obscured mostly in shadow, but she could read what was going on inside his head. He was too old, she'd tell herself. But he had already demonstrated, walking sticks in hands, sheer strength of will just to be able to walk into her room. He was a man, she reminded herself, and therefore was never too old.

As much as he would have wanted to, though, he never touched her. The realisation if he did so would be to throw open a particular door that he wouldn't then know how to close. It was the way he would lean and sway and grip onto his sticks for balance, for dear life, she found this disconcerting enough.

It was the fact that he wanted to. That was all that mattered to him, and to her.

When it came to the moment outside his home, surrounded by his furniture in preparation for his Viking funeral, Mo and Elijah having done most of the heavy lifting, it was up to her to feed him pieces of co-codamol and pour whisky down his throat. She continued up until the point his face muscles relaxed that he could no longer form the expression that peered down at her nightly. The desire to break her as if she was a wild horse. She sprayed on lighter fluid, over his head and body, concentrating in the end around the groin area. She lit the match.

It was strange for her to be thinking of this when she received a call from Sofi, who informed her in a strangely detached way that there would be a service later that morning at Manor Park Crematorium and it would be 'great' if she could make it. He had called her once before; but for this latest call, she idly speculated on how many times he was going to make it before deciding against it, endlessly flip-flopping, never sure of the best course of action. He was probably this moment, having now invited her, agonising over whether this had been the right thing to do. The crematorium was walking distance from her latest squat, so she took this as a sign, not that she needed much persuading, that she should attend.

***

She had some free time on her hands. Yesterday, she retraced her steps back to the street where the kneeling man was killed by an air gun. She was sure she was standing in the correct spot. She looked both left and right to confirm the postbox and local shop were the right distance away. No evidence remained of the dead shouty man, or the blood that pumped out of the wound on his throat and onto the pavement, which was to be expected really. A lot had happened since in the intervening days. A lot to wash over. A lot to wash away.

Her head moved quickly, assuming many angles, searching frantically. From her vantage point she found shouty man's vacated flat, subsequently occupied by her erstwhile partners in crime. It would have been ransacked no doubt before Mo and Elijah got there but still imminently habitable.

But there was something wrong. The outside of the building was black and charred. Windows boarded up; the front door, what was left of it, crooked on its hinges. She had come looking for friendly faces, finding only ghosts instead.

***

There weren't many mourners at the service. She was both surprised and unsurprised by this. Si had given the impression that he kept himself to himself mostly, and the social circle he and Sofi had was a tightly-knit one. It seemed all the more unexpected, then, that she should be asked along. Sitting in the front row she assumed were Sofi and the children. Sofi was dressed in black tie and dark grey suit; a younger, more diminutive, more clean-cut version of Si. She'd been something of a blank canvas before, but now the emotion hit her. To finally be in a position to see his family made her feel unbearably sad.

She wasn't dressed for the occasion—she wasn't sure a duffel coat that had seen better days was appropriate attire for any occasion—but these were the only clothes she had. She sat at an empty row second from the back. From the wall speakers chimed an instrumental version of *Please, Please, Please Let Me Get What I Want* by The Smiths. There was a pamphlet on the chair which she quickly picked up with nary a glance and folded in two.

She thought of her own family; her dear old mum and dad. Two magpies, inseparable, that's what they were. Two lovebirds; never to observe one without the other.

After the coma, her father came to take her home. He was on his own and it was no surprise to anyone that he hated to be away from his wife, her mother. He looked so much older than she remembered. 'Your mother's not well,' was the first thing he said to her. 'I can't be looking after both of you.'

Despite being given the okay to travel from the States, she was still weak—still needed a wheelchair for anything more than the taking of a few steps—too stunned to react to her father's words in a meaningful way. She was a chore, a task, an object to be fetched and carried and made plans for. Dad had only so much love to give and it was all for his wife. Even if he wanted to, he had no control over it; so little in reserve to bequeath to anyone else, including his daughter.

It had been agreed (although not by her) that she'd stay for a while with her gran in Northampton. It was there that full health and fitness was returned, but inside she was divided. She was in pieces and estranged. Never cast adrift, although her gran was situated miles away from her home in Huddersfield. Never truly forgotten, but she drifted away from her family all the same. And she had been drifting ever since. She was in her early twenties, robbed of her past but determined of her future.

In the crematorium, it occurred to her the thing that scared Si the most—he'd let it slip a couple of times—was being burned alive. Now he was dead, she supposed, it no longer mattered. The coffin festooned with white and yellow flowers was in position on the catafalque. At the very least, it didn't matter to her.

A celebrant was up on his feet delivering some Si-themed platitudes. *He loved Sofi, his husband, and children, Alex and Julia. A private family man. Popular among his workmates. A keen supporter of Luton Town. Participated in 10K runs for charity.* With the exception of the first part, she did not recognise the person being described; a fact that made her smile inside.

A normal service from start to finish, measured from the first to arrive through to the last to leave, you'd expect to take around thirty minutes, but the impression here was that it would be over in no more than twenty. The drapes opened, signifying the end point of the ceremony, and the soft drone of a conveyer belt delivered the coffin steadily and purposefully into the furnace. There was a flash of intense light and Si's corporeal frame was released to the ether. Despite sometimes making it difficult for himself, he loved and was loved in return. In the end, who could say otherwise, that this was all that mattered?

Service over, she wanted to put distance between her and everything else. The thinking was, stick around the grounds for the time it takes to smoke a cigarette and then return to the squat.

Between puffs, from a respectable distance, she watched Sofi shepherd the kids towards a woman standing next to a car. She thought it must be his sister, it had to be. Julia's dress was dark green with a floral print.

Alex wore a suit similar to his dad. She hated the idea of any eight-year-old having to wear a suit. He had puffy eyes. It broke her heart to see it. But in all kinds of ways, incalculable and inevitable she supposed, in the fullness of time innocence was there to be broken. Nothing so simple and pure could be built to last forever.

Sofi, in calculated steps, made a beeline for her. She took a deep breath, blinked and braced herself.

'Olivia?' he said.

'Sofi,' she said, a thin smile underlining her face. She recognised his voice, which only confirmed what she already suspected. 'I'm sorry. I don't know what to say.'

He looked down at one of his shoes, which he raised from the heel up, twisting the toecap against the stony ground.

He had obviously been thinking a lot about what he wanted to say. 'I'm sorry, too,' he said. 'I know you've explained, and thank you for that. When it was his time he called, but then he hung up. I got your number from the missed call. He had the chance to say goodbye, but, no, he didn't … I still don't understand why.'

She looked away from him towards the irregularly shaped gravestones in the distance. She recognised these as markers of the past, defying the passage of time, while at the same time remaining faithful shrines to it. Sometimes she viewed herself in a similar light.

She'd heard there were a number of crypts to be found in an adjoining graveyard with stone angels keeping guard, jealously protecting the whispers of the dead. Plenty of places to explore should the mood take her. From this direction, a cold breeze encroached; icy fingers encircled and grabbed her. Her coat was too light for wintry weather. Sometimes she was glad of the fever to keep her from being cold at night.

Sofi could see she was uncomfortable, which wasn't his intention. It was the opposite in fact. 'It's cold,' he said. 'We're expecting snow.'

'Hah,' she said, smiling again, a little wider this time, all the while conscious she hadn't yet earned the right to relax. 'Every winter I've been here in London everyone expects snow, but it never happens.'

'Ceremony was nice,' she said, pushing on the conversation.

'It was quick,' he said. 'Si would have approved. He wasn't for outstaying his welcome.' At this Sofi's voice, his eyes, threatened to break. His own words had tripped him up; multiple meanings and multiple worlds. He coughed once, twice. He pushed against the onset of giddiness.

He kept it together. 'There's less of a waiting list for later in the day—a funeral, the cremation, I mean. People are still adjusting. Don't like being too close to curfew, even though it's lifted. Still coming to terms with…'

He struggled to both finish the sentence and make sense of it.

'Normality,' she said, happy to take on the burden of both.

Right enough, she looked up to the sky and could swear she saw it visibly darken. It was like the hand of a giant had descended, shielding the light, only wanting it for himself and no one else. It was then that she decided, having wrestled with the notion for several days, it wasn't enough to just eke out a living. Not enough to just be a survivor.

Sofi had decided as well. 'We're leaving London,' he said. 'Kids are staying over for a couple of days then I'm taking the guts of the following week to pack.' He looked back towards sister and children. He knew he needed to get back to them.

'You look a lot like him,' she said.

'Everyone says that,' he said. 'It's always I look like him, never him looking like me. It's fucking annoying.'

They shared a smile. There had been a lot of smiling. She was sad. She was happy. Where else in the universe, except right here, could she have experienced anything like this?

'Look,' he said, 'I wasn't sure I wanted you here, right up to—even after if I'm honest—I asked you along. Funny, huh? But I'm sure of this, now. Please come and see us if you can.'

Not waiting for an answer, not looking back, he was already walking back to his family. 'I'll text you the address.' The words floated in the air like a feather caught in the wind, reluctant to ever have to bow to the inevitable and bed down once more on the ground.

Finishing her cigarette, she watched him as he returned to his loved ones. She followed him as he dropped to one knee and cuddled his kids before ushering them into the car. Then she didn't watch anymore.

Normality, she thought. How difficult—how alien a concept these days—this was to grasp. You asked people, that's what they said they wanted. You presented it to them and that's where all the difficulties began.

The crowd control on show at the concourse at King's Cross, the one that swallowed up Si and so many others, was repackaged and exported on a global scale. The world spilled out. The world got kettled. The world was squeezed into a corner. The authorities acted—anticipating a series of events, lessons learned, computer modelling; logarithms already in place. The use of technology, the fail-safes in terms of organisation and surveillance that kicked into place should the *Light* ever fail. The machinations of government planning, some would call it a conspiracy. In any case, order was restored.

Still, it had to be quick. In terms of security forces morale. In terms of planet earth keeping its act together, at least on the outside; at least, seeing past the cracks.

Of everything that was said this time around, the torrent of political and social commentary, even less was couched in terms of Heaven and Hell and God and the Devil. If anything, it was more spiritual; more in terms of what it was to be human. Taking pride of place across Germany, Canada, Ecuador, Fiji, India, Uganda, and yonder, the one statistic pushed out to everyone everywhere. No matter how desperate, frightening, and problematic the world had seemed, there was no change to the suicide rate. No matter how well acquainted we had become with death, we still held onto life and this was why we continued to thrive as a species. In this scenario there was no First Mother and Child. There were no worldwide proclamations. No industry of death. No Church of the Last Day. No First Days…

We already had all of these.

The fault was corrected. The finger of blame was pointed at a rogue group in Russia, which the Russian government instantaneously denied the existence of. There were reports buried away of an arrest in Moscow of a man with an eyepatch and his toeless 'accomplice.'

Whatever, the solution called for delving into a myriad of networks; of diving into a Pacific Ocean of switches and locating, quarantining and killing the errant code responsible.

The *Light* was resurrected and the people were thankful. They were relieved. They were exultant. They were traumatised.

It had vanished. For an actual time it was truly gone, slipped from their fingers. The human psyche wasn't prepared for this. It couldn't deal collectively or otherwise with the shock.

Going forward, emergent from a world precariously off-kilter, there sprang newfound resolve. The *Light*, it was decided, had to be made impenetrable to future cyberattacks. All those borders, the concept of independent states, of national security; all those overlapping firewalls had to make way for an emphatically global singular response. And those states that weren't prepared to play ball, simply put, would be banished. The countries that argued against the change did so from the outside. And exile was such a lonely, dark place to be.

'It is not as if the Light is going to go away. It has become part of us; as important to us as the air we breathe.'

The Church of the Last Day led the call, but in truth it was preaching to the converted.

Citizens of the world embraced the next generation of *Light* implants like lifelong friends.

Lifelong friends in the form of microcircuitry enmeshed under the skin, wireless, emitting a signal, constantly. Every day brought the reality closer of every baby microchipped at birth. Overlay network embedded, configurations in place, global authorisation established. It was the acceleration of the *Light*.

Your readings could be constantly taken. Announced by a ping on a mobile phone, fitness tracker, or smartwatch. There would be no need for something as overt as placing your palm on a panel. No need to worry about straying one minute past a twenty-four-hour period. No need to worry really about anything.

It was its ascension. It had come far from its murky, remote beginnings. No longer under the cover of darkness something your subconscious needed to swim, run, or float to. The *Light* was with us always. It was inside us.

There was no greater advocate of complete autonomy for the *Light*—seeking to make her mark both domestically and on the international stage, and so distance herself from her deceased panda-*worrying* predecessor—than the freshly incumbent President of the United States.

The finances of death were given a much overdue overhaul, brought kicking and screaming into the twenty-first century with the introduction of the *death debit*. Where a Last Day could be financed as an electronic transaction, where no money needed to pass hands. To be fair, death debit was open to a snappier appellation, call it a *rest fund*, *zombie tax*, *death by a thousand transactions*; as yet there was no obvious frontrunner.

The concept of the mattress fund was consigned as a thing of the past. The idea of a shoebox, outside of keeping shoes in, was well on the way to obsolescence.

From death came birth; purple light, purple stars. Al Baumann's last will and testament at last having taken shape and form. Bursting into existence, it had the capacity and reach to touch every living human soul.

The *Light* Web was born.

***

But for now, as all this around her was taking shape, she was standing in the hall and staring at the *Light*. Through all the good, bad, and indifferent times, she had never known anything but the *Light*. Maybe, she was thinking, now was the time to finally embrace and accept it. It had been so long since she'd taken it, though, and for all they knew she had tumbled off the map a long time ago. So she would have to input her NI number and hope for the best. The reality was she'd probably have to go through all the pain and hassle of re-registering and couldn't face that sort of stress, not right now.

Not quite ready to rejoin the human race, she was content for now with staring at the periwinkle glow. She gaped at it, tried to force her thoughts inside it, and she supposed the *Light* was happy to reciprocate and stare back into her also. What would it make of her? It wasn't a case of her being wicked or kind, although she hoped that she had always strived towards the latter. She was in danger of missing the point, though. It didn't decide whether you had been good or bad, rather if you had sufficient breath left in your body. Would the *Light* give her a tick or cross, she wondered—or more likely in her case a question mark.

The shade changed to orchid.

There was no hope, no religion, no second opinion, no referrals. There was only the *Light*. She still wanted to take it, but decided it could wait until tomorrow. What could happen before then?

In the hall there was evidence of packing. There were boxes of various sizes. Also present was the ghost of Geoff, adding to the clutter. Geoff was lying on his back, arms crossed, unshaven, cushions propping up his head, staring at her sleeves, not wanting to give her the satisfaction of a smile.

She had reached the point she was convinced the marks had all but faded from her arms. Still, this morning she hadn't peeked, had kept her arms covered. She didn't want to burst any bubbles. Ignorance wasn't bliss, but was it better than disappointment.

Along with the spare room came a pair of long-sleeved silk pyjamas, which belonged to Sofi. A little on the baggy side, but not impossibly so. She enjoyed the touch of it on the skin, a lightness which followed her as she moved. If she closed her eyes long enough, it helped her forget just about everything. Until it was time, that is, to remember.

She had arrived after accepting his invitation, having decided it was heartfelt. She did so bearing gifts in the guise of a book, *The Magical Faraway Tree*. Si's last act was to pass the book to her so that it would continue on its journey while he himself embarked on a greater one. On being presented with it, Sofi was unsure what to make of it, but Ollie deep down hoped one day she'd get to read it to them.

What could she say to Sofi? That *he* didn't want to say anything? That he'd already said it all. It wouldn't come across as much of a reason why. She didn't have the words to put it across the way it ought to be put across. Mercifully, Sofi did not push, did not pry. What passed between them was a shared sadness, an acknowledgement of the emptiness. A longing for something that could never be returned. And for Sofi, for now, this seemed enough.

Down the hallway, interrupting her thoughts, Sofi's head appeared from the doorway. 'Are you going to stay there all day?' he said. 'I'm making omelette.' He sounded surprisingly upbeat. In fact, it was the first time since she arrived he was anything but borderline morose. Helped no doubt by the rush he was experiencing, unavoidable, completely understandable, which came with the knowledge he and his loved ones had minutes earlier passed the *Light*.

She was a guest in his house, so heeded his summons, stepping over Geoff's ghost as she went.

Leaving one ghost behind, she stepped into the living room. The first thing she noticed was the slats of the vertical blinds were slightly opened, letting in shards of morning light. She diverted her attention as coming from the sofa there was a gamut of noise and entangled activity. The source of the commotion was Julia and Alex, wrestling each other for full control of the TV remote which slipped out of both of their grasps like a troublesome bar of soap.

The TV, so brought to angry life, flicked onto a news channel. It showed a report of two people having been shot dead in Harlesden where curfew was still in force. You could ask with a degree of legitimacy if they knew they were going to die that day, why then would they care about a curfew? But it was a reminder that the government could bring back restriction of movement, and more besides, anywhere and at any time. It made her question, not for the first time, who or what stood to gain most from the upheaval; the seemingly never-ending aftermath.

The fact remained unchanged that death had changed. It was a matter of having dropped the ball, of picking it back up again.

We were better prepared. But such an argument owed more to the past than to the future and did nothing to offset the nagging feeling that the societies of the world, with eyes wide opened, in full view of everybody, were sliding into something unwieldy and authoritarian, which would later give cause for regret.

One man's howls emerged from the kitchen. Omelette preparations were not going well. Ollie took her chance and snatched away the remote. She had control. Adolescent mutant ninja turtles courtesy of one of the kids channels popped up on the TV screen, instantly mollifying the children, leaving Ollie to congratulate herself on a job well done.

Maddeningly, she remained aware of the shafts of light coming from the blinds. For a moment they intersected, interlaced, criss-crossed like duelling Lightsabers, different colours, blues on light reds. It was all a trick of the light.

Julia and Alex talked excitedly and at the same time.

'No shit, Sherlock,' Alex said under his breath, primarily to get a rise out of his sister. In the time since Ollie had arrived, he'd said it at least seven times, but never when dad was in earshot. Julia, face completely crumpled, threatened to tell on her brother for what also seemed like the hundredth time.

'Come and get it,' called the voice from the kitchen, so igniting a stampede. Everything that occurred previously was forgotten. Vacating the living room, the children scampered forth.

Again Ollie, never one to rush, was left to her own thoughts. Not that she was ever truly alone.

Once my eyes popped open, the automatic response was to grab and pull with a flourish the duvet from my naked body. Memories were too precious to waste on the morning. The soles of my feet stood on the bedroom carpet. There was a full length mirror, so I might have flashed a look. I must have showered, dried my hair, got dressed; light stubble, so would have skipped shaving; had breakfast, taken a shit probably.

There were the voices, the external inner monologues; everything from before, but increasingly scrambled. She could not attribute which thought belonged to whom. She could not tell what was what, or for that matter who from whom.

What was the point of a life if you could not turn it around? Why couldn't we remember our memories as an infant? Why not our first word or step, or what it was, say, to be teething? If death was only an end, then the end of what? And at what point, besides her, would there be anyone left to care?

The light still bothered her. She marched across the room. With every intention of tightening the blinds shut, she twisted her hand around the cord. She did not flinch, even though she was aware of a hand on her shoulder. Si's ghost was standing next to her. It was his house after all.

It wasn't that she'd found him particularly enlightening. There was no eureka moment. He just happened to be with her when she learned a valuable lesson. One that was so close to the tip of her nose it was like a sheet of glass was pushed up against it. Sometimes it was the simple things that were the most difficult to distinguish or properly make out. It wasn't that death was all about death. It was the opposite, in fact.

Although he did ask a lot of questions, some even she didn't readily have an answer for.

Si's hand brushed against her arm down to her hand around the cord. She understood his reticence not to allow her out of his sight. He was concerned. He was being protective. She'd just have to show him, have to make him see.

She took a breath and then snatched a look through the open slats and out of the window.

There were so many of them. Beyond the front garden; beyond the road; beyond the gaps between the houses on the other side of the street; beyond the borough, the city borders, from every conceivable part of the globe, crammed in together. They formed a crowd that stretched on forever. It was mind-boggling, the largest gathering she had seen yet. Out in front there was old Charlie, of course, and the shouty *Charlton Heston* guy, not kneeling for a change, but holding the side of his throat. There was Mo and Elijah; their latest squat having caught fire during the unrest, in all probability causing them to die of smoke inhalation as they slept in their beds. There was the forty-fifth (or was it forty-fourth) President of the United States. There was Al Baumann and Heather Carlson, somehow inseparable after all this time but unable to stand the sight of each other. There was Jennifer Coutinho holding baby Daniel. Jennifer appeared happier than at any other time she'd seen her. There was her mum who died of cancer. Her dad who died of a broken heart. Her gran who died of old age. There were the young soldiers Santino and Joaquin. There were so many others.

No one should die alone.

She found herself in a reflective mood. Hers was a difficult birth, or so she was told many years later. She came into the world as the rioting spread perilously close to the hospital grounds. She was born Olivia Susan Frances on the 7th of January, 1998. The day that death changed—the day that everything changed. This was her first day on earth.

'*That was the day*,' they'd say looking back and everyone knew what they meant by this. '*That was the day*.'

Now she'd decided, frankly, she was only interested in the living. She closed the blinds; shut them tight. There was no light.

Noise was coming from the kitchen, some whoops as the first omelette was revealed. With a deep breath and a clear head, more so than was the case for a very long time, she steadied herself and turned away.

She headed towards signs of life.

Editor: Kirsten Murray
Production: Jim Campbell
Cover by Alex Ronald

Thanks to/Inspiration from: Alan Moore, Mike Carey,
Neil Gaiman, Mike Perkins, Dave Hill, John Ridgway,
Richard Corben, Will Pickering, Luke Cooper, David
Lloyd, Jon Haward, Alex Ronald, Eli Winter, Kirsten
Murray, Christian Dunn, Joan Hilty, Jim Campbell

Contact Jim Alexander at planetjimbot@gmail.com
Follow him on twitter @JimPlanetjimbot

Contact Kirsten Murray at hello@kirstenmurray.co.uk

GoodCopBadCop (paperback and digital) by Jim
Alexander available from Amazon, Barnes and Noble,
Kobo, Etsy, and lots of other places

We're on Facebook:
www.facebook.com/groups/planetjimbot
Check out our shop online:
www.etsy.com/uk/shop/PlanetJimbot

Printed in Poland
by Amazon Fulfillment
Poland Sp. z o.o., Wrocław

54377252R00202